Crashing Cassie's Comfort Zone
Jackie Campbell

Ellendale Road Publishing – Novato, CA
ISBN: 978-1-7375684-3-8
Title: *Crashing Cassie's Comfort Zone*
Author: Jackie Campbell
Digital distribution | 2021
Paperback | 2021

This is a work of fiction. The characters, names, incidents, places, and dialogue are products of the author's imagination, and are not to be construed as real.

Dedication

Acknowledgements

Thanks to Kristen Tate and her team at thebluegarret.com for another brilliant editing journey.

Thanks to Travis Simmons at samsdadgraphics.com another cover creation.

Thanks to Erica at newbookauthor.com for all the organizing and publishing help.

Chapter One

Cassie Bryant, a King Kong coffee cup clasped in two hands on her lap, perched on a wooden bench bolted to the Hudson River-end of the High Line pedestrian walkway. It was late September, and the cup warmed her hands. A cold breeze pushed in off the Hudson, fall's way of announcing an early assault on the city. Years before, they'd warned the massive wrecking ball off the old, dilapidated High Line railway route around the new Hudson Yards redevelopment area in New York City. The long-abandoned elevated rail line, supported by a maze of steel beams and concrete, had been redone as a landscaped pedestrian walkway from the old Meatpacking District to the river. The pulverizing ball's fury wreaked havoc on everything else. For months now she'd watched, fascinated, as multiple skyscrapers, civic structures, and art projects sprouted from the ruins.

The rhythmic hammering of pile drivers, the scorched smell of welded steel, and the roar of diesel engines powering an array of heavy machinery didn't disrupt Cassie's focus on one building in particular—the new Grand Manor Hotel. *Soon it will be mine,* thought Cassie. *Soon it will be completed and my years of dedication to the company should catapult me to the general manager position of the new flagship hotel in the Manor Hotel chain.*

A man in shabby clothing hobbled slowly toward her from the left, occasionally grabbing the handrail for support, dragging his small cart with one bent wheel, scattering a few pigeons in his path.

"Thanks for saving my seat, Harold," said Cassie, handing him five dollars.

Harold hadn't saved anything, but it was part of their ritual. Homeless Harold claimed this section of the city. Cassie's friend Vivien ran a nonprofit dedicated to helping New York City's large, unhoused population, and had introduced them months before.

"The weather's going to change now, Harold. You know where to go to keep warm?"

"You're the best, Cassie. I'm good. Vivien's got us covered." Five dollars in hand and some light banter exchanged, Harold tugged on his cart and was off to supervise the rest of his empire.

A set-in-stone New Yorker, Cassie Bryant had been born, bred, educated, and employed right there in the city. The last seven years had been spent with the hotel chain, where she'd added skills and experience to her NYU master's degree in hotel and tourism management. She'd started schooling away her Brooklyn accent in her late teens; it had vanished completely by the time she'd collected that master's degree.

Her dues had been paid in several of the chain's hotels around the city, and now Cassie enjoyed a very responsible position in the corporate office in Midtown Manhattan. General manager of the new hotel would be one of the company's most prestigious jobs, and she wanted it desperately. Chairman and owner Dan Weaver liked working with her, valued her decisions and opinions, and had mentored her since her early years.

A planner by nature, Cassie had money saved and was looking at Upper East Side condos—a large studio to start. She would be in a great neighborhood, just a quick ride on the 6 Train and a fast connection to the new hotel. For now, living at home with her folks in Brooklyn was her best option. After graduate school, she had moved out for two years but soon realized that saving money would be much easier if she were back home paying her parents a more modest rent.

A damp gust of wind off the river played with her long black hair and snuck behind her thin silk scarf, sending a shiver down her neck, drawing her back to the present. The wind had shifted. Time to go; rain was coming. The smell of the Hudson behind her was replaced by scents from the city to the east, along with aromas from the rapidly growing foliage along the High Line.

Cassie gave a parting smile to the scene before her. It summed up what she loved about the city: crowds of people bustling past each other, tourists and locals getting on with their days, massive construction activity heralding the changes coming to tired neighborhoods. The constant energy and electricity, excitement and wonder of America's premier city.

She drained her coffee cup and placed it in the bin beside the bench. Pilgrimage completed, Cassie Bryant shook off her dreams and headed toward the subway station and home.

*

Thursday morning, Dan Weaver stood in Cassie's office doorway. "Ready for the meetings next week? Fall is gorgeous in the mountains out west."

Cassie looked up from her computer. "Boss, if you remind me once more, I'm going to lock you in your office. Yes, sir. I'm ready." Their relationship was such that Cassie could throw a dig at him. "You may be excited, but this is the biggest trip I've ever taken, and it's to the middle of nowhere. I know you love it out there, but this is all very challenging to my comfort zone."

"A simple trip is challenging? Ha! Wait 'til you find out what's challenging." He laughed to himself, then added, "Listen, I'd like you to come out early, before the rest of the team—tomorrow, in fact, if you can make it."

"Tomorrow?" Cassie said slowly, her mind whirring. *Does he want me to come early to talk about the new general manager position? Is that what he meant by challenging?*

"Yes, sorry for the short notice."

"I can do it, no problem!"

"I'll see you in California tomorrow then. I'm flying out tonight." He gave her a salute and left her office.

North to Boston, south to Philly and DC by train was as far as she'd traveled to visit hotels in the chain. She'd only flown once, for a trip to Florida. Childhood vacations were at the Jersey Shore or Coney Island. Other than that, Cassie was a prisoner of the city with no desire to be paroled. She never had the urge to experience what stimulated and fascinated others, never felt trapped, never felt limited by her tightly controlled urban life. When coworkers or friends stopped by after trips, they'd leave little gifts on her desk: a refrigerator magnet from Rome, a snow globe from Alaska, scented soap from France, a poster from London.

Late September or early October was the preferred time for the annual meetings. This year, Dan was having the meeting at the mysterious, old, original Manor Hotel tucked somewhere in the mountains of Northern California. None of the employees knew anything about the first hotel the family had owned for over a hundred years. It was the only hotel not on the East Coast and had never been part of the chain. If anyone asked the boss about it, they would get a vague reply, pleasant but short. The year before, someone in accounting, drunk one Friday night after work, blabbered that the boss held the Western hotel in a separate family corporation. Dan wanted to ensure that, should something terrible befall the Manor Hotel Corporation, his pride and joy in the middle of nowhere would still be safe.

The mystery hotel's website was a half-page long with no pictures. Probably done the first week web pages were invented and never updated. Information was so minimal the operation could be mistaken for a phony CIA front. Speculation around the office about what it looked like ranged from an enormous, scary wooden hotel like in the movie *The Shining*, to a dilapidated stone manor house in the English style, to a glorified Motel 6. No one knew for sure.

Everyone in the Manhattan head office did know that Mr. Weaver spent a minimum of six weeks a year tucked away in the West Coast forest, more in the last two years. He always returned to the corporate offices looking refreshed, energetic, and happy. Why, after years of greedily holding this private jewel to himself, was he suddenly hauling ten or twelve of his managers out there for the annual meeting?

The meetings were arranged for the usual Tuesday through Thursday, but the managers and financial staff could then stay in Northern California—anywhere between Lake Tahoe and San Francisco—for a four-day weekend vacation on the company. Quite a generous bonus from the kind of boss people dream of; it must have been a good year for the chain.

Cassie wondered again why the boss wanted her to arrive the Friday before the meetings started. Had anyone else been summoned early?

*

"Nervous, honey?" asked her mother, hovering in the doorway of Cassie's bedroom. "This is a big trip for you. You've never been off the East Coast before. Heck, you've hardly ever been out of the city.

Getting away will be good for you. You'll see new things, meet new people."

Clothes were strewn all over Cassie's modest bedroom. Packing decisions had to be made. "Just a little nervous, Mom. I can't remember the last time I had to pack for a week. What's the weather like? Will there be dress-up functions? Easy for the guys: they just throw a sports coat in their bag, problem solved. Dan's so cryptic about everything. Everybody's trying to figure out why he wants the meeting out in California."

Cassie sneezed. She was catching something, a given this time of year in a city as densely packed as New York.

Mom gave her a loving pat on the arm. "Watch out for that, honey. You know you pick something up every year." Concern expressed, Mom got back to more important stuff. "It's a shame you're not seeing Herschel any longer. He'd have been nice company for that big bonus weekend in San Francisco. Oh, well."

"Thanks, Mom."

Mom had missed the inflection. It wasn't gratitude for dinner, it was a mildly depressed 'thanks' for reminding her of the ex. Old school, her parents worried that their daughter was now over thirty and still single. Bringing up Herschel Carter, her boyfriend for over two years, was not helpful.

Two months prior, dear Herschel had dumped her. She subsequently found out that Herschel, a stockbroker, had taken up with his boss's daughter. Evidently, he was trying out a new ladder to help him climb to the top of corporate America. Unfortunately, Cassie also found out he was experimenting with the new ladder while still seeing her, hence, her search for a studio on the East Side. They had been planning on buying a place together, a one-bedroom. Cassie unconsciously rubbed her arm, as if she could still feel the sting. She'd loved him, and he'd hurt her. The experience had not disappeared, but merely lurked in the back of her mind, periodically coming out when least expected, like now.

Cassie looked at her suitcase. It reminded her of the small box she existed in, but she was happy with her confined, structured life in the bounds of Brooklyn and Manhattan. Maybe an unfamiliar experience in a new location would be good. California. *God*, she thought, *that's so far west, China has to be nearby*. She'd finally be a woman of the world—jetting coast to coast, winding through the Sierra

Nevada Mountains, drinking champagne on the Golden Gate Bridge. She fantasized about her scarf blowing in the wind on the deck of the tour boat going around Alcatraz, a soft salt spray on her cheeks as the boat slices through the waves.

Herschel had treated her to a weekend on Long Island once.

*

Everything ready for her departure the next day, Cassie rushed out. She was running late for drinks and dinner with her best friend, Vivien Van Houten. They'd met during college and had got on immediately. Vivien had been pretending to get an education at Vassar, the elite school outside New York City, while Cassie toiled away at NYU. Vivien loathed Vassar, but her family insisted. Abandoning the campus every weekend, she escaped on the hour-and-a-half train trip and was back in the city every Friday night. Filthy rich, entitled to the max, and funny as hell, she was a walking advertisement for all the high-end stores in Manhattan. When Cassie called her an elitist snob, Vivien took it as a compliment.

She held sway over the bar when Cassie settled on the stool beside her. Vivien was still in Elitist Mode after grinding money out of wealthy donors at a long lunch earlier. Cassie would have to bring her down to Normal Mode. Vivien eyed her friend up and down. "And how was your week doing—what is it you do again? Work? Yes, that's it. You work. What an appalling activity."

"You work just as hard as I do running your nonprofit, Viv."

"Don't dare say such a thing! I never knew you had a mean streak in you, Cassie Bryant. People like me do not *work*. We... we participate in philanthropic endeavors." She waved a finger in Cassie's face. "Never use the W-word around me again."

Tension and a hint of sadness on Cassie's face prompted Vivien to say, "Oh, dear. You have that look. You're not dragging yourself down over that idiot Herschel again, are you?"

Cassie's eyes fell to the glass of wine Vivien had ordered for her. "Maybe a little. Mom triggered it a while ago. I still don't understand. I thought we really had something. We were planning a future together. What did I do wrong?"

"We've been over this. You did nothing wrong. It simply didn't work out. His loss, as far as I'm concerned. You've got to get over this. Do I have to give you the life-isn't-fair speech again?"

Cassie slowly shook her head as if that was all it would take. "Anyway, that's not why I'm nervous. I'm leaving for the company meetings tomorrow out in Manor Valley, California. My first time off the East Coast, and my second time on a plane. The boss will probably announce the new manager position. You know how bad I want that job."

"Poor you, are you flying private or—oh God, let's not talk about the other option, I haven't eaten yet." Vivien faked a cringe at the thought of flying in a packed airplane. Her façade started to crack. "Wait! Did you just say Manor Valley? You're going to the Manor Valley Hotel in California? No, no. I've heard of it. Very exclusive. They'll never let you in." She gave Cassie her best condescending pat on the hand.

Cassie's head straightened. "You've actually heard of it?"

"I have. My parents went a few years ago. Raved about it. As I say, very exclusive. I'll have father make a call. Warn them what to expect."

"Stop it, Viv. My boss owns it. He keeps it separate from the chain. He grew up in Manor Valley."

Animated now, her aloof façade gone, Vivien gasped. "Your boss *owns* it! The same man who rents suffocating cubicles passed off as hotel rooms to wayward travelers and greedy people engaged in commerce?" Vivien unconsciously brushed dirt off her thousand-dollar slacks, not wanting to be infected by the mere mention of these sordid activities. "Oh, why haven't you introduced him to me? Is he handsome? I might even sacrifice the city for a weekend to stay at *that* hotel."

"Viv, he's happily married. You always thought him slightly better than a street peddler because he has a small chain of, forgive me, *business* hotels. Half the time, you make me meet you outside because you can't bear to be seen in one of his lobbies."

"That's a gross exaggeration. I do stop by now that you're in the corporate offices, not toiling away like you did for years in one of those packing plants for people." Vivien scanned the room, her act over. "Enough of this crap. I feel like slumming it tonight. Dinner at Trump Tower?"

They went next door to their usual modest Italian restaurant.

Chapter Two

The plane was on approach to SFO, lumbering and bouncing around during descent. Cassie pulled a tissue from her bag before stowing it under the seat in front of her and tried to clear her plugged ears. It didn't work. The cold she'd caught earlier in the week was worse. Her nose had been running the entire flight, and she felt warm and achy. She prayed it wasn't the flu; she'd forgotten to get her shot this year. Hell, she forgot most years and paid the price.

At the rental car agency, she requested a compact car. Cassie was happy that she had finally gotten her driver's license two years before. She'd never had any desire to drive. Living in New York, what was the point? She didn't ski, and she didn't beach. She worked. A subway or cab, or Uber or Lyft, were not always available in smaller towns where they had hotels. Her questionable driving skills would now be tested on the long drive from San Francisco to the mystery hotel in the mountains.

Cautiously, she made her way out of the parking garage, across the Bay Bridge, and onto Interstate 80. From there, it was the same highway for several hours until she reached the Sierra Nevada Mountains.

Two hours of driving took her just past Sacramento, where she stopped for a restroom break, coffee, and a snack. Her intense focus on the road was not helping her throbbing head, her runny nose, or the pain in her clogged ears. In the small shop, Cassie placed two packs of tissues and a small pack of cold pills on the counter beside her coffee and snacks. Back in the car she did some head twists, trying to push aside the pain in her neck and shoulders. Gas looked good; she was off again.

Her cell phone rang. It was Dan checking up on her because he knew she wasn't a traveler. Wasn't that nice?

"Are you on the road yet?"

"Just past Sacramento. I've got the place plugged into the car's GPS. No problems so far."

"Okay. Be careful, Cassie. The roads get windy after you get off the freeway, but it's a very soothing ride." He couldn't resist a little jab. "And don't panic when you reach the foothills. Unlike New York, there are more trees out here than people."

"Very funny, Mr. Weaver. I'll see you soon."

'Hang up' pushed, call terminated, Cassie focused. *Foothills? What the hell is a foothill?*

She knew she was in the forest because of all the green forest stuff. The scary green forest stuff of unending bushes, plants, and trees forming unbroken walls on both sides of her. At home she didn't see this much green on St. Patrick's Day. It looked like it was closing in on her, pressing up against the edges of the narrow road leading from the freeway to her destination, adding to Cassie's fears about being one of the few cars on this two-lane road. Dan said it was a *soothing* ride. She felt like she was in an endless green tunnel and it damn sure wasn't *soothing*. Wherever this place was, it must take a week to pump in daylight. After twenty long minutes of twists and turns surrounded by green, green, green, she thought she was hallucinating when she rose up a long incline and crested the hill's top.

Bang! Everything opened up in front and below her, like a massive door at the end of the green tunnel. The rearview mirror checked, she slowed to a stop close to the edge of the road. It dropped off quickly. Cassie blew her nose again, took a sip from her water bottle, and surveyed the scene below. It was like driving onto the top corner of a beautiful picture-postcard or stumbling out of the spiral binding holding up a landscape wall calendar.

Manor Valley, California, smiled up at her from below, an intimate valley entirely surrounded by hills turning into mountains. The focal point was a large lake. It appeared to be about two miles long and half as wide. Sun winked back at her as it came off the water undulating in the breeze. She was nervous about getting out of the car, but all great explorers had to take photos to document their journeys.

Fearful of this remote location, she scanned the woods around her like she'd seen special ops guys do on TV. She got out of the car, left the door open on purpose, and shook off some lightheadedness before hurrying around the front of the car to get a better look.

Cassie wasn't stupid; she was from New York City. Predators were a way of life. She'd read that mountain lions were sly and quick out here in the wild. Her guard was up. She opened the passenger door just in case one was watching her, getting ready to pounce before she could get back to the driver's side. If the animal came for her, she'd jump in the passenger's side, climb out the driver's side and slam the door, trapping it inside. The scene played out in her stuffed-up head. The lion pounded on the windows trying to get out. Massive claws ripped the upholstery to shreds while gargantuan teeth tore off one of the head rests before mangling the steering wheel and swallowing the rearview mirror.

Nothing to worry about. It was a rental; they had insurance. Better get the photo quick.

There it was, its back to her, filtered through the trees on the near shore—the Manor Valley Hotel presiding over this gigantic oil painting. It was a magnificent eighteenth-century, Georgian country home plucked out of an old romance novel, plopped down here in the middle of nowhere. A large lawn with a circular driveway was partially hidden on the building's front side, leading down to the water. The trees limited her view, but she saw a lot of construction activity at the back of the old building—the only thing marring this perfect image. She took a picture. Thinking of her parents and Vivien, she switched to video.

Back in the car, her approach took her down the western slope on a long, relatively straight descent. A sharp bend at the bottom turned her back onto the road toward the hotel. It meandered a short distance before it became the main street—the only street—through the small town: a single short block with stores and shops on both sides close to the lake on her left. Another minute, and the road passed in front of the hotel entrance. Sporadic rooftops of houses popped out on her side of the valley, camouflaged in the trees. The distant slopes appeared to be preserved in their natural state.

When she stopped at the hotel entrance, a doorman immediately assaulted her—a well-mannered and enthusiastic young man who greeted her by name. He informed her with a big smile not to touch her bags or he might lose his job. Evidently, she was expected.

She might have been expected, but she wasn't expecting anything like this.

Inside the lobby door, Cassie stepped into the past. A large, circular, three-story-high entry hall welcomed her. She paused to take it all in. Elaborate historic moldings and a painted interior dome drew her eyes up. Looking straight ahead, she had an unobstructed view through the hotel to the spacious rear exterior, but the back appeared to be screened off from view, probably to mask the new construction.

Through a doorway to her left, she glimpsed a wood-paneled bar with comfortable upholstered chairs and polished wooden tables. To her right, a spacious dining room. Her eyes followed the intricately patterned marble floor across the circular space to the left past the bar entry. A massive fireplace had several people comfortably seated in front of it. The circular line of the room was interrupted by the hallway leading to the back. To the right of this was the curved reception desk.

Proudly holding the center of the grand lobby, below a massive brass chandelier hanging from a chain running all the way to the top of the dome, was a large round marquetry table with one of the most beautiful flower arrangements she had ever seen. The sheer size of it grabbed her attention. Delphinium, larkspur, hollyhocks, garden roses, and lupin shot skyward from an oversized Asian vase. Never having received flowers from a man, Cassie thought she'd marry one if he gave her a bouquet like this. She drew close and noticed a discreet card propped against the vase: LILY'S FLOWERS AND CHOCOLATES, right here in Manor Valley. Her fingertips absently ran across the polished table's surface as she moved around it, marveling at other lobby details.

"Good afternoon, Ms. Bryant. We won't be bothering with check-in today. Let me take you to your room."

Startled, Cassie jumped and snatched her fingers off the grand wooden table like a child before her mother reprimanded her about touching things that weren't hers. A cheerful young woman this time, dressed in a dark-blue suit with a rose-colored blouse.

In the four-story elevator, her escort continued, "We hope you had a pleasant trip. You must be tired after your flight and the long drive from San Francisco."

Who are these people? Were they tracking my car?

On the top floor, they walked down a long hall to a corner room. The guide held the door for her, and Cassie noticed the young lady give a quick glance around the room, checking that everything was in order before presenting her with a key.

"Enjoy your stay, Ms. Bryant. If you need anything, just call downstairs."

Still in awe, Cassie needed some clarification. "Thank you so much for escorting me to the room. What's your name?"

"Nelly, Ms. Bryant."

"Well, Nelly, we can drop the Ms. Bryant. My name is Cassie. I work with Mr. Weaver back in New York."

"Yes, Cassie, we know."

We know? Who the hell is 'we'?

"How long have you worked here, Nelly?"

"Well, I'm from the valley, so I've had various jobs at the hotel all through high school. During the summers, I've worked in the kitchen, the restaurant, even did maid work in the rooms one year. After college, I came back, and now I'm training at the front desk and in the office. I love it here."

Not wanting to seem too curious, Cassie asked, "Is it busy this time of year?"

"Business is always good here at the hotel. Thankfully, we are having our quieter few weeks before the fall crowd gets here."

Bewildered by these answers, Cassie could only muster, "Well, thanks again, Nelly."

When the door closed, Cassie looked at her hand; it was a key, an actual key attached to a fob. She'd never seen one. Every hotel in the world now had electronic cards. Carrying the old-world theme through, the room was decorated in the elegant English Georgian style. A richly colored Persian rug covered a large section of the hardwood floor. Polished mahogany chairs flanked a small leather-topped writing table under a window, which framed a view of the lake and hills beyond. The furniture all looked like pricey antiques, and the room was bigger than the studio condos she'd been looking at in New York. She thought she should be dressed formally just to walk around in a room like this.

Was that really a four-poster bed? With a down comforter? Where were you supposed to put all those pillows when you went to sleep? A trained eye took in the details. Business must be good, everything was crisp and neat—no frayed linens, no chipped paint. Dust wasn't allowed in these rooms.

Period moldings and historic paint colors added warmth to the room. No prints on the walls—they were all oil paintings. A quick check of the spacious bathroom revealed a striking contrast. It was brightly lit, with ultra-modern tiles and fixtures. A separate tub that a shark could swim in took up one wall. A shower the size of a walk-in closet, complete with several showerheads and a built-in seat, finished the space.

Cassie slumped down on the side of the bed, blew her nose, and shook her head in a vain attempt to unclog her ear, trying to comprehend it all. She'd read about grand old resort hotels like this in school: The Broadmoor in Colorado Springs, The Greenbrier in West Virginia, The Point in the Adirondacks, the Grand Hotel on Mackinac Island in Michigan.

God! How did this place even get here? It was magnificent—from another time, like steam engines, fountain pens, and teenagers with manners. How could Dan not blatantly brag about this hotel? Elegant seemed a paltry word to describe it all.

A beautiful, violet orchid resting on the writing table by the window drew her attention. Admiring it, she rose to get a closer look. A sealed note on expensive stationery with her name rested beside the plant.

Dinner tonight at our house.
Come at 7:00. Casual.
Ask at the desk for directions.
It's ten minutes.
You couldn't get lost if you tried.
Dan & Rita

She opened the small drawer in the writing table wondering if she'd find a quill and inkpot, maybe some parchment paper.

Casual, coming from her boss who was always in a suit. "Dapper" is what her mother called him. Pocket-square handkerchiefs, tie clips, even cuff links. Dan had manners that should shame the younger generations. A direct talker, he had a terrific sense of humor that would put anyone at ease. With his perfectly combed salt-and-pepper hair, he reminded Cassie of a mature Cary Grant. When Dan's wife, Rita, visited New York, she was always dressed tastefully. Cassie tried to picture her version of casual.

No time for a nap. She laid out a short-sleeved dress and a thin sweater. She'd skip the pantyhose. Thank God there was time for a bath, not just a short shower.

Tired and sore now, she'd been feeling worse on the drive up. She'd hardly slept the night before, puzzling over the coming meetings. Her left ear refused to unclog from the plane's descent into San Francisco. A glance in the mirror confirmed her fears; her wide-set blue eyes, probably her best feature, she thought, were bloodshot, and it felt like the drummer from the band Have a Little Pain was practicing behind them. Even her nose was red.

Strength needed to be gathered. She admonished her reflection in the mirror with a pointed finger and—what was it they said out here in the wilderness?—"Cowboy up, girl." She smiled, remembering her father's occasional reproach to his younger employees when she was growing up—"grow a pair." To her father's great amusement and saddened wallet, she'd been polished in the politically correct atmosphere of an East Coast university, so neither of those phrases would ever cross her lips in public. At times like this though, she had to admit they packed a stunning amount of clarity and motivation for so few words. She missed her dad already. A loveable, gruff New York City plumber, he had a mouth to match. She loved sparring with him, loved reprimanding him about his antiquated manner of talking with people. One of her goals in life was to shepherd him into the politically correct twenty-first century. So far, he was having none of it.

Cassie took two cold pills, shivered slightly, and felt a spot of lightheadedness again before settling into the warm oversized tub. She'd seen a hair dryer in the closet, so she had time to wash her hair. She soaked an extra face towel in the warm water and placed it over her forehead and eyes as she slipped down to her neck and listened to—nothing. No hotel activity, no distant chatter. Not even her constant companion in New York, street noise, interrupted. Simply nothing.

*

When Cassie came down to the lobby, cheerful Nelly was at the front desk. She didn't even have to ask the question.

"Your car is out front, Cassie. Drive out to the main road and take a right. Go along the lake to the end, and you'll see some vegetable allotments and a big white greenhouse on the left next to the water. Just follow the bend around them and head up the hill. A half-mile up, you'll see a big log cabin on the right. That's the Weavers' house. Believe me, you can't miss it."

How do these people know where I'm going?

Cassie set off, spare tissues in hand, a spare in her bag, and an assortment of pills at the ready. It was definitely flu, not a cold. Her head ached, and her nose was running. Dark clouds had replaced the sunny day over the lake. It started to drizzle, and she switched on the wipers. She knew what a greenhouse was. She'd ask later about what an allotment was.

Dan was right; you couldn't get lost. Drive to the bend at the end of the lake. Yep, there was the greenhouse. Now up the narrow, windy road to a big log cabin on the right.

Why couldn't they build *straight* roads around here?

Chapter Three

Dan Weaver, always full of surprises, had her bewildered again. It was a *large* log cabin, not a Western movie log cabin. These logs were massive, two feet plus in diameter, and going up two floors. Before she got out of the car, he was at the door with two large dogs, both intent on getting their own share of welcoming her. They bounded down the two steps from the porch, ran over to the car, and waited for her to get out, tails wagging. She'd read about the West and knew they weren't wolves because they came out of the house. Never having been around dogs much, she got out slowly and stood there. From the porch, Dan said, "Just pat their heads. They won't jump on you."

Dan quickly ushered her through the front door, out of the wet weather. He had on a V-necked sweater over an open-collared, plaid shirt with jeans below.

God, he really meant casual. Where did Mr. GQ even find a pair of jeans?

"Welcome to Manor Valley, Cassie."

It surprised her when Dan gave her a big hug. Back in New York, he was formal and elegant, always with the old-world manners, a gentleman in every sense of the word.

As he released her, he said, "I know there must be some politically correct rule about physical contact and hugging these days, but you're not in New York anymore, Alice. We're much less formal out here." He stepped to the side and motioned with his hand, allowing her to go first. "Come on back—Rita is in the kitchen. She can't wait to see you. It's just five of us for dinner. My oldest friend and his wife."

As she walked back to the kitchen, the home again surprised Cassie. It was nothing like the traditionally furnished hotel. Large contemporary paintings hung on the beautiful exposed-log walls in the living room. Exotic hardwood floors were partially covered in elaborate area rugs. There were leather sofas and chairs, and custom-made cabinets and end tables in a country style. As she approached the kitchen, she could see it was large and modern with pricey appliances and a big Wolf range. The back wall was all glass, framing a large yard with a swimming pool and forest beyond.

Rita, Dan's wife of close to forty years, embraced her as soon as she entered the kitchen. The two women had developed a close relationship since Cassie joined the company. Rita had few friends in New York. When she visited, she would commandeer Cassie as her companion for a day or two. Her husband knew better than to protest. Their days usually started with a pleasant lunch, after which it was shopping, museums, galleries, or the newest theater productions, all of which Dan was happy to beg off.

"You have no idea how happy I am that you've finally come to our home," said Rita. "When my husband finishes with his work nonsense, we'll ride around, and I'll get you oriented. It's the polar opposite of the big city, but I think it will grow on you."

The others were around the kitchen island having wine, ignoring the dining table set for five off to the side. Introductions were made. Ann and Jim Walker were lifelong friends who lived nearby.

Rita, noticing Cassie's condition, whispered so the others wouldn't hear. "I hope that's a cold, dear. You don't have allergies, do you?"

"No. It's just a whopper of a cold. Luckily, I've never had allergies."

Rita ushered her to a stool. "Sit, dear. Get off your feet." She turned to her husband. "Dan, get Cassie a glass of wine. She's had a long day traveling." She then raised a finger toward her husband. "And she'll be sleeping in tomorrow, so whatever your schedule is, change it."

Looking at her boss, Cassie knew he understood this was not up for debate.

Cassie tried desperately to take it all in stride. Dan had mentored her, been like a second father to her for years. Now, in front of her, was this man she didn't recognize in a home she would never have pictured him in. Back in the city, he took her to lunch every few weeks. He'd bounce questions off of her, quiz her on different problems, and ask her opinion about the hotel business's future. She felt that he valued her views. At the same time, she always felt like she was being evaluated, her knowledge and decision-making ability tested. She'd never seen him out of a suit. She'd never seen him this relaxed and casual, never a clue about this second life.

Whenever Rita was in New York, she dressed to the nines, regal and elegant. Here she looked like a typical homemaker, running around in her apron making dinner. Cassie knew it was just the two of them. They had met in college and never had children. Rita preferred Manor Valley, didn't like traveling much, and her time was full with community activities and charity work in the area.

Eventually, the group made their way to the table. The neighbors were friendly and attentive toward her.

Jim Walker explained that he was also a longtime employee at the hotel. "My son and I do our best to hold up the construction and maintenance end of things around here." He nodded toward Dan. "But this guy should be home more to lend a hand. Did you know that your boss is actually an excellent carpenter?"

Oh my God, how many more surprises?

But it made sense. Dan was remarkably fit for a man in his late sixties. Thinking back, she remembered that he always had time for all the workmen at his hotels. He understood what they were talking about and enjoyed the friendly banter.

They tried to school her in the area's history and the hotel; most of it passed over her head. She wanted to know why she was here tonight with no other employees. Was he going to offer her the job or not? Nerves made her gulp down her wine. It was quickly refilled. She was getting lightheaded again, even a hint of dizziness. She needed to be careful.

Nine o'clock arrived, and Ann and Jim made their goodbyes. The men were getting an early start in the morning to play golf if the weather cleared. Fall was creeping in fast, and the remaining season would be short.

The three of them cleaned up the kitchen before Rita said goodnight. "Dan, don't keep Cassie late. She's not feeling well, and you know how you like to talk."

Cassie could tell by Rita's manner that whatever they were going to discuss was important.

The two of them moved to his quiet study and settled into two leather armchairs flanking the small fireplace in front of his desk. Floor-to-ceiling bookcases crafted in a dark wood covered two walls.

A fire in the small fireplace took the evening chill and dampness out of the air.

"You're wondering why you're here tonight, aren't you, Cassie?"

"I am, sir." Smiling but nervous. *Is this it?*

"I'll get right to it then. I know that you want the new Hudson Yards hotel. You're not going to get it right now." A hand rose to ward off the shock he'd just delivered. "You can have it later if you want it. I have something very dear to my heart to offer you instead. It's something much more important to me personally, and something much more challenging for you. That new hotel you want so bad—don't think I haven't noticed—is just a big, alternative version of what you can do in your sleep. I also know you're a New Yorker to the core. Forgive me, but I want to change that too. Expand your horizons, as it were."

Much more important? Dear to his heart? Expand horizons?

Cassie took a big gulp of wine, a stall to digest the shock. She was not going to be the general manager of her dream hotel. Devastated, she remained silent, a neutral look on her face, waiting to hear whatever was on the boss's mind.

"Did you notice the construction down at the hotel?"

"I did." Simple. Fast.

"In your master's degree program, you focused on event management, marketing, and tourism development. Others in the company haven't studied those things. Not a problem, since most of our hotels don't do big events or depend on tourism much. We're primarily small business hotels." Dan casually waved a hand in the air. "Out here, it's very different.

"Where you're staying is the first hotel in our family, going back a few generations. I'll sing you that long song later. The point is, we're doing a major addition to the hotel itself, and we're updating all the related outdoor operations with it. You've probably already sensed that we're currently targeted at an older, more affluent clientele. Changing times means it's time to address the newer generations. I want to do it without losing the old-world grace and dignity of the place. This is not an urban hotel. It's a destination resort with special parameters, which makes it unique. I'll explain it all later." Dan warmed to his subject. He shifted to the edge of his chair, rested his elbows on his knees, and focused intently on Cassie.

"The point is that I want someone I can trust to oversee this transformation. I need someone who understands the younger generations, knows what they're doing, can get it done, and can put in the hours. I want you, Cassie. I need you for a two-year commitment, and then you can have whatever you want in New York—the new hotel, or vice-president of the whole chain. Either way, I'm not losing you. You know that you're like a daughter to Rita and me, and, quite frankly, you're my most valued employee. You're loyal. If you don't want to do it, I'll find something you'll like back in New York. But please give me the weekend and Monday to lay it all out for you before making a decision. I know this comes as a big surprise. The two new wings are almost finished, and the interior work can continue over the winter. We're shooting for opening late next spring, and that's just the hotel part. There are a lot of hotel-related outside operations also." Dan gave her an imploring look. "Please tell me you'll at least hear me out over the next few days."

She had little choice. "I will." What else could one say after Thor just wedged his hammer between your ears?

Cassie excused herself, asking directions to the bathroom. She needed a few minutes of privacy to digest all this. Even with the flu clogging her head, the devastating news had gotten through loud and clear.

In the powder room, Cassie had another chat with a mirror. *This. Is. Not. Happening. To. Me. What would I do trapped out here in the wilderness? I'm a New York girl.* She paused long enough to wipe a cold towel over her face. Her head was hot. *Okay. Okay.* This disaster had to be thought through. Dreams had been dashed before. Get a grip. What the hell was even going on at that hotel? All the construction? What were his plans? And what the hell were these 'outdoor operations'? In New York, it was simple—there was no *outdoors*. You were either in the hotel or out on the street, fumbling through the jungle on your own, and good luck to you.

The flu was cresting. Her head was killing her, every joint ached, and the shock of the last fifteen minutes was overwhelming. She reached into her purse and took out an old bottle of Valium. When things started bumping against the overload line, which was rare for Cassie, she would take a Valium to settle down. She checked the date on the old prescription. It was three years old. *God, I hope they're still good.* She popped two to be sure. She was starting to feel dizzy from the weight pressing down on her.

The perfect storm was brewing, creeping in, biding its time before consuming Cassie Bryant. A cornucopia of things swirled around and mixed in her brain: the cold pills, the aspirin, the Valium pills meant to settle her, the tension from the plane trip, the stress of the car drive, and the earth-shattering news. Stirring it all was the fatigue from lack of sleep the previous night, and the extra wine absently consumed due to a distracted mind.

She returned to the study, and they chatted a bit more. Ten thirty was upon them, and she was wrecked from the long flight, the long drive, and the long day. They made arrangements to meet for lunch at one the next day in the hotel dining room.

Dan walked her out to her car. Nervous himself, he failed to notice Cassie's condition; he wrote it off to exhaustion and surprise from the news he had just given. Scanning the area, he cautioned her, "Drive slowly." The early drizzle had progressed to a windy rain. "Remember, there are no streetlights around here, and it's a narrow, windy road going down the hill. Be careful."

When she reached the bottom of the drive, Cassie stopped before turning left onto the road. Woozy now, it was finally hitting her. Hard. She almost leaned forward to rest her head on the steering wheel. The perfect storm was about to pounce.

She drove very slowly down the hill, mimicking the speed of her head and body. The rain intensified. The wipers tried to keep pace with the cascade of water obscuring her view. Bends in the road were hard to see. Hunched over the steering wheel, she was managing—barely.

As she neared the bottom of the hill, approaching the last bend around the lake, the perfect storm crushed down on Cassie's splitting head. Her foot slid off the brakes. Momentum already at a minimum, the car moved in slow motion toward the right shoulder. It slipped neatly through the two wooden posts that marked the entrance to the allotments' small gravel parking lot. Snails had time to get out of her way. At the far edge of the lot, a grand old cedar tree tried to swing her hips out of the way, but naturally couldn't. A sigh of relief whispered through her branches as Cassie missed by inches.

The car nuzzled its way through the chicken wire fence that surrounded the allotments to protect them from deer. A last gasp took the car six feet down a slight embankment where it assassinated several tomato plants and dinged a corner of the stately greenhouse, breaking several of the white painted glass panels. Spent, stuck in the mud, the car surrendered and stalled.

Chapter Four

At the bottom of the hill from Dan and Rita's, right where the road curved around the lake, a mismatched row of six allotment sheds stood sentry over their modest farming plots next to the old, white-glassed greenhouse. Some were prefab, some hand built. They varied in size from a basic four-foot by eight-foot tool storage unit up to Cliff Walker's twelve-by-twelve mansion.

The community gardens had been set aside for the valley residents soon after the hotel went up. A British family had started calling them allotments in the 1940s, during the Victory Garden era, and the name had stuck ever since.

Cliff and his dog, Tank, had spent the afternoon and evening cleaning up the outside growing beds and the small metal-roofed allotment shack for the coming late fall and winter. Hours of work went into repairing irrigation pipes outside and the heating system in the greenhouse next door before the winter snow. Everything was now ready for the approaching cold.

Cliff stood in the doorway watching the dog sniff around the growing beds searching for one of his balls as raindrops started falling. "Come on, Tank. Inside. It's time for dinner."

It had been a long day and several hours of work remained, but a break was long overdue. Cliff's day job had been brutal lately, denying him time to maintain things at the allotment. Tired now, he was going to take some me time.

The soup simmering on the two-burner hot plate was ready. With the dog fed, Cliff unfolded the lone plastic chair and sat at his makeshift table of an orange crate with a piece of plywood on top. Muscles relaxed as he ate his soup. *Finally,* he thought, *peace and quiet. No more people grinding on me for the weekend.* Just a few easy things in the morning and then his lounge chair, football, and *Game of Thrones* reruns would be waiting for him at home.

His back was acting up a bit and he decided to lie down for an hour and read with no distractions. He rummaged through his camping gear in the corner and pulled out his sleeping bag. A folding aluminum cot was unhooked from a ceiling rafter and laid out in front of the small pot-bellied stove radiating warmth into the room. A new espionage novel by Mick Herron had been delivered earlier in the day from Amazon. The first decent autumn rain was music as it spattered off the metal roof. Eight thirty. Time to let Tank out for a quick pee and then relax with the book and another beer before getting back to it for a few more hours.

The camp light on the stool beside the cot gave sufficient light to read by. Boots and flannel shirt off, he laid his weary six-foot, one-inch frame down for a well-earned break, comfortable in his unzipped sleeping bag. Tank curled up a few feet away on his mat.

Suddenly, headlights flashed across the single makeshift window of the allotment shed. Tank jumped up and started barking. The headlights bounced up and down and stilled. Glass broke, and a car sputtered.

Cliff jumped up, pulled on his boots and jacket, snatched his flashlight off the workbench, and rushed to the door. The twenty feet to the near edge of the greenhouse were covered quickly; seconds more had him at the other side below the parking lot. Headlights bounced off of the unbroken glass panels of the greenhouse, illuminating the scene.

Stopping a few feet in front of the car, he shined the flashlight through the rain onto the figure of a woman stumbling unsteadily out of the driver's door. She was all dressed up as if she'd been to a party. Disheveled, long dark hair falling everywhere, the heavy rain dripped off her.

The woman stood facing him, a zoned-out look on her face, with one hand reaching back on the open door, an attempt to maintain her balance as she swayed slightly.

Cliff thought she looked like a woman who hadn't remembered her safe word. Her pale face matched the color of the white car. The woman bobbed up and down in small spasmodic motions like her knees were telling her they weren't quite up to the job.

He could see her unfocused eyes trying to zero in on him through the flashlight's beam. In a high-octave, slurred voice, she said, "I'm *supposed* to be in New York. I'm *supposed* to be the general manager."

Speech over, her eyes rolled back in her head. Her head rolled back to match them. Cliff figured the only reason she was still standing was because she hadn't decided which way to fall.

Then she did.

The woman slowly sank to her knees, her collapse broken by a few inches of muddy mulch in the garden plot. The grand finale ended with her upper torso falling forward on top of one and in between two other tomato plants.

Cliff thought the sound of the rain and wind bouncing off the surviving tomato plants sounded like a roar of approval—in all, a truly brilliant performance.

Christ on a bike!

Cliff ran over, reached down, and turned the stranger on her side so she could breathe. Synapses firing away, he reviewed the scene in his mind. She had nothing broken; she was mobile when she exited the car. She couldn't have hit her head; from the scene, the vehicle couldn't have been doing but a couple of miles an hour, and the airbag hadn't even released.

He decided quickly to get her out of the mulch and lashing rain. It was cold out, and she only had on some kind of fancy thin sweater over what looked like a pricey dress. He lifted her into his arms and carried her the short distance back to the shed. Once inside, he saw that her front was literally covered head to toe in muddy mulch, not so bad on the sides and back. No towel was going to wipe this off. She was soaking wet already, so he hauled her back outside the door to the nearby hose. Propping her up against the wall as best he could with one hand, he gave her a quick spray to get the bulk of the muck off and muscled her back inside.

Drenched, he knew he had to get her dry and warm quickly. Hesitating, he evaluated the situation, but knew he didn't have a choice. The dress came off, revealing frilly, green, weapons-grade underwear. That's how he would slip her into the sleeping bag. Wet or not, he wasn't about to remove *them*. He grabbed a nearby rag and wiped off most of the water. She wouldn't catch pneumonia from damp, skimpy underwear.

Slipping her into the sleeping bag on the cot, Cliff couldn't help but notice the flawless pale skin, the body's subtle curves. After all, he was a man. She had been easy to carry. He estimated the woman to be about five foot six or seven inches tall, slim, and light. He also noted the beautiful, shiny, black hair, and soft, long-fingered hands with painted and well-cared-for nails. Between the clothes, the hair, and the nails, he deduced that this woman had a few bucks and took care of herself. And she definitely wasn't from around here.

Cliff spread her dress and sweater out on the battered chair by the pot-bellied stove to dry. Satisfied that she was safe for the moment, he went back out, reexamined the scene, and turned off the ignition and headlights.

He thought about taking her to the hospital. It was a half hour away, more like forty-five minutes in this rain. Reentering the shed, the woman was snoring—a child wrapped in its baby blanket, comfy and oblivious to the world. He'd seen no cuts or bruising earlier: no need for a hospital trip; she was just drunk. More like completely toasted. It must have been a hell of a party.

She'd stay the night or until she came around. He had no idea who she was or where she was staying, and he couldn't very well go casually knocking on doors with this woman draped over his shoulder asking, "Do you recognize this person?"

He went back to the greenhouse where there was a stack of burlap bags.

Back in the shed, Tank watched while he fashioned himself a bed for himself on the floor.

*

Cliff woke early to the first rays of the rising sun coming through the window. The storm had passed. The woman was still out, but at least she wasn't snoring. He put water on for tea before grabbing his jacket and going out to check the damage done the night before.

He took pictures with his phone. Nothing major, thank God. After checking the exterior of the car, Cliff got in and rummaged through the glove compartment. He found a rental agreement and a driver's license.

Who leaves their driver's license in the glove compartment?

The woman was Cassie Bryant from New York City, age thirty-one.

His four-wheel-drive pickup truck was just above in the small gravel parking lot. It cranked to life, and Cliff positioned it above the woman's car. He spun the cable winch out and connected it to the vehicle. It easily pulled the car up the small incline. It now looked as if it had been correctly parked, except for the absent fence in front of it. The entire process took less than fifteen minutes. Cliff didn't want everyone seeing that the car had hit the fence and the greenhouse. It was a small town, and gossip tended to magnify itself.

Back inside, he made two cups of tea. Black would have to do for the Demon Driver of Manor Valley; there was no milk or sugar. He couldn't resist taking a picture of her, a child still wrapped up in her comfy sleeping bag, oblivious to the world. He sat with his tea and watched the patient.

She stirred. Light through the window, the sound of birds in the trees, and unfamiliar smells must be registering. Eyes opened. Cliff and his big smile were there to welcome Cassie back. "Good morning. Don't panic. You had a small accident last night and then decided to take a mud bath in my yard. How do you feel?"

Recognition of her surroundings registered. Cliff saw confusion and alarm shimmering across her face. She flinched when she turned and saw a massive dog lying beside her with an inquisitive look on its face. Tank had sensed that something was wrong with the female human and had been standing guard over her all night.

The woman, Cassie, glanced from the dog to the room. She looked up at Cliff, pain oozing off her face. "Who are you, and why am I in this hovel?"

"Hovel? That's a little cruel." Cliff swept his hand around the room. "It's an allotment shed. Historically accurate. An architectural jewel."

The confusion was not going away. He watched as Cassie glanced at her dress neatly folded on a stool to the side. Panic was getting ready to knock. She discreetly lifted the flap of the sleeping bag a few inches and seemed relieved that her underwear was still on.

"Don't worry," he said. "Nothing happened. You were soaking wet and I had to get you dry and warm."

A hand raised in Cliff's face, palm out like a veteran traffic cop. "Stop. What happened last night? Who are you? And how did I get here?"

A somber, serious mask replaced his smile. Why not have a little fun with this out-of-towner? Recklessly driving around while on a mega bender—she deserved it. "Are you Cassie Bryant from New York City, age thirty-one?"

"Yes, how do you know that?"

Ignoring the question—that's what the cops did on TV—Cliff continued, solemnly summarizing the situation. "Well, you've got a problem, a *big* problem. It seems you were *racing* down the hill in your car late last night, intent on your mission. You're obviously well trained. You aimed perfectly at our *maximum-security* fence and crashed through. You then *murdered* a large section of agriculture and finished your attack by *annihilating* a historically preserved town structure. Fortunately, no lives were lost."

Eyes were wide open now. Even her mouth was gaping.

"I've opted not to call the sheriff—there's no reason to make a big scene out of this. It's a small town. Why don't you get dressed now, and I'll quietly drive you down to the sheriff's office where they can get you fingerprinted, take your mug shot, and have you booked. Then they can get you shipped off to Washington before anyone even finds out."

New York defiance pushed past the confusion. "Mug shot? Booked? Washington? What the hell are you even talking about?" Not sounding as confident as it should.

"Well, this was obviously a well-orchestrated, blatant attack on the great American agricultural industry."

"I remember nothing about attacking agriculture. Why am I getting arrested?"

"Ha! I'm sure that's how all you terrorist trainees start. First something small like this, and then what? The entire California wine crop? The wheat harvest in the Midwest? No, no. Ecoterrorism doesn't go down well around here. I'm sure Homeland Security can sort it out once they have you in Washington. You know, find out about the other members of your cell, stuff like that."

"Ecoterrorism?"

Confusion was evident on her face. He sensed she remembered nothing of the night before. Tears started welling up in her eyes. She began to shake. Cliff knew he had gone too far.

"Whoa! Whoa! I was only kidding. You're good. There isn't any problem. You just had a minor accident. Everything is going to be fine. I'm sorry. I'm sorry." All orchestrated with a symphony of placating gestures. "Relax. Look, I even have some tea ready for you." He motioned to the dress folded by her head. "Your dress is dry. I'll go outside for a bit. Take your time, get dressed, and I'll explain everything while I drive you to the hotel. Unfortunately, your car isn't going anywhere right now." As he went out the door, he said over his shoulder, "My name's Cliff, by the way."

After thinking about it during the night, he figured she must be one of Dan Weaver's people from back East out for the meetings. She must work for one of the hotels. From the driver's license, it was obviously in New York. This was not a country girl. The last time she saw a tree, it was probably painted on the side of a red brick building.

The woman grappled for some dignity. "I'll just call for an Uber."

Cliff laughed to himself as he made for the door. "There's no Uber here. I'll get you a Lyft." Watching this woman was more entertaining than watching *Game of Thrones* reruns.

Chapter Five

*H*orrible man*, thought Cassie as she fumbled to her feet and watched him giggle his way outside, bathing in the amusement value her ordeal gave him. Unsteady—her head felt like someone was moving furniture around in it—she put on her clothes. God, they were a mess.

What the hell happened last night? Why am I almost naked? What accident?

The creature with the appalling sense of humor came back in.

"Have you seen my shoes?" she asked.

"They must have come off while you were taking your mud bath last night. I'll look for them later, as soon as things dry out."

Mud bath?

Cassie, again attempting to regain some dignity, declared that she was ready and staggered to the weather-beaten door. She would have held her head high if it wasn't killing her. The man—Cliff, he'd said his name was—stood there with an amused smile on his face. Exiting the shed, she shrieked loudly and crashed back through the door, almost knocking over the man behind her.

Thirty feet away, defiantly standing in one of the neighboring allotment patches and banqueting on some plant leaves, stood a massive buck deer. Standing at a side view, frozen in place with his head held high and turned toward them, he was regal and magnificent in the low, rising morning mist after the rain. Massive antlers were motionless on his head like a crown, proclaiming his royalty among the species, as he stared them down.

Cassie had never seen a live deer and ducked behind Cliff's back. "He's not going to hurt us, is he?"

Cliff glanced over his shoulder at Cassie. "He probably wants to buy you a present for knocking down the fence."

Cassie nervously scanned the area. She looked at the backwoodsman, down at the massive dog being held back by the backwoodsman, and then to the monster deer in front of the backwoodsman. "How many other vicious predators live around here?"

Cliff shrugged his shoulders. "I'll go back in and get my gun. *You* should probably shoot him. He could be a witness if Homeland Security questions him."

"WHAT!"

Cliff snorted in amusement. "Come on, let's get you back to the hotel."

He led her to the edge of the greenhouse and pointed out the furrows in the ground from her stalled car. Then he directed her in front of him up the curved gravel path, which normal people used to access the plots from the parking lot. After a few laborious steps, Cassie flinched. Her shoes were lost somewhere in the mud, and her bare feet were suffering on the sharp gravel.

Behind her she heard, "I should carry you. Your feet will get cut up."

She turned back to the man. Arms shot out at him with straight fingers on both hands, a karate move they taught to seven-year-olds. "Don't touch me! I'm trained."

Both arms raised in surrender. "Okay, but yesterday we killed an eight-foot-long rattlesnake on this path. Venom is probably all over the gravel. If you step in that with scratched feet—well, it's a slow, agonizing death."

She almost jumped into his arms.

Cassie looked around as he carried her toward his truck. "Where's my Lyft ride?"

"I'm it. I'm giving you a *lift* back to the hotel. There is no Uber or Lyft around here."

After she was ensconced in the truck and Cliff had turned on the heater, he pointed out her route the previous night, sweeping his hand around to highlight the devastation she had inflicted on the area. She thought he looked like he was conducting an orchestra with all the drama he was stuffing into the story.

"I pulled your car out early this morning, so any passers-by wouldn't be making a big fuss out of this. I think we can safely assume there will be no criminal damages, no incarceration. You will be accountable for the substantial property damage. It could run into the thousands."

Incarceration? Thousands in damages?

As he put the truck in motion, Cassie surveyed the scene. Comprehension of what happened the previous night slowly sorted itself out in her mind. None of it even remotely on the level that this man was trying to assign to her. Her wits were returning.

"It looks to me like I knocked down a wooden post with some kind of screen on it, ran over a few tomato plants, and broke a couple of white glass panes on that so-called 'historic' greenhouse. Where does 'in the thousands' come from?"

'You're a city girl, aren't you?"

"I am." Defiant.

"Well, that fencing is not a screen. It's chicken wire. Very expensive. Imported from France. And those small white glass panes on the greenhouse, special thermal hand-blown glass from Denmark, also costly."

Chicken wire from France? Old painted glass from Denmark? Does this moron think I'm an idiot?

The suppressed directness of a born-and-bred New Yorker was forcing its way through the polish and veneer of Cassie's carefully crafted life.

Best to keep quiet until I figure out what the hell is going on.

As they drove along the empty, early morning road, she asked, "How do you know where I'm staying?"

"There's only one hotel here. Not real tough."

She sat up straight. She would not humiliate herself by yielding to the temptation of looking in the rearview mirror. That would only earn her another rude comment. The coming walk of shame through the massive lobby permeated her thoughts. An assortment of guests' remarks jostled in her head: "She looks like a wild one." "That girl knows how to party." "Who dug her up?"

Hell on earth was interrupted by the man beside her. It was as if he could read her mind. Maybe he was one of those backwoods shamans.

"I'll drive you around to the side service entrance. Walk down the hall, and you'll see the service elevator on your left. It's before the kitchen door. You might get lucky, and no one will see you."

Christ, do I look that bad?

"Later today, after I check out your car, I'll leave a message for Cassie Bryant from New York City, age thirty-one."

*

As soon as she fastened the security lock on the door, Cassie bolted straight for the bathroom. The mirror. She needed a mirror.

Oh my God! Her beautiful black hair was flecked with mud and hanging all over the place. The expensive dress trashed. Makeup was everywhere but on her face. Her expensive Louboutin shoes lost in the mud, never to be seen again. *What is that red stain all over my chest? Is that blood? Jesus wept! No. I really fell on top of some damned tomatoes.*

That man. His parents probably found him in a dumpster. She didn't know whether to kill him for his questionable help or kiss him for suggesting the service elevator. She should be safe; this catastrophe could never get out. He was obviously some local itinerant squatting in that vile shack. It was so small you'd have to go outside to change your mind, and the only way to clean it would be arson. He'd acted like he owned the place. She thought it might be the dog's house, but why would a dog need a hot plate and a cot?

Focus returned to the mirror. Time for another chitchat. She forced a smile and addressed her reflection. "Talk about making an impression, Cassie! Compared to other national disasters, this one is right up there with 'Well, aside from that, Mrs. Lincoln, what did you think of the play?'" Her scowl returned as she leaned closer, holding the edge of the sink with both hands, and continued. "How do you spell mortified? Come on, Cassie. You can do it. Mortified, M – O – R – T – I – F – I – E – D, mortified. Good girl."

She raised one hand and shook a finger at herself. "Wait. Today, Cassie, you even get to use a capital *M* in front. Now, should we try some synonyms? How about *humiliated* to start? Why not add *disgraced*? *Catastrophe* would be a good one to wear."

Suddenly, she bolted for the bed and her bag. *How did he know I was Cassie Bryant from New York City, age thirty-one?* He must have gone through her bag and the car. She upended the bag on the bed and checked for anything missing. A glimpse of the man and his vicious attack dog bounced off her synapses. A seasoned member of the New York City community, Cassie knew the odds of any cash being there was negligible. But, there it was, the wallet with credit cards and cash. Also, her unread book from the flight, her mobile phone, and even her can of pepper spray bought off the internet—a necessity in New York when she worked late, which was most of the time. All there.

Huh.

It was only nine o'clock in the morning: four hours until lunch with the boss downstairs. Back in the bathroom, Cassie shook her head at the image in front of her, expressing her disappointment. A couple of steps to turn on the shower, and then she undressed.

She felt like she'd fallen down the bad luck ladder and hit every rung on the way to the bottom. The shower helped, as did lying still on the bed for a half hour. She'd actually slept—crashed rather—the night before in the backwoods hovel, completely out for seven or eight hours. The headache diminished and she was surprised that she didn't feel that bad. Maybe the worst of it was over. Maybe crashing on some filthy hovel floor was a new leap in modern medicine. She dressed in a pair of deep-blue slacks and a white blouse with a sweater on top.

When she worked in the various hotels, before being placed in the corporate headquarters, Cassie never enjoyed taking breaks in her office. There were always distractions: the phone ringing, the emails her eyes would drift to, coworkers sticking their heads in with questions. She would head for the kitchen, have a fresh cup of coffee, steal a breakfast bun, settle herself on a stool, and chat with the chef and staff. The chefs took care of her, and she did likewise. Breaks like that helped clear her head for a few precious minutes.

This morning, she needed something in her stomach before lunch. There would be no aspirin, no pills, no alcohol, ever again; Cassie Bryant would tough it out. Armed with a fresh pack of tissues she left her room to seek out the kitchen. She'd introduce herself, a member of the company here for the meetings, and beg for some coffee.

Chapter Six

When she entered the kitchen, a stoutly built, gray-haired woman looked up, smiled, and asked, "May I help you, young lady?"

God, did everyone always smile in this place?

"Yes, please. My name is Cassie. I'm with the company back in New York, and I'm out for the meetings. I'm having lunch with Mr. Weaver at one, but I didn't want to take up a place in the dining room, and I wanted to see more of this grand hotel. Is there any chance I can get a cup of coffee and maybe a bun?"

The mention of Mr. Weaver said it all. Everyone in the hotel wanted to make an impression on the company people from back East. The stout woman motioned Cassie to a high table with six stools; it was a break area for the hotel staff.

"You sit right there, luv. I'll get you a cuppa. Some nice pastries should carry you over 'til lunch. It's a bit slow right now. My name is Ethel and I'm the chef. Do you mind if I join you? I'd love to get off my feet for a few minutes."

"I'd love the company," said Cassie.

Are those fresh cinnamon buns? Nobody has cinnamon buns like this anymore.

Conscious of her figure, Cassie decided on one. When she returned to the table there were two on her plate. *Oh my, how did that second one get there?*

She cast her eyes over the kitchen while she waited for Ethel and her coffee. Ultramodern, well-lit, with the latest equipment, the kitchen was spacious. Stainless steel sparkled everywhere. There was plenty of room to move about, unlike the cramped kitchens in New York. One of the cooks had just finished three tempting-looking breakfast plates and set them under the heat lamp for pickup. Another busied himself with prep work for lunch. The staff she observed going about their tasks all seemed young and energetic.

Ethel came with the coffee. "You look a little pale, luv. Coming down with the flu, are ya? Get this down ya, pet. Not like tea, but it'll do the job, perk you right up."

Don't I wish that was all it would take, thought Cassie.

"I'm impressed with the kitchen. It's all state of the art. Will it handle all the business from the new expansion?"

"Without a problem," said Ethel as she swept her hand around. "Mr. Weaver plans ahead. As soon as he got approval for the new wings, he started improving all this. I've been here twenty years, and, at my age, I was nervous about what all the new work would bring, but Mr. Weaver promised me I'd have lots of additional staff, and I'd even be able to relax a little. Told me I could leave the physical work to the young ones and focus on keeping the place running smoothly. He's a dream to work for."

Ethel was originally from London but had never been to New York. She peppered Cassie with questions about the city and the company's other hotels.

A voice coming from behind her said, "There's my Ethel. You've been at the beauty parlor again. I'm not going to let Hollywood steal you away from me. Look at what I've brought you."

A cardboard box full of tomatoes, leeks, and other goodies plopped down between the two women. A bundle of flowers found its way in front of Ethel.

Ethel beamed; Cassie almost threw up—it was *him.*

As he slipped into view she noticed he'd cleaned up. The stubbled face had been shaven. Hair combed. He wore clean Levi's and a flannel shirt. In his hands he carried some kind of orange vest like road crews used in New York, which he placed on the stool beside her before he—presumptuously, Cassie thought—sat opposite her. She logically deduced that he probably wore the vest at night while he was going about his business rummaging through trashcans, so a car wouldn't accidentally run him over.

"Oh, you're such a dear!" said Ethel. She nodded toward Cassie. "This is Cassie. She works for the company in New York. She's out for the big meetings. Cassie, this is Cliff. The biggest gentleman in the whole valley next to Mr. Weaver himself."

Gentleman? Who edited her dictionary?

She looked around the kitchen for something clean and quick. A cleaver? No, be realistic, a guillotine? *I can simply slip in my head, pull the lever, and this whole horror show would disappear.*

Cliff gave her a big grin. He dragged it out. "Cassie... from New York City... age about... nineteen... An absolute pleasure, Cassie." He extended his hand along with that sick grin. "You look familiar. Have we met before?"

"No, no. I don't think so."

Ethel laughed. "Ha! Nineteen! He's such a kidder."

Cliff's focus turned to the chef. "These will probably be the last of the vegetables for the season, Ethel. There would have been more, but the allotments were *attacked* last night." He glanced at Cassie. "Some *shifty characters* raided the plots, crushing plants and stealing tomatoes. They even broke some windows in the greenhouse."

"Oh, my. What's the world coming to? Well, you two sit here." She looked at Cassie. "I know what *he* wants with all his smooth talk. Food." She moved to the stove a few feet away.

Out of the corner of her eye, Cassie watched Cliff as he got up, helped himself to some coffee, grabbed some silverware nearby, and casually walked a few steps to another counter and grabbed the salt and pepper before sitting across from her again. He seemed to know where everything was, acting like he leased half of the kitchen.

Was there no security in this place? Could anyone just roam in off the streets and trade raw vegetables for a meal?

In a low voice, so Ethel couldn't hear, Cliff said, "So, you're Cassie Bryant from New York, age thirty-one. Is that Kassie with a *K*?"

Perplexed, Cassie had never heard of a Cassie with a *K*. Was this guy stuck on stupid or just a few fries short of a Happy Meal?

"With a *C*."

"Well, Cassie, how are you feeling after your recent ordeal?" he asked.

Pride be damned; might as well double up on the humiliation. "Please, you're not going to say anything, are you?"

"Relax. You had an unfortunate accident. No need to make a big thing out of it. Never happened as far as I'm concerned."

The gasp was almost audible. "Thank you. It's very important to me. I'm so embarrassed as it is. I don't need it compounded." Relief almost smothered her as hunched shoulders released from her neck.

Mortification returned, and she lowered her eyes and attention to her coffee and buns, unable to meet his eyes.

As Ethel turned from the stove, he smiled and quietly added, "Well, if I ever need one, you owe me a kidney."

Ethel rejoined them, set an omelet down in front of Cliff, patted his cheek, and wrapped her hands around her cup of coffee. Just then, Dan Weaver bounded in through the kitchen door.

"Good morning, everyone. Oh, great, Cassie. I see you two have already met." He glanced at Cliff. "Cassie met your parents last night." His attention was redirected to the chef. "I'm just getting a cup of coffee, Ethel. You stay right there. I'm going to work a bit in the office before Cassie and I have lunch."

Dan pulled down a mug from a nearby cabinet and poured his coffee. As he passed the table again, he said to Cassie, "You're mine today. Tomorrow, I hope I can talk Cliff into showing you around the valley. See you in the dining room in a bit."

God, this person is Mr. Walker's son? His father is Dan's best friend!

Cassie watched as Cliff vacuumed up his eggs. He then jumped up and helped himself to more coffee. "Not afraid to eat, is he?" Cassie asked Ethel.

"Poor lad's been under the cosh. It shows on him sometimes. He's even been working Saturdays for the last few months." Ethel smiled proudly. "It's my job to keep him healthy. That boy could eat for England."

Ethel might have been here for years, but the accent and idioms were foreign to Cassie. She asked. "Under the cosh?"

Cliff plopped himself down on his stool. "It means 'in a difficult situation' or just plain overloaded."

A probe wouldn't hurt, thought Cassie. The man had no idea about the job offer, and she had no idea how someone this free and easy could possibly be under any 'cosh,' whatever the hell that was. "Do you work here at the hotel?"

"Odd jobs here and there," he said as he gulped down his coffee and stole half a bun off her plate.

Nervous, not knowing what else to talk about, she said, "Well, I hope things are going well."

"What is it you people say in New York? Hunky-dory? Yeah, that's it. Well, everything is going hunky-dory."

Many years ago, Cassie had heard her father use the expression. From her political correctness training, and knowing her father, she knew it must be offensive to *some* group. Her father could offend a mailbox. She sat up straighter. "I've never said hunky-dory in my life."

That grin again. "Another of my feeble forays into humor, Ms. Bryant." With that, he winked at Ethel. "Got to go, ladies. Empires to build."

As he disappeared out the door, Ethel sighed. "What a fine young man. Isn't he a dream?"

More like a nightmare. "Yes, he seems delightful."

Chapter Seven

Her life so far in dear old Manor Valley could be slipped in somewhere between *C* for catastrophe and *D* for disaster. She didn't want to think about what the rest of the alphabet would yield. There was still time before lunch with Dan, and she needed some fresh air to help her rebound back to something resembling normal.

Outside, the weather was brisk. Fall was on them. Cassie wrapped her sweater around her and headed outside to get a good look at the exterior of the hotel. She'd been preoccupied with driving when she'd arrived the day before and wanted some privacy to gather her thoughts.

Smiling staff greeted her as she moved through the lobby and out the door. Arms folded across her chest, the breeze off the lake playing with her hair, she walked to the end of the circular entrance drive, looked both ways, and crossed the road. It was still about a hundred and fifty feet to the water's edge. She thought she'd never smelled air so fresh and clear. A paved path ran parallel with one of bare earth along the lake. Cassie noticed two horseback riders approaching on the dirt one and assumed the asphalt one was for walking, jogging, or biking. A manicured lawn as wide as the hotel covered the rest of the space. Back-to-back benches flanked by decorative shrubs were placed along the path, giving people the option to appreciate the beautiful lake or the grand old hotel. A mother and her toddler were feeding ducks on the grass by the water. In the distance, a couple was throwing a Frisbee for their dog. On one bench, a girl around high school age sat engrossed in doing a charcoal drawing of the hotel. Cassie chose another bench and studied the building.

She'd seen pictures of old Georgian-style structures like this. It was a grand country home snatched from an English TV show. Sure, back in New York, the Metropolitan Museum and other buildings were as elegant, but not like this: proud, alone, overseeing this beautiful landscape and lake. No horns, no buses, no sirens. Here, the whisper of the wind through the trees and the clopping of hooves from the horses passing behind her replaced the city's clamor. At home, multi-story buildings pressed up to each other, locked in acres of asphalt and concrete, being bullied by a forest of cranes and netted scaffolding pressed up against them.

Impressed. Definitely impressed. What she'd seen and heard about the hotel so far had an impact. She still did not understand what went on outside. God, move all this to New York, and she'd have signed up this afternoon.

Reality pushed the fine old building aside. The shock of it all muddled her thoughts: no new job as general manager in New York, this bizarre new offer on the table, and a decision needed to be made in the next few days. Could it get any worse? She had to pull herself together before lunch.

*

Dan swept a hand toward the dining room window facing the lake and far hills, keeping his eyes on Cassie. "I know all this out here, in this quiet valley, must seem bizarre to you. I'll give you a short history. It'll help as a starting point for you."

White tablecloths, sparkling silverware, and perfectly folded, high-quality linen napkins complemented the magnificent room. The ceiling had to be twenty feet high. Each table had a small flower arrangement off to the side. Beside them, antique-looking silver salt grinders had matching mini pepper grinders. The grouping looked like they'd been lifted from a Dutch still-life painting. The tables were spaced far apart, privacy assured. Cassie could imagine them pushed closer together during peak seasons. Ornate crown moldings framed the high ceiling and oversized moldings framed the windows and doorways, all done in white. Historic oil paintings hung from the period beige walls.

Dan Weaver let his eyes drift out the window as he began his story. "Some level of great-great-grandfather arrived here in the valley around 1855, near the end of the Gold Rush, about five years after California became a state. The transcontinental railroad opened between Sacramento and Omaha in 1869. No one knows exactly how he made his money: gold, timber, mining, a supplier to all the expansion, a combination—no one knows. He came from poverty in England and made a fortune here. Evidently, he always wanted a grand country house—the kind he would never be allowed to approach back in England when he was a child." Both hands opened to his sides. "He found this valley during his travels and built the building we're sitting in now. A realistic man, he knew it was remote and way too big for his needs. He lived in a large section but made it into a hotel, plus a hunting and fishing destination, for others in this middle region of California who had also prospered in the boom.

"The lake is over two miles long now. It was tiny at the time. Tall evergreen trees went right down to the water's edge. Ex-miners and Chinese railroad workers provided cheap labor. Massive trees were cut back across the flat area next to the lake, and partially up the hills. He dammed the small river at the lower end of the valley to create the lake you see now. All at the same time as they were building the house."

It fascinated Cassie. She watched Dan pause and sip his coffee. She also noticed that it was refilled immediately and silently. No 'Would you like a refill, sir?' No fuss, very discreet.

"Is all the surrounding land a state park?"

"No. After the First World War, when the concept of vacations became more widespread, the range of guests grew. Still affluent, but more bodies. By that time, the place had a reputation in San Francisco and even Los Angeles. Large-sized lots on the tree-covered lower hills were created. A few were sold off and built on. It also became a fall destination for the moneyed people in California who were from back East. Hunting and especially hiking were popular.

"After years in the area, when he started building, the man lost his taste for the ubiquitous evergreen trees. He replanted around the lake and up a distance on the hills with the deciduous trees of his youth. The ones he remembered from England, and those he saw in his few years back East. Some aspens and cottonwoods were the only deciduous trees in the area. He paid a fortune bringing in saplings of maples, chestnuts, sycamores, and others and planted them in the areas he had stripped. It's an autumn ring of brilliant color, a jeweled necklace around the lake. Hiking and riding trails wind their way around the entire valley. If you take the job, get blinds for your office window, or you won't get any work done for two months when the colors change."

The scene sounded lovely to Cassie until he snapped her out of it by mentioning *the job*. The job here—in nowhere California. God, couldn't he find something a little closer to civilization? A tent park around an oasis in the Sahara? Maybe a yurt retreat in Outer Mongolia?

Their food arrived. Silently. No 'Here you are, folks.' She watched the waiter. He set her dish down from the left, walked around the table, and did the same with Dan's. *God, did he just do that?* She had read about proper food service from years past. The rule was 'down on the left, up on the right.' She couldn't wait to see if he did it when they were finished.

"Enough of the history for now. You'll get more as we go. By the way, dinner tonight at our house. Rita wants you back, and I want more time to sell you before the meetings start on Tuesday."

He started his sales pitch. "The level of challenge around here, unlike the rest of the chain, goes far beyond the front door. But let's stick with the hotel for now. Unlike our other locations, this is a *destination resort* hotel. The old building is in great shape and will remain the same. It's geared to an older crowd: affluent, educated, with a sense of history. They like the old-world touches and the outdoors. The new wings are for the younger generations with money. As you can now see, they are a modern, understated design but do not take away from the old building's elegance. The wings are only two stories high—their exterior color and new plantings will help them disappear into the landscape. They don't have lake views. They *will have* all the amenities: state-of-the-art internet, full-service business center, and first-class spa and gym. Between the wings, at the back of the old structure, will be a large pool. Lake swimming doesn't appeal to youth these days.

"Cassie, bringing this all up to speed and maintaining the level of service will be a major challenge. Jim Hanson, the current manager, wanted to retire two years ago. Like me, he's not a kid, and the younger generations' needs and wants are, quite frankly, difficult for us to grasp. He promised to stay on until I found the right person for the job. Unfortunately, he's home recovering from an operation. He's close by and a phone call away. Most of the others in the company are older and have little marketing experience, especially with a facility like this. Six months ago, we brought in a new assistant manager, Justin Banks. He's young, twenty-seven, and energetic. He'll be a big help getting you up to speed if you take the job."

Cassie was keeping up so far.

"It gets even more complicated. We are very integrated with the small communities in a twenty-five-mile radius. Hell, to give you an example, if they come here for dinner, which few can afford, they show their driver's licenses and get a twenty percent discount. Many of them supply services to the hotel or the outside activities. Their kids work here. Local jobs are paramount to us."

Dan paused as the waiter arrived to clear the plates.

Wow, he actually walked those extra paces to pick up on the right.

Coffee arrived. Dan wrapped up his presentation. "One last thing for now before we take a tour. I'm going to work out a management agreement—not a sale—with the chain. We're going to include the hotel in the Frequent Stayer rewards program for the chain. It should thrill our customers. They can use the points for a nice vacation, and we'll be putting the hotel on the website. An investment is being made: it has to be repaid."

A quiet moment passed as they finished their coffee, taking in the view. Dan put his napkin down. "Let's go look around."

After a tour through the hotel, Dan walked Cassie out to the construction work outside. They stood on the rough concrete by the new, empty pool, and Dan swept his arms around at the two new wings. "You can see the exterior of the additions are finished. We're moving fast on the inside work."

Cliff was at the far end, wrapping up a talk with two other men. He walked over and addressed Dan. "Jim and Chris finished the gunite on the pool last week. They're starting the coping around the top today, so we're ready to do the stone patio whenever we want. With the cold coming and all the work going on out here, they don't recommend the final pool plasterwork until spring. I think they're right. What do you think?"

"I agree. Tell them we appreciate them getting the concrete and coping done." He smiled and turned to Cassie. "I couldn't have picked a better project manager. Cliff was born to do this. All the subcontractors love him. The two of you will be working closely together if I can talk you into taking the job."

Her face went blank. *Yes,* she thought, *absolutely, no question, definitely things could get worse.* This *person*—the hovel dweller, the meal scrounger, the terrorizer, was the *project manager* in charge of all this?

Snapping out of it, she looked at the face with the complacent grin.

The same two thoughts shot through the same two minds.

This is the man Dan entrusted with building this project?

This is the woman Dan wants to hand my baby off to after it's built?

*

Back in her room, a larger scope of knowledge lodged in her brain, Cassie lay down on the bed. Tempting. Very tempting. She felt like Eve toying with the apple in the Garden of Eden.

The elaborate dining room easily held its own with any high-end hotel in New York. The wine cellar, a real cellar carved into granite rock underground at one end of the basement, was another surprise. The spa, gym, and business center were just skeletons, but she got the idea.

The expansion would definitely be a challenge. Actually exciting. If she took the job, it would occupy all of her time. She could switch off any thoughts about dear old Herschel, that slimy pig. *Well, let's not go there right now.* Still, this was a foreign country to Cassie. She didn't even know if the place had a zip code. No friends, no family. Granted, she'd be working 24/7, but what would she do with her twenty minutes of free time each week? Skeet shooting? What the hell was a skeet? She'd seen polo on TV. That looked interesting. But then she'd have to get up on one of those massive hairy things with saddles on them. Kill that idea. Fly fishing? Get a life.

The gods allowed her a desperately needed nap before dinner. In the shower, she watched the water circling the drain. A premonition of her future life?

Cassie panicked slightly in the elevator. With everything else clogging her mind, the rental car had been forgotten. How would she get to Dan's house and back? How could she explain this away to Dan and Rita? When she reached the desk, they handed her a sealed note. "Cliff Walker left this for you, Ms. Bryant."

She moved a discreet distance off to the side and opened it.

Out front. Keys are in it.

I'll feel better if you have a staff member drive you around the curve by my allotment and greenhouse.

The car gleamed. He'd even washed it.

How did he know where I'd be going?

Uncomfortable with the credits young Mr. Walker was racking up, Cassie set off. When she reached the bend in the road, she noticed he'd repaired the imported French chicken-wire fence. Pieces of plywood covered the missing panes of hand-blown Danish glass. She scowled at the scene of her disgrace, tightened both hands on the wheel, and focused ahead.

Chapter Eight

Dan, Rita, Cassie, and Cliff moved to the dinner table. Rita had given Cliff a loving jab about how Ethel spoiled him.

"If the president stayed here, and some have over the years, Ethel would see that Cliff got *his* omelet before the president," said Dan as the four of them settled around the dinner table. He explained so Cassie would understand. "Cliff trades with the other people on the allotments and makes sure Ethel has a steady seasonal supply of fresh vegetables and herbs, and *he* has an endless supply of first-class meals."

Everyone laughed.

A large picture window opened another view into a picturesque hollow beside the Weavers' house. Cassie was glad her back wasn't to it. After the deer incident, she was fearful about what other wild creatures might come up, break the glass, and devour her. In New York, she only had to worry about burglars, who would take things when you weren't home and leave you alone. Out here in the wild, she knew the creatures wanted to take your liver, your heart, or your kidneys. It didn't take a genius to figure out why raccoons wore those little black masks. Weren't they the ones who stole lumber and built dams in the rivers?

Settled at the table, Cassie wasn't relaxing. Why was Cliff here? Would he let something slip? This had the potential of turning into a Titanic night. She forced herself to calm down and focus.

Cassie glanced at her right when Cliff asked her a question. It registered that it was the first time she had looked at him. Mortified earlier this morning at the allotment, she had kept her eyes cast down. Terrorized later on in the kitchen and meeting him again outside, she had looked anywhere but at him for fear of what he might say. Both incidents guaranteed minimal eye contact when she'd seen him on arrival tonight.

Now, she took in the disheveled, shortish, blonde hair, the clean-shaven face, tan from being outside in the wilderness, the fit figure from whatever kind of manual labor he performed—God, he picked me up like I was a twig off a tree. An appraisal now forced her to admit he was actually handsome, now that he'd shaved and had some clean clothes on. A shame his other attributes did not measure up: that outrageous relaxed attitude, that appalling sense of humor, the gross insensitivity to her plight the night before. She would maintain a more formal air with this one.

Dan looked at Cliff. "Speaking of the allotments, I saw you repairing the fence by the greenhouse. What happened?"

Some water caught in Cassie's throat. She grabbed her napkin to cover her mouth.

"Probably some teenagers partying, maybe a cell of ecoterrorists, or shifty undesirables. Not much damage. I'll need to have some custom-blown panes of glass flown in from Denmark for the greenhouse."

Dan and Rita laughed. Cassie suddenly focused on the view outside. She'd been promoted from ecoterrorist to shifty undesirable. Were there no limits to the depths she could sink? Was he going to pull the pin on the hand grenade and blow up last night here at the dinner table? *Change the subject—quick.*

"These potatoes in the cream sauce are delicious, Rita," said Cassie.

Cliff, seated to her left, said, "Not potatoes. It's real mountain food—baby fawn's ears with a sauce of wild boar snot and cream."

Cassie gave him a tolerant look, careful not to make it reprimanding, for fear of public revelations best left to rest.

Cliff was the son that Ethel never had. Cliff was the son that Dan and Rita never had. Since his childhood, they were all used to his warped sense of humor and loved it. He lit up any room he walked into.

Dan said, "It looks like you two have hit it off. Be careful of his humor, Cassie."

Cliff beamed. "Hit it off the minute we met this morning, Uncle Dan. Cassie's probably a little prankster herself."

Uncle Dan?

Cassie looked down at her dinner knife, wondering if it was sharp enough to slit her wrists. How far would the blood squirt? Would it gush and splash all over everyone at the table? Should she hold it over the soup bowl?

She pulled herself together and thought it time to get some answers. She had seen enough to ask some professional questions. A huge life decision would be made in the next few days. A ton more information was needed.

"I've yet to see a maid's cart in the hallway. When do they clean the rooms?"

Dan set down his fork. "You'll love this. We borrowed it, years ago, from a few of the posh, old English hotels. Each of the four floors in the main hotel has a maid's room by the service elevator. When people come down for breakfast, they are recognized by the staff. This is a small hotel. The fact that they're eating is relayed from the dining room to each maid's room, and we do some cleaning then. Otherwise, the staff keeps a watchful eye on their comings and goings. No carts are littering the halls. Everything is hand-carried to the rooms. All very understated. The new wings, unfortunately, will have the usual carts.

"You'll appreciate that we also don't apply the quota of rooms a maid must do in a day like normal hotels. You've seen your room—lots of pillows, comforters, and blankets. It's heavy, hard work. Think about my earlier comments about the community. We want to keep our employees as happy as our customers—no backbreaking work at minimum wage. Our people are invested in client services. We recheck all the rooms in the late afternoon and evening. If a bed needs to be remade after a nap, it is. In the evening, if the clients are out, the beds are turned down and chocolates are placed on the nightstand."

God, am I on a different planet?

More questions were put forth about the operations and answered before Cassie realized all the talk had been about the hotel. One last point and she'd change the subject.

"The wine cellar impressed me," said Cassie. "It's massive. There must be a fortune down there."

Dan said, "There is. The only keys beside the manager's and the maitre d's are with me, Rita, and Cliff's father—a perk he has for being a lifelong friend and watching out for things around here when I'm gone so often." He smiled. "Thankfully, Cliff drinks beer."

A thought struck. Cassie remembered her dress, deceased now because of rain, tomato stains, and mud. *Did he really spray me down with a hose?*

"Rita, I need a new dress for the meetings. One of mine is stained. Is there any place nearby?"

"Oh, did something happen to your dress?" asked Cliff, now all Mister Concerned.

Cassie stiffened. If the night continued like this, she'd need a chiropractor to sledgehammer out the tense muscles knotting up in her neck and shoulders. "Probably just some red wine from the last time I wore it."

"I did that to a white shirt once," said Cliff. "It wasn't that deep *tomato* red, more like a pink. Is that what happened to your dress?"

A slight blush confined itself to her neck. Cassie wondered if that big buck deer from this morning would be interested in taking a contract to kill this person.

She pictured it in her head—those massive horns pinning him to a tree, grinding away deeper and deeper, antlering him to death. She'd be sitting on a stool off to the side, listening to him screaming and flailing his arms. "Please, please, Cassie Bryant from New York City, age thirty-one, forgive me!" Blood would be squirting everywhere and dripping down the tree bark while she casually picked some lettuce off her teeth from her pastrami sandwich.

She turned and gave Cliff a big, satisfied smile.

Thankfully, Rita jumped in before she could respond about the dress. "Oh, yes. You can try Mellissa's Fashions in Auburn. You can be there in less than forty-five minutes. If you can't find something there, Sacramento is just a little farther." She turned to Cliff. "I'm busy tomorrow. Can you take Cassie down to Auburn?"

Cliff smiled. "I'm your guy, Cassie. Anything for Aunt Rita and Uncle Dan. We'll do the outside tour in the morning, like Dan wants, and I'll run you down in the afternoon."

The evening wound down and Dan said, "Cliff, can you help Rita clear the table? I want a few words with Cassie."

They retreated to the study.

"I know this job thing is a shock to you, Cassie. Please let me lay out some more thoughts." Dan shifted to get comfortable. It was time to highlight some of the pluses. "You are not trapped out here. You can go home regularly. I know your family is important to you. It's nearly October now. You're going home after the meetings. Thanksgiving is in a month, and Christmas the month after that. Heck, you can go back for long weekends every month. Do this for me for the two years, and you can be executive vice-president in New York after that. I'm going to be stepping back soon. Rita and I want more free time together. The whole thing can be yours." He then threw an obscene salary at her. "Don't say anything now. Give it a few more days to get the idea of what goes on around here. Think about the changes necessary to bring us into the modern age after all this construction is done. I know it's no easy task I'm asking you to do."

Cassie shifted in her chair, focused now, armed with more information than the night before. "Dan, this hotel is a quantum leap from what I'm used to with the modest hotels back East. The restaurant, wine cellar, spa, gym, pool? And I don't even know what these 'outside operations' that you talk about are." She sat back and waved a dismissive hand. "I don't think I'm qualified for something this large with such a high level of service."

"That's exactly why I want *you*. You are qualified. You're creative, responsible, energetic, and bright. Most important is that we work well together. I'm not throwing you to the wolves. I'll be spending more time here, and I'm only a phone call away, just like when you were learning back East. Yes, there is a learning curve, but you'll get past that quickly. Tomorrow, Cliff will make all the outside operations clear. Justin, Cliff, and I can get you up to speed in no time. I need your creativity and management skills for the future.

"One more thing," said Dan. "If you take the job, you'll stay in our guest house. It's a one-bedroom with a kitchen and living room. You can't see it from here. It's down a dip where the driveway continues past the house. Very private." He paused, remembering another item on his checklist. "And we'll get you a car. Subway service is spotty around here."

*

Back in her room, Cassie took an Excedrin PM to help her sleep. The flu was dissipating, and her head felt like it was returning to earth. The exhaustion from the previous night's ordeal, compounded by the long day, caught up with her as she pulled the down comforter up to her neck.

Way too tempting, she thought. Traveling home whenever she chose took one of the significant edges off her reluctance. If she performed, the other side of purgatory, in two years, would earn her a quantum leap in her career. The added pay incentive still shocked her. She pictured the expanded size of the condo awaiting her on the Upper East Side. No romantic ties to worry about—Herschel might have done her a favor by dumping her. Tomorrow she'd discover more about the small town and whatever the hell 'outside activities' were. Pitch and putt? Miniature golf complete with the windmill like at Coney Island? Maybe that game where you throw sacks of sand through a hole in a piece of plywood? Out here in John Wayne country, one of them had to be horseshoes. Hopscotch? Competitive skip rope?

Her head shifted on the pillow. She realized she had no 'outside activities' in her own life—no hobbies, no outside interests, just work. Being dragged off by Vivien to various openings, charity functions, and fundraisers were the high points of her social life. Otherwise, it was subway-work and subway-home. That would have to change too if she were to take the job and keep her sanity.

Chapter Nine

Cliff had chosen ten o'clock intentionally. The night before, he'd noticed that Cassie was exhausted. Not quite on the level of an eighty-year-old grandmother shuffling home in the pouring rain after a two-hour funeral, but not far behind. Let the poor thing sleep in. Get some breakfast into her first at the restaurant in town and then do the tour. She reminded him of a fawn: alert, nervous, struggling to comprehend an unfamiliar environment. Today he'd try to notch back his sense of humor, get her to relax a little, maybe even enjoy herself. Dan was counting on him to help win her over. The valley had given her a rough start, and he'd contributed his share. She was waiting in front when he drove up.

The Mall, as the locals called it, was on the lakeside of the road a few minutes from the hotel. It consisted of two large barn-style buildings joined together years ago by a twenty-foot, glass-covered walkway between them. They stopped in the spotless, beautifully planted parking lot beside the nearest structure. As they walked to the first building entrance, Cassie gestured to the row of locked dumpsters lined up against the wall.

"Do people steal trash around here? Why the locks?"

"Bears. The dumpsters have to be metal, sturdy, and locked. They'd shred wooden containers or trash bins just to get at any scraps inside. Never leave food in your car overnight. They know how to open car doors, or they'll break your window. Unknowing tourists find out the hard way."

The look on the city girl's face was priceless.

Not pausing, they walked straight past the little shops and stands inside the first building to the restaurant at the back. Tables were lined up all along large windows overlooking the deck outside and the lake beyond. It was late September, the large summer crowds were gone, and half of the deck dining furniture had been placed in storage for the coming winter.

Cassie scanned the menu. "Eggs Benedict? You have eggs Benedict here?"

"Yeah. Unfortunately, raccoon is out of season."

Raccoon? said the look on her face.

"Okay, let's get you oriented," said Cliff. "Time for our New Yorker to have a laugh on us." He swept his hand around. "We call these two old buildings the Mall."

Cassie almost spit out the coffee she was sipping. "The Mall! Where's the Louis Vuitton and Chanel—in the other building?"

Good for her, thought Cliff—*finally a smile and a laugh.* "We'll look around after breakfast, but right now I want to go over what Dan called our 'outside activities' and some of the restrictions put on the use of the lake and the surrounding areas."

Their eggs Benedict arrived. Cliff noticed Cassie was enthralled by the lake view, watching two distant canoes paddling side by side against the background of changing fall colors on the far slopes. He thought he'd start there.

"Boats—visitors can bring their own, or we have a rental concession down at the end of the lake where you drove into town. No powerboats or jet skis allowed. In winter, no snowmobiles. We don't want the constant noise bouncing off the surrounding hills, disturbing the peace and quiet. The hotel leases out the concession to maintain control and quality. They rent small sailboats, kayaks, rowing shells, canoes, even rowboats. In summer, local college kids give lessons to earn some money for school. Next to the concession is a loading ramp. Beside that is a large RV park where guests can rent space. We don't want the RVs constantly driving through town. There are several small beaches around the lake for sunbathing, picnics, and swimming. Some are only accessible by boat. The boat concession is responsible for keeping them all clean. A large section on the lake's far side where the stream comes in is marked off limits by buoys—no boats allowed. It's great for fishing, and we stock it each year to make it a fruitful experience. Parents love taking their kids there. Well, that's it for the lake activities."

Cliff stopped briefly to enjoy his breakfast. He observed that Cassie registered everything. She must be in business mode. Questions would probably come later, so he got back to it. "All the shops and services in town serve the surrounding area for a ten-mile radius. These two buildings plus the small shops on the other side of the street are supported by the locals, as well as the tourists and guests. We have various seasonal activities and promotions to keep them coming back.

"In a hollow opposite the allotments, at the other end of the lake, is a large area of stables and horse training rings. It's another concession rented by the hotel. They rent horses for riding on the trails up in the hills and rent stalls for locals and nearby residents. The trails are all owned by the hotel, and we see to their maintenance. Horse competitions go on from spring through fall. They're great for business here at the Mall."

Breakfast finished, they went on a tour of the Mall. Small shops and moveable stands filled the space. It was Sunday, and even though it was the slow time between summer and winter tourists and hotel guests, the place was busy. An event was going on at the stables, and the hikers were arriving for the fall colors.

Cassie looked up at the massive, exposed beams and joists three stories in the air. "Why are those beams so big? You could hold up a skyscraper with them."

"Snow. They span a vast area and have to hold the weight of the winter snows. Don't forget, we're in the middle of a forest. Back when they built these buildings, lumber was nearby and cheap."

He continued Cassie's introduction to the valley. "The portable stands are for the locals in the surrounding area who come and sell their arts and crafts. The hotel owns these two buildings. Locals get preference, and they can rent stalls just for a weekend. During hard times, like recessions, Dan sees that none of the permanent shop tenants get evicted because they can't pay the rent. He's very aware of the interdependence we have on each other."

They moved through the passageway to the second building. Cassie stopped at one stand offering handmade wool scarves, hats, and sweaters. Cliff noticed his sister, Lily, standing outside her shop and walked ahead to talk to her.

"Who's that, brother dear?'

"One of Uncle Dan's from back East."

Cassie approached a few moments later.

"Cassie, this is my sister, Lily. Cassie is here from New York for Uncle Dan's meeting." Cliff pointed to the shop behind them. "Come on in, Cassie. This is Lily's shop."

Lily smiled warmly. "Nice to meet you, Cassie. Everyone is excited about Uncle Dan's big meeting. We hope you'll all find time to come over here and support the local economy." She looked down at the bag with the new wool scarf sticking out. "I see you already have."

"Is business good?" asked Cassie.

"We'll be swamped in the next few weeks with hikers coming to see the fall colors. We get a lot of people escaping Sacramento for the day. The hotel is a great client. We supply all the flowers and small chocolate boxes for the guest rooms, and the flowers in the dining room."

"Yes, I saw that magnificent display in the lobby. It rivals anything I've ever seen. It's breathtaking."

Lily beamed at the compliment. "Thank you."

"Lily employs high school kids on weekends and afternoons when they're out of school," said Cliff. "She spends a lot of time at her greenhouse next to the allotments on the way to Dan's. You remember seeing the greenhouse, don't you, Cassie?"

Cassie studiously ignored him, giving Lily her rapt attention as she explained, "We grow a lot of the flowers we need. The rest we buy from growers down in the Sacramento Valley. Local artisans in a neighboring valley make some chocolates, soaps and candles—some we import."

Cliff checked his watch. Time was pressing. "Well, we need to move. Got a lot to see."

He noticed Cassie's eyes drift to the back of this second building as they left the shop. A grand view over the lake mimicked the other building where the restaurant was. This building had a large, casual seating area with sofas, chairs, and various-sized tables. A giant stone fireplace of rounded stacked river rock interrupted the lake view in the center of the back wall. A crackling fire threw out an invitation to all.

She gave Cliff a questioning look. "What's that area for?"

"A break area for people who don't want a full meal in the restaurant." He poked a hand over his shoulder. "Supports the bakery and the coffee stand, and it has free high-speed internet. Locals and hotel guests flock to it when they need to get out or meet some friends. Probably like a giant Starbucks in New York. The bakery also makes the confectionary items for the hotel."

Well, she seemed to be focusing and asking pertinent questions, thought Cliff, still in the early stages of sorting out this rural America thing, but starting to come to grips with it all. He'd sensed her mind wrapping around the outside activities when he went over them. Maybe she'd buy into it, maybe not.

*

Cassie rolled around everything she'd seen and heard as they walked back to the truck. The interdependence Dan spoke of was taking shape in her head. She was getting the idea that the hotel and the valley helped support a lot of the local inhabitants. It was reinforced as they drove past the village sports store and an all-around general store, which looked like it housed a small pharmacy.

With a clearer vision of what was going on, Cassie, as the years had taught her, tried to anticipate problems. "I have a question," she asked.

"Shoot."

"This is a small community. The hotel expansion will bring a lot more people and business. Was there much opposition to it during the planning and permit stages?"

"Good question. Yes, as would be expected, there was opposition. The environmentalists obviously, and some other small factions resisted. Change is rough on some people. But there was overwhelming support for the expansion from the locals and the surrounding communities. This affects their livelihoods. The expansion will create jobs, stimulate the whole economy around here, help people send their kids to college. Overall, it's created excitement, not dread. There should be no problems when it opens."

When they got back in the truck, Cliff handed her a roll of paper towels. "Here, I brought this for you."

Cassie frowned. "What exactly are these for?"

"Your cold. It's a long day and your tissues will probably get all soggy and gunky."

Soggy and gunky? She quickly covered the tissue in her lap with her hand. This man's warped and dated sense of humor was right up there with her father's. It was a thoughtful gesture, and, like her father, he had to cover doing something nice with a smart remark.

58

A passenger now, sitting high up in Cliff's truck, Cassie marveled at the view of the surrounding forest, catching glimpses through the trees of open fields and scattered houses on their way to the freeway. No traffic here—they were the only car on the road. This time it was a relaxing drive through the mountains, an experience Cassie hadn't had before in her urban life. On her drive up, it was all tension and focus.

Finally, Cassie looked at her hands. She'd always been proud of her long, graceful fingers and nails. Clean now, they were still battered from the misfortune at the allotment. "Is there a nail salon back in town?"

She looked up to see one of his grins. "Nail salon? We have a great dog groomer who does pet nails. Would that do?"

So much for sympathy.

Cliff amended his comment. "Yes, we have a salon that does women's and men's hair, also nails. I'll point it out to you when we get back."

Soon they were in Auburn, and Cassie found a lovely dress in the first shop she tried.

A few minutes into the drive back to Manor Valley, Cliff said, "So, Cassie Bryant from New York City, age thirty-one. You might be the big butt on the throne around here, huh? Our very own Daenerys Targaryen or Cersei Lannister."

"Excuse me?"

"Oh, sorry, that came out wrong. You might be the butt on the *big* throne around here. I know you don't have a big butt. I've seen it. No, no. You have a nice butt."

Did he just say I had a nice butt?

Another tidbit of wisdom from the founder of the Inappropriate Academy. Thank goodness this fool was locked away out here, deep in the woods. He was more out of touch than her father. Someone really should start a political correctness school for all the Neanderthals that encroached on her—up until this week—perfect life. Then again, Herschel never told her she had a nice butt.

"How do you know about the job offer? And why do you call Dan and Rita uncle and aunt?"

"They're Lily's and my godparents. They're a second set of parents. My dad and Uncle Dan grew up together and were in the service together. Rita and Dan never had kids. If you take the job, we'll be working closely together. Dan wanted me to spend time to feel you out." He hurled another smile at her. "Unfortunately, aside from the additional construction work, I'm also the one who oversees the outside activities." He added a pointed finger. "Under watchful supervision from the hotel manager, of course."

Oh, God. Cassie's head started spinning—again.

"I'm supposed to help sell you on the idea, impress you with the tour." His voice lowered, a confidential tone. "Does Dan know about the, ummm... drinking problem? Are you in a program back East? May I ask when was the last time you fell off the wagon?"

Cassie almost flipped. "WHAT? What drinking problem? I don't have a drinking problem!" Anger turned to confusion. Suddenly she saw how she must have looked flopping around in the mud—of course, a drunk driver. She was mortified—again. She turned in her seat to face him. "Please, Cliff, you have to understand, you've got it wrong. I was sick with the flu, had no sleep the night before, and my head was killing me from the flight. I'd taken cold pills"—she'd skip the Valium, or he'd add drug addict to her image—"and drank too much when Dan shocked me with the job offer." Pleading now. "Honestly, I'm not a drunk."

"Okay, okay! Sorry. What was I supposed to think after that performance? It's a tough job running that hotel. I hope you're up to it. I won't hint at it again. Case closed."

They drove silently for a time. Cassie's mind spun at her conduct and how this person must see her. He probably felt like he was driving around with the new Manor Valley Monster, terrified about what she might do next. Maybe she should just ask him if he knew where to score some crystal meth.

Of course, being so close with Dan and Rita, he'd worry about her competence. Of course, after spending all that time bringing those new wings out of the ground, he'd worry about who would take the reins after his job was done. Tonight, he'd probably have the villagers lighting their torches, swarming the street, herding her out of town.

When they pulled up to the hotel, Cliff reached behind the seat and presented Cassie with her lost shoes, now sparkling after he'd cleaned them.

Cassie beamed. "Oh my, I thought these were gone forever. Thank you so much."

"Did you see that?" said Cliff.

"What?"

"You just smiled. That was your second smile in Manor Valley. It really made your eyes pop, even made your hair shine. You should do it more often. It'll take practice, but you can do it."

*

So much to take in, so much to process. Safely back in her room, Cassie lounged in a hot bath, trying to drive away the tension permeating her entire body. The exotic hotel aromatherapy bath oil scented the air, easing her stress. Uninterrupted quiet and a warm towel on her head helped her concentrate.

Everything she'd seen and heard today ran like a film clip through her head. Fine, it wasn't New York, but the entire valley definitely reeked with charm. The slower pace had its appeal: not the tense hustle and bustle she was used to. The Mall, as they called it, was impressive, warm, and inviting. Smiling, well-mannered people milled around offering 'excuse me' or 'pardon me' whenever they bumped into each other. Even some bikers with tattoos, bandanas, and Levi's vests with club names on the backs displayed their manners. It was not the glum, combat atmosphere of moving around or shopping in New York.

She pictured herself sitting on a sofa in the Mall with a cup of coffee, lost in the view. Subtle landscape colors hinted at the coming change; a few weeks and it would be brilliant around the lake. The massive fireplace fascinated her. Had she ever seen a real fire burning in a fireplace?

Dan's comments about the interaction with surrounding communities, minimized by Cassie during their first talk, now resonated. She now understood the responsibility of the hotel in the combined effort. 'Outside activities' still needed a lot of thought. 'Outside activities' seemed to involve *him*, and her attention now drifted there. No one had ever questioned her competence. And what about him? What about his competence?

She had to admit she was begrudgingly impressed. After their tour, Cassie thought Cliff quite capable. When it got down to business, his smart-alecky, abrasive, full-of-himself behavior was replaced by a serious, well-spoken, organized mind. His descriptions were precise, his way of explaining things well thought out. All of her questions were clearly answered. If he didn't know something for sure, his reply was, "I'll find out."

She'd settled a little after the drinking and competence accusations. God, she hoped he believed her.

Perhaps it was time for her to find out more about young Mr. Walker? Her friend Vivien was always vacuuming up as much info as possible about a man—business or personal, it made no difference—trawling the web and querying mutual acquaintances. Vivien used the excuse that it was simply background information so she could be more sensitive to them and communicate in a shared language. "Just checking to see if there's any skeletons in the armoire," was how she put it. It was an appalling breach of privacy as far as Cassie was concerned. The very thought of it was anathema to her principles, a violation to the core.

Cassie propped herself up on the bed with her laptop and cautiously looked around the empty room just in case. What the hell, she'd Google him.

She opened a private browser so she could erase her tracks. Why had she remembered that little tip when Vivien had showed her? Name, city, state, and Google led her to LinkedIn. No profile photo and so little else it wouldn't get him into a 7-Eleven, much less a job interview. Facebook next—nothing. That made sense, a friend request from him would be laughed at and dismissed by any rational human being. Let's try Instagram. Another zero. Well, she reasoned, the only followers he could get would be himself and Ethel. Maybe TikTok—he had a warped sense of humor. Again, nothing. Who the hell didn't do some social media these days? She gave up, refusing to check Vivien's ace-in-the-hole, Venmo, where she'd try to track what his money was spent on. Way too invasive for Cassie, and this guy probably still wrote checks. *God!* She could have found out more about a monk cloistered in a monastery for half a century.

Chapter Ten

Cliff was under orders. Dan told him that he didn't want to smother Cassie with a continuous barrage about the job offer. He also didn't want her alone in the hotel, didn't want loneliness and homesickness creeping in. He assigned Cliff to entertain her Sunday night after their tour. By Monday night, her workmates would be in town, and aloneness wouldn't be a factor.

An attraction was niggling at Cliff. The strange woman from New York was confused about Manor Valley, and he was confused about her. Nervous, no way was he going to dinner with her by himself. He called upon his sister to help. Dinner would be at Lily's, and Cassie could spend time with another woman near her own age in what might be her home for two years. Clever Cliff.

Definitely attractive, Cassie aroused long-suppressed feelings in him. He must take care, or she could become another woman who would leave him in Manor Valley, another woman who would leave him empty. All of his previous girlfriends had moved on—life in the valley not for them.

Way out of my league, anyhow, he thought.

After getting his degree in construction management, Cliff had taken a job with one of the big firms in Sacramento. He stuck it out for ten months before realizing it wasn't for him. Managing big projects required a lot of moving around, and he loved Manor Valley. The valley was home. He missed the hands-on part of construction, the part he'd learned from his dad growing up. He'd just have to wait until he found a woman who loved the valley as much as he did.

He had no problem seeing that Cassie was on the fast track in the hotel business. Two years and she'd be gone, back to New York and her comfortable lifestyle. Manor Valley was a different planet to her. Her shifts between fascination and fear at what she encountered amused him. She'd never seen a deer? She'd never seen a real fire in a fireplace? In the truck she'd gazed at the forest like a mesmerized five-year-old.

The decision she has to make must seem monumental, he thought. *Uprooting herself and adapting to a lifestyle so foreign to her.* She hadn't verbalized how she felt about the job offer, but he sensed she was on the fence. Fear or no fear, he sensed she had a tough side. He thought if she took the job, she'd stick it out. No mention of a boyfriend, but Dan did hint at a recent breakup.

Lily lived in a cozy, small house tucked up in the hills. On the drive over, Cliff supplied Cassie with Lily's background. Twenty-six years old, she'd only been away from Manor Valley for college and working a year in San Francisco. Lily had taken over the hotel flower concession and a small stand in the Mall from their mother. It took Lily only a year to expand it to the current shop, where she added the chocolates and candles. His summary was, "She's like you—works a lot."

*

Cassie looked around appreciatively as Lily gave her a tour of the house. It consisted of one large, open, vaulted-ceiling room with the kitchen at the back, two modest bedrooms, and one bath down a small hallway. It invited you in, full of feminine touches and pieces picked up in her travels. It was a mild night, and a table out on the deck was set for three with a view of the mountains.

As they sat for dinner, Cassie said, "I shudder to think what this much square footage would cost in Manhattan. And I can guarantee you the view wouldn't be like this."

The two women bonded well at dinner. It was almost as if Cliff wasn't there. The women exchanged stories about their childhoods and college years. He noted the surprise on Cassie's face when Lily told her she'd gone to UC Berkeley near San Francisco and traveled a lot during the slower times.

Lily was privy to the job offer. "What are your thoughts so far about the job, if you don't mind me asking?"

"It's so sudden. I've barely had time to think about it. Everything here differs from what I'm used to. And I don't mean just the job. It's the lifestyle, too. Forgive me, but what do you do around here besides work?"

Lily sympathized. "When I lived in Berkeley and San Francisco, urban life was a shock at first. Like you now, but in reverse. I slowly got into the flow, experienced all the exciting things the area offered and enjoyed it all. I still go down to San Francisco every few months." She thought for a moment while sipping some wine. "Believe me, there's plenty to do here. We have different things that you can't do in the city: riding, hiking, swimming, snuggling by a fire on a winter night, enjoying the peace and quiet. I like the slower pace, the closer interactions with people you work with. I speak from experience. What's that expression? Don't knock it 'til you've tried it."

Encouraging. Cassie hadn't had time to think about any non-work options. The view from another woman, who'd experienced similar trepidations, put a better perspective on her situation, eased some of the tension.

Talk continued over coffee, while the invisible man washed the dishes.

"What did you major in at Berkeley?" asked Cassie.

"History."

"Wow, not botany or horticulture?"

"Didn't Uncle Dan tell you about the history of the valley and the hotel?"

"He said it was built by some ancestor who moved here around the Gold Rush."

"Oh, my God! Just some ancestor? Do I have a story for you." Lily pushed the coffee cups aside and poured them both some wine. "It's the reason I chose history. I did my senior paper on the mysterious hotel's builder, his wife, and life at the time.

"The summer after my first year—I still hadn't declared a major—I asked Uncle Dan If there were any old papers about the hotel and the man who built it. He said there were tons of old account books, ledgers, receipts, and letters along with God knew what else in a storage facility in the next valley. He gave me the keys and told me to help myself. History was never his thing." Lily was rising to the story now. "Forget all that accounting stuff, I found the diaries of Travis Weaver, the man who built the house, and those of his wife. Talk about a historical romance! Danielle Steel could have written it."

It drew Cassie in. "You've *got* to tell me."

Lily sipped her wine and dove in. "Travis Weaver was a complex man—self-educated, driven, brilliant, never ceasing from physical work in the day, or mental work, reading, and planning at night. He was a fair man with looks and personality. 'A bloke's bloke,' as Ethel would describe him.

"In 1869, the year the transcontinental railroad opened, he stood outside his completed home. Swelling pride dampened when he realized there was nothing and no one in it. The structure was his area of expertise; what went inside, he wasn't so sure about. He'd never been inside, much less lived in, a house like that. And he had no one to share it with.

"I have to say," said Lily, "the frank details that went into diaries at the time fascinate me. I now understand why they were so sacred and private. Travis more or less wrote that what he now needed was help and a wife.

"A five- or six-day horse ride to San Francisco was miraculously cut to five or six hours with the opening of the railroad. Travis decided to go and seek help from some of his friends who had migrated to the city. They were not on the wealth level of the famous big four of San Francisco—Collis Huntington, Leland Stanford, Charles Crocker, and Mark Hopkins—but they were a long way from starving. His friend Clive Ostler eagerly awaited him.

"At a lavish dinner his second night, eight couples joined them. Travis didn't need advice from the men; he needed a woman's input, and during the meal, he confessed his shortcomings and pleaded with the women for help. He was so self-effacing, they couldn't wait to advise. Travis's head was a mess with all that needed to be considered. Late in the discussion, Mrs. Ostler suggested, and all the ladies agreed, that Janet Wilson, the Ostlers' inimitable housekeeper, the envy of the other ladies, would be the choice to escort him around in his shopping trips to furnish the house. Their task would be to find him a wife.

"Janet Wilson's life, comfortable in her youth, crashed around twenty. An only child from an upper-middle-class family in England, she moved with her parents to Hong Kong when she was seventeen. Her father worked for one of the big taipans, the heads of wealthy English trading families based in the Orient. At nineteen, her parents died from sickness or an accident—the historical record isn't clear. Janet had no desire to return to England. She was comfortable with the money left to her, but at twenty took a job as governess for a wealthy English family. The short version is that she was seduced by the oldest son a few years later, had a baby out of wedlock, and was dismissed from her job.

"She would not return to England as an outcast with her bastard child. Any lies about a husband would follow her. She would go to San Francisco, the booming town across the Pacific in America. Awash with new money, not as stifling and strict as her homeland, she would have an opportunity there for a new life with her son.

"Janet visited an employment agency her first day; she had her job on the second. Since she had a child of her own, a governess position wouldn't work. Janet told people that her husband had died in China. Instead, she became housekeeper to the Ostlers. A real English gentlewoman—well-bred, smart, graceful, with knowledge of the mysterious Orient—they snapped her up immediately.

"Travis later wrote that he remembered the lady when he had arrived and she greeted him. Attractive, well-formed, she was formal and distant without being cold. He paid little attention."

Lily had set the stage. She leaned back and sipped her wine.

"And?" said Cassie.

"Enough for now," answered Lily. "This story is too good to give you the short version. "I'll tell you some more next time."

"You can't leave it like that!"

"Next time, I promise." Lily turned to her brother. "Do you have anything you'd like to contribute tonight, brother? You've been awfully quiet."

"Nope, I'm good," said Cliff. "It is a terrific story. I remember reading your paper. I remember how Uncle Dan almost cried when he read it."

As she walked them out, Lily said, "I hope you take the job, Cassie. It would be great having you around. My advice—give it a chance."

Chapter Eleven

Monday morning Cassie leisurely woke from the best night's sleep she'd had in ages. She stretched out in bed before she suddenly snapped upright and looked at the clock. She hadn't set an alarm. Relief settled in as she saw it wasn't late. Why was it so quiet? Had the Living Dead finally arrived in Manor Valley and dispatched everybody? Her normal alarm at home was the steadily rising volume of early morning garbage trucks, with their constant hydraulic whoosh as they stopped and started their way down the block. Or the procession of early morning delivery vehicles, taking advantage of the relatively quiet streets before they were clogged by traffic. Where was the sound of the laboring buses wheezing away from the stop at the corner?

Her mood dampened as the impact of the coming day registered. Monday, when the rest of the New York staff would begin arriving ahead of the meeting scheduled to start on Tuesday. Decision time. Dan would want to announce the plan to bring the Manor Valley Hotel into the chain, boast about all of its improvements, and reveal who would run it under the reorganization. Still undecided, Cassie wanted some peace before Dan assaulted her with his final day of pitching her to take the job.

Skipping the dining room, Cassie went down to the kitchen to con an omelet out of Ethel. If Cliff could do it, so could she.

"Good morning, luv. How's the cold?" said Ethel.

"Much better, thank you. Ethel, is there any chance I can get an omelet? I don't want to sit by myself in the dining room."

"Get right over to the table, luv. I'll fix you up." As Cassie sat down, Ethel added, "Not there, luv. That's Cliff's seat. He had breakfast a couple of hours ago and is out back working on the new wings, but he'll sneak in for a coffee anytime."

Cliff's seat? Will he have his own massage table when the spa opens?

"Sorry, is it okay if I help myself to coffee?"

"Make yourself at home, Cassie. You're one of the family."

It was a busy time for Ethel, so Cassie left her to it. She was meeting with Dan in an hour and wanted to review things in her mind. On her phone, Cassie made notes: pros and cons. After the original shock, she had calmed down and now had a basic idea of what went on around the hotel and Manor Valley. It was so different from her job in New York. The sheer scope of the challenge still hadn't fully registered. She smiled at the skill of Dan Weaver; he should have sold air-conditioners in Alaska. After a few minutes, the pro column looked big, the con column sparse. Cassie almost flinched as her eyes bounced back and forth between the two sides. The sparse side was mainly the emotional downside of being away from home for the first time in her life, away from family, away from New York. He trumped that by expense-paid trips home almost every month.

Ethel came over with her omelet. The smell alone distracted her. "Enjoy, sweetheart."

This wasn't a bad perk, either. Cassie decided to get Ethel a small gift before she left.

After breakfast, the pro column surprised her again. It expanded while she ate: free rent in a spacious guest house—with a fireplace. Free car, just about free rein over a very challenging enterprise. Prominent on the list was that obscene paycheck. Two years didn't seem *that* long for the reward at the other end—executive VP in New York. The learning curve would be significant, but she knew she'd have help along the way. Everyone she'd met was friendly, and the area was growing on her rapidly.

Upstairs, Dan gave her a hard hat and dragged her out to the back of the hotel, where they met Cliff to review the new construction. Cliff tilted his head as he looked at Cassie. The hard hat was down over her eyes, and she couldn't see well. He took it off her head, adjusted the straps, and put it back on. "There. The concrete is safe now. If you fall over, you won't get blood on it. It's tough to get off."

Did he just invade my personal space, taking that hat off my head? She thought it a nice gesture, in any event. She now understood that personal space to him was probably anything within ten feet of his big-screen TV on game day.

Her mind buzzed as the two men explained details of the new pool area between the wings. She pictured the view from the lobby, as a guest would look out over it.

They maneuvered over cables, air hoses, and subcontractors' equipment, roaming the halls and rooms inside. The size of the gym and spa shocked her. In New York, square footage was so expensive that everything was reduced to its minimum possible dimensions. Cassie was on war footing now and barraged the two men with questions about everything.

They walked around the exterior hotel perimeter. "What's that?" asked Cassie, pointing to an area to the left.

Dan took this one. "For years it was lawn bowling. We're replacing it now with bocce ball courts. Keep up with the trends."

At the back, tucked against the hill down a slight slope to make them invisible from the lobby and pool deck, were tennis courts. "Gosh, where's the golf course?" asked Cassie.

"We decided against one. We want nothing taking away from the impact of the valley landscape. There's one about twenty minutes away."

When they approached the area to the right of the hotel, Cassie was flabbergasted. Her room was in the front of the hotel, and she had never seen this side. A massive six-foot-high hedge maze loomed in front of her, replicated years ago from an English country home. It drew her like a magnet before Cliff put a light restraining hand on her elbow. "The kids love it. What you want to ask is what's *under* it." Cassie gave him a questioning look, and Cliff continued. "Have you wondered where all the cars are? Why the entire property looks like it does without a parking lot intruding on the picture? The parking lot is down there. We wouldn't want guests scraping ice off their windshields, would we?"

*

Dan, clearly nervous, took Cassie back to his office. His pitch was winding down. Two coffees were placed in front of them, and he started to wrap things up.

For the past three days, Cassie had been sorting out all the 'what ifs,' a cloud of mosquitos pestering her, pushing her this way and that way. Suddenly, she said, "Stop. Enough." Language slipped. "The hell with it. You win. I'll do it."

Oh, what have I done!

The pro column had won out. Cassie Bryant would spend two years in the wilderness breaking bread with the locals, learning their language and customs. She would bring light to the provinces. She would return triumphant to New York, like Stanley to London after finding Livingstone, her place in hotel history assured. Cassie Bryant was a warrior. Battles had been won and lost before. If people in the military took overseas postings to Iraq and Afghanistan to help their careers, she could do a tour in the outback of California. Born to fight in the trenches, she vowed to soldier on and confine her depressing thoughts to days ending in *y*.

Ecstatic, Dan jumped out of his seat. "Thank you, Cassie. You will *never* regret this." Relief melted off him. "Stay right there." He went to his desk, saying over his shoulder, "I have to call Rita."

When his wife picked up, Dan said, "Cassie just said yes!"

*

Cassie was left to see her co-workers Monday night, cautioned by Dan not to say anything. He wanted the honor at the first Tuesday meeting when he told all the managers and key home office staff about the hotel's plans.

The week passed in a blur. There was a lot for Cassie to go over concerning the hotel: changing staff, small remodels underway, cost-effectiveness, marketing strategy, and a depressingly long list of other items.

She left a minor meeting on Wednesday morning and tracked down Justin Banks, her new assistant manager. He would be a big help with Cassie's job, a massive right hand since he had been settled in for six months and must know the subtleties of how things worked. Hopefully, he would be easy to work with and hadn't aspired to the manager job himself.

She shouldn't have worried. The interview, if that's how one described it, was encouraging. Twenty-seven years old, from Oklahoma, Justin was bright, although somewhat shy. Dan had stolen him from one of the competitive chains when he was making a name for himself in Los Angeles.

"All Dan does is rave about you, Cassie," said Justin. "I'm thrilled you've taken the job. I love doing the behind-the-scenes stuff. I've always wanted to be part of a high-end resort hotel, and now I'm here. You're welcome to the weight of being the boss."

Quick questions revealed that he was thorough and perceptive. Curious about her own impending move, Cassie asked, "What made you leave Oklahoma?"

Justin theatrically pulled his glasses down his nose and peered over them at Cassie. "Have you ever been to Oklahoma? Seen how flat it is? Some people pray for rain. I've prayed for mountains since I was a kid."

Huh, a sense of humor too.

She hoped he didn't hang out with you-know-who.

*

The final night's dinner arrived, and Dan was bent on impressing all the staff from the East Coast. He wanted everyone to return home and sell the merits of the Manor Valley Hotel, especially to every customer in the Frequent Stayer Program when they checked in to any chain hotels.

They held the function in the grand dining room. It was cocktail hour. Everyone milled about, relaxing after the last day of meetings, all talking about the hotel or their plans for the long bonus weekend ahead.

Cliff leaned toward Cassie as they surveyed the crowd from their spot by the entrance. "I'll get us drinks, and you can mingle with your friends. What would you like?"

"Thank you. A glass of pinot noir, please."

He couldn't resist taking a jab after the scene in his truck on the way back from Auburn. "Perhaps a Diet Coke might be a better choice?"

The glare he got in return ushered him away. "A glass of pinot it is."

When he returned, Cassie asked, "Why are you here tonight?"

"Dan wanted me here to work the guests from the East Coast. After I gave them the tour of the new wings yesterday, he thought it would be good if I were here to sell the merits of the valley, answer any questions about the other things going on with the new wings or outside activities." He stopped scanning the crowd and turned to her with a beaming smile on his face. "You know, impress them like I've impressed you." He shrugged his shoulders. "Besides, Uncle Dan told me there'd be some hot strippers later."

Cassie shook her head in amazement, sipped her wine, and returned her attention to the room.

They sat for dinner. Cassie watched waiters in tuxedos drifting noiselessly around the dining room, catering to everyone's needs. Dan had told Cassie that they only wore them on holidays, but tonight was special. A string quartet played off to the side. Dim chandeliers glittered overhead, candles and flowers on every table. The endless wine list impressed the New York staff, who'd toured the cellars the day before, especially when Dan told each table to order whatever they wanted. Overall, everyone was in awe of the magnificent mystery hotel—everyone imagining the marketing power it would bring to the chain, everyone lauding Cassie for her good fortune.

For intimacy, they limited tables to four people. Dan, Rita, Cassie, and Cliff occupied one near the entrance. Dan wanted as many visiting staff as possible near the windows to enjoy the view.

When dessert and coffee were served, the string quartet shifted to more contemporary tunes, encouraging dancing. Dan held Rita's hand as they got up and looked across the table. "Come on, you two. We have to set the theme."

Taken by surprise, Cassie and Cliff exchanged nervous glances.

Slightly behind him as he led her to the floor, Cassie gave him another review. The fashion police would not be busting through the doors hauling him away tonight. She'd noted the suit and tie as soon as she entered the room. It looked perfect for his usual casual way of standing around. Neatly combed hair accented his tanned, lightly lined face. She liked the way it lit up with a playful smile when she came in. He hadn't been around since Sunday, and she'd somehow missed the comfort of his presence. Getting used to his ways, Cassie felt protected when he was near in this new environment.

He slid his hand onto her lower back as they moved to the slow song. "Sorry, I don't know if I'm allowed to say that you look beautiful tonight."

She could only muster, "Thank you."

Cassie hadn't been this close to a man in months. He smelled good. He moved well. His hand softly on her back gave her an unanticipated shiver. At various points during the dance, she discreetly moved her hand around and felt nothing but muscle. This was different than dancing with Herschel, inexplicably more comforting and sensual.

Like teenagers at a prom, they moved about in silence for a time, pleasantly uncomfortable at this closeness.

Cliff said, "I told Dan that you wanted a country band so you could practice your square dancing, but he nixed the idea."

His breath on her ear felt good. She gave him a mildly reproachful look, lowered her face, and pulled herself closer. When was the last time Herschel told her she was beautiful? She enjoyed the closeness, the security, didn't want Cliff talking right now.

*

Friday morning, people scattered for their bonus weekends to various destinations like Lake Tahoe, San Francisco, and the wine country in Sonoma and Napa. No such luck for Cassie Bryant from New York, age thirty-one. The task ahead had fully settled on her. She'd meet with Dan this morning and catch the night flight home from SFO after returning her car. A lot needed to be done.

On the plane, she filled her laptop with lists: what to pack and take back, should anything be shipped? Tasks to jump on were listed, among which was a whole new website for the Manor Valley Hotel, since the existing one was almost nonexistent. Marketing ideas followed—she'd have to check with Dan, Cliff, and Justin to see what they did now. Holidays and vacations were a big part of this hotel: almost irrelevant to the chain's other properties. More ideas and questions filled her screen.

They had advised her to fly back into Reno the following week, where someone would pick her up. A hint of happiness crept in when she realized she'd be home again in a month for Thanksgiving.

Tiredness finally won out as she closed the lid of the laptop and allowed her thoughts to drift.

It was an incredible final dinner: another perfectly orchestrated event by Dan Weaver. She'd danced with Cliff—more than one would think appropriate. Well, thoughts in *that* direction would be cast aside, written off as a pleasant interlude, not to be pursued. A professional relationship would be established and adhered to. Complications like that would not be added to her problems. Technically, he worked for her now. He would supervise construction and outside activities, but she was the boss now—the final say.

Chapter Twelve

Cassie was a gift late in life for Ed and Nancy Bryant: their only child. They'd brought her up well; doting was well balanced with discipline. Bad grades in school were not tolerated. She would go to college and surpass her parents, both of whom were children of immigrants whose education stopped at high school. Ed and Nancy continued the plumbing company left to Ed by his father, serving Brooklyn and the neighboring boroughs of New York City.

Cassie and her parents sat around the dinner table the evening after her return. Ed and Nancy listened attentively to Cassie's animated description of her adventure, the first time their baby had been west of Pennsylvania and gone for more than a few days.

"In the early morning, deer walk all along the front of the hotel by the water. The lake is so beautiful. It's all different colors depending on where the sun is—green from trees, blue from the sky, gray when it's cloudy. Sometimes, if it's windy, the water is etched with white strips like mini ocean breakers. Some mornings there's a breathtaking low blanket of fog covering it up until the sun strips it back and wakes it up for another day."

Nonstop during the meal, Cassie enthusiastically covered the people she'd met, the inside and outside of the hotel, and the little town.

"Well," said her father, "it sure sounds as if you liked it out there."

Cassie snapped out of it at that remark. "No, no, certainly not. I'm simply describing it to you. God, it's in the middle of nowhere. It's over twenty minutes from a freeway." Said like she thought the moon was closer.

Cassie looked at her mother and knew her defensive tone was not well hidden.

As her mother took the dishes to the kitchen, she asked over her shoulder, "And this Cliff gentleman you talk about. Tell us more about him. How old is he? Is he good looking?"

Dad piped up. "What your mother wants to know is if this is some poor, unsuspecting guy that we can unload you on."

Dad would love meeting Cliff, thought Cassie. *Birds of a feather from the Stone Age who both flunked sensitivity.* "Dad! You can't say to your daughter that you want to *unload* her on some *guy*. That's so insensitive. Haven't I been coaching you on how to communicate with the younger generations? You and that Cliff person certainly have something in common—you share the same sick sense of humor and disregard for modern forms of social interaction."

"Whoa, honey." Ed raised his palms in mock surrender. "I've been studying while you were away. I'm totally *waked*." A condemning finger shot out. "You just *mini aggressed* or *marginalized* your own father because of his lack of formal education. I'm going to have to build a *security* room in the basement if you keep this up: a place where I can mend my crushed feelings after your attacks. Also, I sense some *age discrimination* there."

Ed was up on all the political correctness terms and intentionally distorted them. Half the time he thought he was in a re-education camp in Maoist China. He enjoyed winding his daughter up when she went off on these tangents.

"First, *father dear*, you can't even get the terms right. It's microaggressed, not mini aggressed, woke not waked, and safe room, not security room. Second, even if you got them right, you have no idea what any of them mean. You're a cultural nightmare, Dad. You are the poster boy for political *in*correctness."

"Poster boy? That's got to be a good thing, right?" He smiled and folded his paper over to the next page.

Knowing that she was being baited, Cassie sighed and went to help her mother in the kitchen. Hopeless was hopeless. She might as well be speaking Aramaic to her father. She was waiting for the 'you kids sure have a lot of free time on your hands.' His normal response when she tried to enlighten him.

"Leave her alone, Ed." The warning from her mother in the kitchen.

Well, now is as good a time as any. Might as well just spit it out. "I've taken a job out there for two years. Dan wants me to get everything up and running and up to date when the new wings open next spring. When I come back, I could be executive vice-president of the whole chain."

Anyone got a hand grenade? Two stunned parents stared open-mouthed at their child. It took an hour for Cassie to placate them, convince them it was for the best, and that she'd be okay. "I'll be home every month. This isn't a big deal."

*

It had only been a week since Cassie had seen her friend, but it seemed longer. She sat across from Vivien at a quiet catch-up dinner around the corner from her friend's massive penthouse on the Upper East Side. Vivien wanted to hear all about the hotel and its surroundings.

Detailed descriptions were dispensed before Cassie dropped the bomb.

"I've committed to move there for two years. The new wings will be done over the winter, and I'll be the new general manager to help bring it into the twenty-first century. We have to market it to a much larger clientele, integrate it with the chain. Then, I can come back and be the executive VP of the whole chain."

Stunned, a few moments passed before Vivien spoke. Granted, her response was somewhat different than Cassie's parents'. "Are you completely out of your fucking mind! Move to the mountains in the middle of nowhere? God, just buy a ski package to Aspen and get the great outdoors out of your system!" She paused for a second, knowledge surfacing. "Oh, I forgot. The family has a place out there. It's a chalet or something. You can stay there—I've never been. I prefer skiing in Europe. I think wines are cheaper there."

Vivien Van Houten never checked the price of a bottle of wine in her life.

"Viv, It's my job. Some of us have to work for a living."

"But what about me?" Viv was getting depressed. "This is very disconcerting news, very distressing."

Cassie had to share it with somebody. Despite her act, she knew that Viv was one of the most discreet persons she knew; confidences were confidences.

Her voice went up an octave. "Distressing? You want to know about distressing?"

She launched in on her disaster at the allotments her first night. A full confession, she left nothing out: the flu, the pills, the wine, waking up in a scary shack right out of *Chucky Kills Everyone on Elm Street*, or whatever those chainsaw movies were called. How she'd been branded an ecoterrorist, a shifty character, and all the while, Backwoods Chucky grinning at her with Cujo, the killer beast at his side.

Vivien almost howled in the restaurant as she pushed her plate away. Nothing would stay in her stomach after that story; she'd be laughing for a week. The vision of her sheltered friend living through the ordeal played in her mind. She reached into her purse, retrieved her black American Express card, and slapped it down in front of Cassie. "I have to meet him. Buy that Cliff person a ticket right now. First class. I want him here tomorrow." She sipped some water to stop from choking. "Take the whole two years out there— I'll still be laughing when you get back."

Sympathy wasn't one of Vivien's endearing qualities.

*

The morning flight from Newark arrived in Reno slightly early. A week preparing things at home and working from the New York office had Cassie reasonably prepared for her adventure out West. The Lewis and Clark expedition had nothing on her. Fears had diminished, and confidence had risen. She should have bought a buckskin jacket, fringe included.

There he was, standing on the other side of the security barrier, all smiles, holding the hastily composed cardboard sign like he didn't know who he was picking up—CASSIE BRYANT FROM NEW YORK CITY, AGE 31.

Were those flowers in his hand?

Cassie suppressed a smile of her own. It registered that he had given up his Sunday to come all this way and pick her up. She was actually happy to see the idiot. At least until she passed through the security barrier.

Ten feet away from her, the crowd milling around, Cliff said in a loud voice, "Cassie Bryant, over here. I see the police took the ankle bracelet off. Congratulations!"

Cassie turned red. People snuck sidelong glances at her as they hastily moved away, gaining space from who knew what type of criminal.

Forget happy to see the idiot.

Why was he allowed out without adult supervision?

Cassie thought he should have been a jester in some medieval royal court, but they would have fired him after a week, or drawn and quartered him, not wanting to waste valuable firewood burning him at the stake.

Three large suitcases hastily thrown in the back of Cliff's truck, and they were off.

"Sorry," said Cliff, "Dan wanted you to come into Reno so I could show you Lake Tahoe. It'll be a full afternoon. Good flight?"

"Until now."

A drive through downtown Truckee first, and then a quick stop at the Ritz-Carlton hotel outside of town. Truckee surprised her. An old mill town from before the last century consisting of a few blocks of old Victorian buildings converted to shops and restaurants. The railway, also from the eighteen hundreds, ran through the center of it all. One look told you it was all about tourism now.

Ten minutes outside the town, a long, crooked side road climbed a mountain to the Ritz-Carlton. "This is the premier hotel in the area," explained Cliff, as they did a tour of the lobby and outside. "Dan wanted you to see the competition."

It would impress anyone. Cassie registered it as the competition right away and made mental notes of everything. Snow had yet to fall, but she got the idea that the whole area was based on skiing in winter and leisure activities in the summer.

"We'll head over to Lake Tahoe now," said Cliff.

A quick detour into Squaw Valley, the 1960 Winter Olympics site, confirmed her conclusions about the area. Even she'd heard about Lake Tahoe. Cassie felt herself getting excited about seeing it live.

In Tahoe City, she got her first look. She was surprised at the contrast between the roads with the mountains pressed up against them and how everything opened up instantly around the massive lake. Not intimate like Manor Valley, massive mountains surrounded this mammoth body of water. Pointed peaks still held snow from last year.

A quick drive down the lake's west side and they arrived at Sunnyside Restaurant and Lodge. They lucked out with a table next to the window overlooking the lake.

"God, it looks like a sea!"

"It's the second biggest alpine lake in the world next to Lake Geneva in Switzerland." He pointed toward the distant south. "See those paths carved in the mountains? Those are the ski runs at Heavenly Mountain Resort, above South Lake Tahoe. Impressive up here, isn't it?"

"It's beautiful."

"Over there is the Nevada side of the lake. Gambling is legal there." It was a clear day, so Cliff pointed again. "Look close. See those bigger buildings close to the shore? They're hotels with big casinos." Blowing off an entire Sunday gave Cliff permission for a little jab. "Dan didn't want me to take you over to that side because of your, umm, gambling issues. Were you in a program back home for that too?"

Cassie was learning when to ignore him.

Finally, they arrived in Manor Valley. Cliff drove up to the Weavers' guest cottage and parked beside a brand-new Honda CR-V. As they muscled her bags around, Cliff nodded at the car. "That's yours. Keys are in it. I suggested a pickup like mine, but Dan and Rita overruled me."

Thank you, Jesus.

Inside, Cliff oriented her. "I'll leave you to it. There's a big game on tonight, and I don't want to miss it."

Cassie slumped down in a chair and surveyed her new home. Eyes registered disbelief as she took everything in. It was a mini version of Dan and Rita's home and two or three times as big as the condos she was looking at in New York. Natural log walls and a high open-raftered ceiling made it inviting and warm. Nothing she'd even imagined before. A large sliding door opened onto a deck and a small meadow, which quickly disappeared into the forest beyond. So foreign after gazing out at another building's wall or a crowded street at home. A small L-shaped kitchen took up one corner.

She rose and moved one bag down a short hallway to the bedroom. Comfortable and cozy, a picture window opened to another view. The bath offered both a shower and a spacious tub, easily three times the size of her parents' cramped bath at home.

"Only Two Years" was her new mantra, and this wouldn't be a bad place to pass it in.

*

Her job officially kicked off today, Monday. First, breakfast with Ethel.

"Well, Miss Bryant, I hear you're the boss now," said Ethel as Cassie came in.

Time to lay down some ground rules. This spot in the kitchen and this woman were going to be her oasis, her sanctuary. "Ethel, call me Cassie, luv, dear, or hey you. Call me Miss Bryant again, and you're fired. Are you busy, or can you take a break and sit with me?"

Cassie addressed one of her areas of ignorance. She could get specifics from Justin later. Right now she wanted a broad overview, a woman's viewpoint. "I'm going to need some help, Ethel. And I know you know everybody and everything that goes on around here." Too excited about starting, Cassie passed on a big breakfast and settled for a cinnamon bun and coffee. "Back East, our staffing is consistent. We don't have the seasonal fluctuations a resort like this has. How is the staffing handled here in the kitchen, up in the restaurant, or with housekeeping, and lobby personnel? Whose responsibility is it?"

"Well, dear, the fluctuations aren't as big as you might think. Yes, there are four-day weeks for some staff during the year, but they're happy to have them. During busy times, they can have six-day weeks. You're sharp. You've noticed all the young people around. The whole town is big on employing them during the summer and holidays. Kids get through college with what they can make in the summer—earn even more if they work the holidays too.

"Justin is your man. He has the list. Since he's been here, he's got it down. All of us call him with our needs, maybe ask him to check the youngsters we like. Even people at the Mall and the stores in town call him. The young people register with him and let him know when they can work and what they can do. Local kids going to college in Sacramento or the Bay Area will drive up just for weekend work."

Dear Justin, thought Cassie. A significant worry off her plate. She knew what a typical assistant manager did; she'd done it herself for years. God, what else was the poor man saddled with that she didn't know about?

Curious, Ethel had a question. "Is there a husband coming, or are you single?"

Cassie rolled her eyes. "I'm single. Just ask my parents."

*

Cassie commandeered one of the meeting rooms as a temporary office. Dan told her to take Rita's office across the hallway from him, but Cassie wanted space to start with, space to lay out things and organize herself. She wanted to familiarize herself with the new wings, and the plans for them would take up a banquet table by themselves. A few hours passed, and she knew she'd need another table.

Like she'd conjured a genie, Cliff came in carrying a yellow hard hat. It was the same one he'd fixed the straps on the day she did the tour with Dan, the day she'd accepted the job. He placed it in front of her. It had EL JEFE stenciled across the front and hand-painted flowers all over it.

"You'll have to wear this whenever you're out in the construction area. My sister painted the flowers, and I did the stencil."

Puzzled, Cassie asked, "And that means?"

"*El jefe* means the boss in Spanish. Spanish speakers are the backbone of construction in California now." He scratched his temple. "Maybe it should be *la jefa,* since you're a woman."

Violations danced through Cassie's mind—*Cultural Appropriation* using Spanish, blatant *Female Gender Bias* with the flowers. She was sure the Political Correctness Police could also find something wrong with the color yellow if they thought about it long enough. She loved it. It was considerate and thoughtful. Hell, she'd wear it. After all, she was the boss now.

Suddenly, her eyes opened wide and she flinched slightly. Her father must never see her wear it. She'd never hear the end of it.

Focusing again, Cassie said, "Can you get me another table like this?"

"Sure thing, Jefe."

Chapter Thirteen

Cassie had been drowning herself in the job for two weeks as life continued in Manor Valley. Autumn wrapped her arms around them. She had settled, but not to everyone's satisfaction.

Rita had to do something about it. Dan was in Boston, conferring on some minor refurbishments at the hotel there, so she called Cliff.

"She's at the hotel twelve hours a day, and when she gets home, she's locked away with her laptop. I'm surprised the damn thing hasn't broken yet. She's doing too much. I try to give her space, some privacy. I pried her out of the guesthouse a few times for a break or a meal, but all she talks about is work. It's not good for her. She needs to get out."

"Leave it with me, Aunt Rita. If she's going to live here, she should learn to enjoy it."

The next morning, Cliff interrupted Cassie in the office. "You've been putting off inspecting the riding and hiking trails, and it's past time. It's part of your job. I can walk you through it the first time. How 'bout tomorrow?"

Cassie looked up from her mini mountain of paperwork and printouts. *Rita is right,* thought Cliff, *she looks haggard.*

"Inspect what?"

"The safety of the trails. You're supposed to do it once a month. You're the boss now. Has rain washed out any of them? Have any trees blown over? Rockslides? We don't need any big liability issues."

Cassie had no idea what he was talking about, but 'liability' got her attention. "How exactly do I do that?"

"I'll pick you up at ten tomorrow morning. Wear jeans, a warm jacket, and stout shoes." And then he spun and left.

*

Opposite the allotments, they turned onto a narrow dirt road flanked by dense underbrush and tall trees. Fifty yards on and it opened onto a flat mini valley bigger than two football fields. Cliff could see nerves prickling and apprehension looming as they drove up, another Manor Valley surprise for Cassie. They drove slowly past paddocks and a roofed, open-sided training ring, then a U-shaped stable building complete with cupolas on steeply pitched roofs and small trimmed hedges framing the central cobblestone yard. Beyond it, there was another riding ring with no roof. The whole place was sectioned off by white fencing, the same color as the stables.

"How do we inspect these trails again?"

Cliff pointed at a horse. He suppressed a smile as her eyes expanded, and one hand shot, palm out, toward the horse and the other pressed against her heart.

"No, no, no. You don't understand," said Cassie. "I've never been near, much less on, a horse. No, definitely not. I can't do this."

Cliff was casual as could be. "Relax, you make it sound like you're going to be waterboarded. There's nothing to worry about. I'll be right beside you. This is the only way to do it." He turned to her. "Unless you want me to call Dan. Tell him you can't do it. Hire someone else."

He knew this was checkmate. She was trapped.

Cliff had come out before picking Cassie up and saddled his horse and Old Molly for the New Yorker. Tank usually accompanied him on these rides, running back and forth across the trails, occasionally chasing after a deer, which would disappear before Tank even got started. Today, Cliff wanted no distractions; all focus must be on getting Cassie through her first ride. He knew he had to get her up and moving before she chickened out. Before she had time to think about it.

Old Molly had moved more tourists around the trails than she cared to remember. Gentle as could be, she missed going out in her later years, ignored by people who wanted younger, prettier, livelier horses. A looker in her youth, gray was now pushing through her blonde hair. One ear drooped to the side from a fight years ago. A visiting show horse had given her some attitude. He had about two hundred pounds on her, but Molly had a go at the arrogant bastard anyhow. *Those pompous, egomaniac, dressage thoroughbreds are all the same,* she thought. Ah, those were the days!

It was a crisp morning, and Old Molly was up for a walk somewhere besides the paddock. Cliff had always been good to her. She saw that his companion was a beginner; Old Molly could feel the apprehension as Cassie approached. Not too heavy, good. She hoped she wasn't a kicker. Old Molly had scars from all the inexperienced ones kicking her sides over the years. This one would let her go at her own pace—slow and easy. If she was good today, maybe the woman would come back and take her out again.

"Old Molly is the gentlest horse I've ever seen. She'll be good for you. She likes women." Cliff almost had to drag Cassie over. "Let her smell your hand and softly stoke her forehead." Before she knew it, Cliff had helped her into the saddle and was standing beside her, going over some rules. "Keep your heels down, you don't want them slipping through the stirrups. Hold the reins in one hand. You can hold onto the saddle horn if you want until you feel how to move. I'll coach you on the way. Don't pull hard on the reins. Molly knows which way you want to go just by the weight of the reins on her neck. If you want to stop, just pull back lightly."

Cliff looked at his charge. She'd be fine on Old Molly. He suppressed a smile, not knowing which was heavier on the horse: Cassie, or the sheer weight of all the visible tension. Get her moving. Get her relaxed.

Unlike the steep, narrow hiking trails, the riding trails were wide and gentle, winding up into the hills. The weather was fall crisp and perfect. They rode side by side.

*

All very nice, I'm sure, thought Cassie. But this stuff was supposed to be seen from inside an air-conditioned tour bus, with the teenager in the aisle seat next to you, crushing you against a very thick window, trying to take a selfie. Yes, she knew that there was a branch of *Homo erectus*, or whatever they were called, who liked stuff like this, but she was definitely not from one of those branches. Fearful thoughts of what lay hidden in the dense trees and hills ahead filled her mind. They should be playing Jason Bourne music in the background: that suspenseful strumming of strings on the violin, viola, or cello, or whatever the hell it was. She should have taken bomb-chucking lessons before she arrived, or was it grenades they flipped into the jungle to kill the bad guys and vicious predators?

"You've got it already, Cassie!" They'd gone a few hundred yards. "Try to sit straighter, not lean forward. Keep your shoulders back and loosen up. Take your hand off the horn, and let your midsection move with the horse, feel the rocking motion. You're going to be a natural."

A natural? thought Old Molly. The woman was trying, she'd give her that, but Molly felt like a mule carrying around a tightly wound pack of camper supplies on her back.

Taking her mind off the horse for a moment, Cassie spotted a hawk—if it had a hooked beak, it was a hawk, right? It sat on a limb staring at her, not twenty feet away. It was at least a thousand times bigger than a New York pigeon, sitting there sizing her up, a licensed killer thinking about upgrading from mice to her, like Gordon Ramsay sitting on some stockyard fence in Oklahoma checking out the beef. As they got closer, it mercifully flew away.

Cliff's horse wanted to bolt on some of the long flat sections and pick up the pace. He'd been stabled and paddocked for over a week and tried to let it out. Cliff easily controlled him, but all the snorting, head rearing, and dancing about made Cassie nervous. Old Molly just enjoyed her walk.

Fall colors were all around them. Birds sang. A gentle breeze, warmed by the sun filtering through the trees, followed behind them. The first half hour, Cliff had to reassure her: no, no hunters would shoot her by accident; no, no pot growers in tracksuits wearing oversized medallions would attack her; no, no pythons or tarantulas hung from the trees. Bears wouldn't eat her, and the satanic cults usually stayed down by Sacramento.

Eventually, she settled down and let her focus wander from the horse and take in more of the surroundings. Suddenly she was in a romance novel, a princess riding through her realm in a fairy tale, a duchess out for a morning ride on her estate. Only books and movies before, but now this was the real thing. High up in the hills, they stopped at a lookout spot with a clear view through the trees, over the lake, and down to the hotel.

"I hear the wind and the birds, but it's all so peaceful and calm. I had no idea." Smiling and excited, she pointed up. "Look at this!" Autumn leaves of red, orange, even brown, were swaying slowly to the ground around them, like colorful mini kites broken from their strings.

They were sitting on a bench positioned just for the view. Cliff took a leather bag off his horse and surprised Cassie with two battered cups and a thermos of coffee. "How are you doing so far?"

"Better than I was when we started. This really is an experience." She pointed to Old Molly. "She's so nice and gentle for something that big."

"I know it's a burden, but unfortunately, you'll have to do this regularly. Usually after rain or a big storm."

"Oh my, I get to do this again?" said Cassie before she caught herself. Trepidation still held sway. "I don't have to do it alone, do I?"

"I'll come with you the first few times. After you're used to it, you may prefer to come alone. It's calming, gives you time to sort stuff out, think about things."

Eventually, they made their way down and back to the stables. "Okay," he said, "time to learn to unsaddle Molly." He walked her through it. After watching her struggle with the heavy Western saddle, he showed her how to take the bridle off and put on a simple halter.

"Now, you have to give her a treat," said Cliff. He gave part of a carrot to his own horse so she'd get the idea.

She didn't like the idea. Saw nothing but teeth, big teeth, like Jaws in the movie, getting ready to attack her hand, maybe take it off at the wrist.

"It's okay. Just hold your hand flat, like this. She'll take it right off your palm."

Scared to start, Cassie was thrilled when it worked. "Can I do it again?"

"Now, the most soothing thing you'll do all week—stable bonding." He handed her a brush. "Brush Old Molly down. She loves it, a reward for a job well done. It'll help you bond with her."

She started tentatively and then found herself enjoying it. "Remember, be careful behind her," said Cliff. "You can brush a little harder."

Soon she was engrossed in it, stroking the horse, in awe at the scale and muscle of the thing. "You were so nice to me today, Molly. I know we're going to be friends."

Encouraging grunts from Molly pushed her on when the brushing slowed. Cliff was forgotten now as the two of them nattered on, two girls at Starbucks after a run in Central Park. Rita wanted her distracted and relaxed. Cliff was doing his job.

He put his horse away and walked the short distance to the office, where Leo, the stable manager, was waiting on the bench outside with a cup of coffee. He could relax for a bit while watching Annie Oakley tend to Molly.

Cassie was excited and refreshed when she returned to the office. Almost a local. Forget that, now she was a frontier woman—battle-hardened on the trails, at home with the elements, an equestrian master. She had to call Dan.

"I saddled up and rode out"—she was learning the lingo—"and checked the riding trails today."

"You did what?"

"Cliff told me it was part of my job, checking to make sure the riding and hiking trails were safe. He went with me since it was my first time." Pride bolted through the airwaves. "And then I learned how to do stable bonding."

Dan was struggling not to laugh. "What kind of stable bonding?"

Her voice bubbled. "Brushed Old Molly down after the ride."

"Cliff had you brush down a horse?"

"Yes. Old Molly."

She could barely understand him through all the laughing. "Cassie, you don't have to check the trails. People who work at the stables do that." He giggled merrily on. The last words sounded like "*Stable bonding!* I love that guy!"

Cassie let the caldron boil until the lid popped off. Not bothering to grab a coat to ward off the fall air, completely oblivious about wearing her hard hat, she marched down the stairs, through the lobby, and out the construction door to the new pool area. She walked purposefully across the rough concrete surrounding the unfinished pool. Cliff was leaning against a wall reviewing some notes.

Tank ran up to her. He was always around outside but never allowed in the hotel or kitchen. Anger radiating off Cassie told him it would be best to go search for a ball. Better yet, chase a squirrel. He could get farther away.

"Are you happy with yourself? Had a good laugh at my expense?" A finger shot out toward Cliff's face. "It's not my job to inspect the trails. People from the stables do that. You must have really enjoyed my 'stable bonding.'" He stood perplexed, so she clarified for him. "I called Dan and made a fool out of myself. You must be thrilled!"

Cliff half smiled at her—the kind of smile that never reaches the eyes. A few moments passed while this barrage settled on him. He'd never seen her like this, couldn't comprehend this level of anger. He held his own in check; ice could be chipped off his voice. "I apologize. I'm very sorry. It won't happen again." With that, he slowly turned and walked back into one of the new wings.

Chapter Fourteen

"There should be no eggs for him at Easter, no candy at Halloween. Coal is too good for *his* Christmas stocking. I'm going to kill him. Skin him alive. Feed him to those big ugly birds—vultures. That's it. Feed him to the vultures. I'll stick a stake through his heart on Valentine's Day. Drive it in with a sledgehammer like a tent peg."

Cassie sat at the island in Rita's kitchen, nursing a glass of wine while Rita cooked. Her butt felt like she'd been riding a kangaroo rather than a horse. Muscles she didn't know she had begged for mercy.

She explained her day and wrapped it up with Cliff's deception.

Earlier, Cliff had called Rita with an update after the angry encounter at the hotel. "I tried to help but, evidently, it didn't sit well with her. I could tell she enjoyed herself on the ride. I guess it was my method that upset her. I'm through."

"Sorry, dear," Rita said now to Cassie. "I'm afraid it's all my fault. I called Cliff because I worry about how hard you're working. You needed something to take your mind off the job, help you relax and enjoy life around here." Rita shook her head and smiled. "I have to give it to him. He did what he promised. You look so refreshed and alive now. You have some lovely color in your face, not that glum, preoccupied person who's been around for the last few weeks. Admit it. You had a good time. It distracted you, gave you back some energy. You should do it more often."

"Okay, yes, it scared me at first, but I enjoyed it." Cassie rubbed her forehead. "And, yes, I wouldn't have dared do it if he hadn't tricked me. I didn't know you put him up to it."

God, how am I going to get out of this one? Both of them just wanted me to relax a little, enjoy myself.

Rita changed the rules. "No business talk tonight. You've been here long enough. What other things do you want to try? What do you miss that you did at home?"

Cassie wound down as they ate. They had a wonderful conversation about things besides work. Her body was sore but relaxed; her usual evening tension dissipated along with it. Reflections on her outburst were temporarily shelved in the back of her mind.

"This Friday night is the town's Fall Party at the Mall. Dan will be back. We never miss it. As the new manager of the hotel, you should go. The town needs to see us present. The hotel has nothing to do with the party. It's organized by the people at the Mall. The hotel makes a contribution of soft drinks and wine. Everyone celebrates a good summer and fall before the busy holiday season starts in a few weeks."

*

On the short walk to the guesthouse she mumbled, "Only two years." She felt like Tank with his tail between his legs after knocking over a water dish or leaving something on the carpet that didn't belong there.

"Well, Cassie, you handled that one a little rashly, didn't you?" She was reprimanding herself in the mirror again, preparing for bed. Toothpaste ran down her chin as she shook her head yes. She wiped her mouth and pointed the toothbrush at her reflection. "Why don't you go lay down, young lady, and think about how to fix this?"

Chastised, she climbed into bed and pulled the covers up to her chin.

Rita was right. All I do is work. The mechanics of the hotel and its complex relationship with the valley and surrounding communities were clearer now. She and Justin had had some great brainstorming discussions about going forward after the opening. She couldn't be happier with all the department heads. Was the constant working becoming a habit to cover other things: justifying her obscene salary, trying to guarantee she wouldn't fail? There were other things to do around here after work, fun things, distractions to put some normalcy back in her life. Hell, today was a colossal example.

Her thoughts drifted back to today's outburst and Cliff.

It had been a glorious day before she called Dan. The sights, the sounds, the smells were still vivid in her mind. *I rode a horse! God, all Cliff was trying to do was make me enjoy myself, spin me down a little. And he did a blockbuster job.* Rita had called out to him, and he delivered the best way he could. It was a new, wonderful experience, and she'd thanked him by berating him, jumping down his throat with recriminations. All he'd ever done was try to help her since day one at the allotments. He'd covered for her, tried to minimize her embarrassment. He was more than entitled to have a laugh at her expense.

Why was she so confused by him? She was used to the New York City social tap dance. Men and women, restricted by new social norms, fencing around each other during getting-to-know-you encounters. Rarely direct, never blunt, were the rules. Be careful about personal questions, very cautious with humor so as not to offend. Politically Incorrect Cliff Walker couldn't care less. Woke to him was something you did after sleeping. Yet, there he was, a nice, considerate person with an amusingly twisted sense of humor. Casual as could be, everyone loved him.

Cassie's pleasantly aching body demanded sleep. She'd work on her apology in the morning. Before nodding off, she felt the chill of the night and thought about Old Molly. Had someone put her blanket on? She'd seen pictures of horses wearing blankets.

*

She hadn't slept that well since she arrived. Molly had pounded her perpetual tension away, and she had to force herself to get out of bed. Stretching in the bathroom brought her back to normal. First, breakfast with Ethel, and then she'd prostrate herself in search of forgiveness.

Cliff was in the new spa, his temporary construction office in the back of the west wing. Empty but for two portable banquet tables full of plans, the walls recently covered in sheetrock, the floor still bare concrete.

Cassie entered and walked up to him, hands clasped in front of her. He looked serious as he studied something on a set of plans in his bright-orange safety vest. "May I speak with you for a moment?"

Cliff looked up, a look of mild apprehension on his face, his voice flat. "Of course, you're the boss. How can I help?"

Not a good start. Her apology would have to be profound. "I'm so sorry about my outburst yesterday. Rita explained everything. I was out of line. I overreacted. You've been more than good to me since that first night. I never even thanked you for that. And then you went and made that big effort yesterday when you also have a lot going on. All just to make me feel better, more at home here.

"I've always been a little introverted. Nervous about how people perceive me. At work, I tend to be a little bit of a control freak, always wanting to do things by myself, be in control. Yesterday, doing something new and out of my envelope, started out being so far out of my comfort zone that I was petrified. It ended up being exciting and wonderful. As you can probably tell, I get a little prickly when people make fun of me. It's my fault. Please, Cliff, I feel awful about how I barked at you. Please accept my apology."

"Apology accepted." Accompanied by a formal smile, not the usual impish one she'd grown to like.

"Thank you," said Cassie. "I should get back."

Sadly, she made her way back to her office. He'd forgiven her, but it didn't seem like he'd forget. Why was she so sensitive about what he thought of her?

Back in the office, Cassie called her confidant. It was noon in New York.

"Are you up yet?"

"Who is this and what do you want?" said Vivien.

Cassie ignored her. "What exciting things have you done this week? A ship christening? A fundraiser for polar bears? Fox hunting in the Berkshire hinterlands of western Massachusetts?"

"Hilarious, Cassie dear. You must have found your sense of humor in the bottom of the Grand Canyon where you lost it a few weeks ago. No, it's been quiet around here. You have no idea the strains people put on my life."

Cassie knew she'd have to be patient and listen to Vivien's trials and tribulations for a bit. She was always like this. The act had to wind down before she was normal. Vivien Van Houten ran one of the biggest charities in New York City. Friends cringed when invited to her cocktail parties. They left with empty wallets. Viv led by example. Years earlier, she'd worked three months at one of the soup kitchens before administration faltered. She went back to supervision and fundraising, her strong points. A day shopping with her took hours. She'd stop at every corner, dispensing cash or admonishing a homeless person to get to a shelter because the weather was changing fast. Half the homeless in New York knew her by name.

"I'm caring and considerate," lamented Vivien. "I don't clog the subway at seven in the morning, robbing your kind of a seat on the way to daily purgatory."

Enough. Time to cut her off. "Viv, you've never been on a subway."

"Not true, young lady. There was a cab strike about ten years ago. You have no idea how courageous I was. Now, why are you calling? You've abandoned me."

Cassie imparted her latest adventure with Cliff and her first horseback ride.

"My family wanted me to play polo," said Vivien. "Unlike you, I am coordinated. On a horse in the mountains? You? I'll fly my shrink out tomorrow. We can get you through this." Suddenly Viv started laughing. Vivid pictures of Little Miss Sheltered formed a reel in her head. "Stable bonding! You have to text me a photo of this Cliff person. I want it on my mantel. And he taught you how to always place your hand on a horse's backside when you walked behind it so it wouldn't kick back at you?"

"Yes."

"Do you think he wants to get his hand on your backside?"

"Vivien!"

In the midst of her giggling, Viv managed, "Sounds like love is in the air to me."

"So is Ebola, Miss Van Houten."

"Call me every few days. Your life is better than the opera. Oh, and stop worrying. Your little outburst will roll right off his back. He doesn't sound like the over-sensitive type."

Chapter Fifteen

Cassie was heading for the front desk to review some things with Nelly, when she noticed Lily in the lobby redoing the spectacular flower display on the center table. This time it was to be a magnificent burst of fall with all the muted colors. She approached her new friend. "Coffee when you're done?"

"Absolutely."

Cassie leaned over the end of the registration desk, going over a document, when she noticed Justin whisk by, buttoning his jacket and pushing his hair back. He was always pushing that hair back. Cassie was going to tell him to get a haircut or buy him a barrette. The cliché finger came up and pushed his glasses up his nose. *Cute,* Cassie thought. He'd jump to handsome if a good woman did some work on him. He scurried to a halt in front of Lily and the flower display. Cassie couldn't hear them, but his animated face and body language were a complete giveaway. Justin Banks had eyes for Lily Walker.

The exchange was quick—his nerves, probably. When he left, Cassie caught Lily's eye, smiled, and gave her the tilted head and raised eyebrow signal for 'What's going on there?'

Lily smiled back and shrugged.

They took a table in the back of the dining room. Cassie wanted to take a break, have a little gossip, and didn't want to disturb Ethel in the kitchen.

"I'm not in this room often—magnificent, isn't it?" said Lily. "I usually send one of the girls to do the tables in here and the guest rooms, but I enjoy doing the lobby display myself."

"You probably change that display a couple of times a month. Find me when you do. We'll make this a thing."

They settled for coffee and a sweet from the dessert trolley.

"Forgive the curiosity," said Cassie. "Is there something going on with you and Justin? He appeared very pleased to see you."

Did Lily just blush?

"I have no idea. He's so nice and attentive when I'm here. Occasionally comes into the shop and buys flowers or chocolates he doesn't need. Tries to make small talk but is a disaster at it." Lily raised her hands. "I think he likes me, but he won't make a move."

"Oh, from what I just saw, he likes you. Everyone I've talked to thinks he's great, but the word 'shy' always pops up. I'm afraid the ball is in your court."

Cassie garnered tidbits about the town, people, and places, before getting to it. "I snapped at your brother the other day. All my fault. I apologized, but I don't know how forgiving he is."

"Good for you. Mister Free and Easy needs a good snapping at once in a while. He's been alone too long. Don't worry, Cassie, he'll take it in stride. My brother is competent at work, but after that, he's everybody's five-year-old. Rita dotes on him, my mother dotes on him, Ethel dotes on him—hell, he's even got me conned. You interested? Please, take him off our hands. He'd be a great hobby for you. Nobody needs grandchildren to pamper, they've all got my dear brother." Lily figured an example would help. "A couple of years ago, he had a date, had her over for dinner. His culinary skills extend to a microwave oven. Ethel cooked him a gourmet meal for two, even sent him home with silverware and china. It was probably the last time he got laid."

"That bad, huh?" said Cassie.

"Okay, maybe I'm a little harsh. Everybody does call him when they need help. Rita needs something fixed at the house—Cliff's there. Ethel misses crucial supplies on a delivery—Cliff's in his truck going to Sacramento. He worked nights redoing my shop."

Curious and confused, Cassie probed. "Why doesn't he have a girlfriend?"

"That one's easy. They all move away. Most kids raised in a quiet place like this can't wait to get out. Some come back after a few years. I even thought about staying in San Francisco. His high school sweetheart left. A girl he was serious with three years ago left. I think he's just given up. Doesn't want to be hurt anymore."

Digesting that, Cassie got to her other curiosity. It had been niggling at her for the past few weeks. What woman wasn't up for a good romance story? "Now, Lily, you have to tell me more about Travis Weaver and his wife."

"Okay, where did I stop last time?"

Anticipation dripped off of Cassie's voice. "Travis had arrived in San Francisco. He'd met Janet when she greeted him at the Ostlers' door. You said he wrote in his diary that he paid her no attention."

"Okay," said Lily. "Remember, I tell this like a romance novel, but my made-up conversations are all based on facts from the diaries."

Cassie nodded and settled back in her chair.

"So, the next day, Mrs. Ostler invites Janet into her study and introduces her to Travis. The situation explained about his empty house in the middle of the mountains, she left them together to sort it out. Watching Janet Wilson while things were explained to her, Travis knew he would be a massive burden on her already busy day, but logic prevailed. Who better to help with his house problems than a housekeeper? Mrs. Ostler and her friends had more important things to do—find Travis a wife.

"When Mrs. Ostler left, Janet asked Travis to describe his house. He wrote that night that the housekeeper—unsmiling, proper and severe—intimidated him for some reason. Travis gave a very understated description of the house out of modesty. He jotted down that she had a poker player's neutral look and noticed that she had lovely dark-blonde hair and a very erect posture. She appeared to be about ten or fifteen years younger than him. How could a young, attractive, graceful woman be so severe?"

Lily collected her thoughts, drank some coffee, and ate some of her pastry before continuing. "From reading her diaries, I deduced that Janet was lively and happy in her youth, but had now drawn inward. The difficult years took their toll. Her son was now her universe; every thought was about securing his future. She'd touched very little of her inheritance.

"Her diary explained she knew from his accent and speech that Travis was no aristocrat from the homeland. No 'your grace' or 'your lordship' would apply. She addressed him as Mr. Weaver. She had to start somewhere.

"'What are your tastes, Mr. Weaver? English furniture? French furniture? Italian paintings? Asian touches? Do you want to mix styles? Perhaps one room in chinoiserie?'

"'Chinoiserie?'

"'It's very popular in London and back East with the well-to-do. It's an interpretation of Chinese and East Asian artistic traditions.'

She noted the blank look on Mr. Weaver's face. 'Why don't we go out and see some shops?' she suggested. 'You'll know if you like it or not.'

"Not an architect, nor an interior decorator, Janet could better them all in this category from her life in Hong Kong. It was a comfortable place to start for her, and she could feel him out more about his house and tastes."

Lily gave some background. "San Francisco had a large Chinese population. Years of immigrants came to work on the railroad and settled there, and it was the biggest port on the West Coast for Asian trade.

"Janet took him to the heart of the sprawling Chinatown. They maneuvered through the maze of tiny, almost hidden streets and alleys behind the small shops on the main roads, back to the larger warehouses. The array of smells from the densely packed community struck Travis. Various incenses floated out of the shops, exotic food smells he could almost taste from the restaurants and food stalls. He identified aromas of varnishes and sawn wood as they ventured deeper into the maze.

"No one knew that this was Janet Wilson's retreat, her hideaway on her days off. She and her son would enjoy wonderful Chinese meals westerners didn't appreciate nor even know about. They would browse in exotic shops and dark, mysterious warehouses full of imported goods. She would relive memories from happier days in the Orient. Americans were fearful of this area; she felt nothing but security.

"Janet almost smiled at the bewildered look on Mr. Weaver's face as they wove their way through fabulous Chinese artworks, exotic furniture, and bolts and bolts of intricate silk fabrics in the cluttered warehouse. Janet wondered why he was always asking what did *she* like?

"'Why don't you just make notes, Mr. Weaver? You can always come back.'

"One massive, elaborately painted, folding silkscreen impressed him. 'I'd like to buy that now, please.'

"He started to negotiate with the merchant. They were close to a price when Janet interrupted. In perfect Cantonese, she took over. Later, Travis wrote that he was dumbfounded. Before him was this now animated woman gesticulating with her hands, which rarely moved at other times. Scowls and smiles went back and forth between the two combatants. Finally, she turned to Travis and declared that they were leaving, spun around, and headed for the door, the merchant scurrying after her.

"'But my screen, Mrs. Wilson?' pleaded a confused Travis, as he too scurried after her.

"He was ignored while the other two continued their—was it a conversation?

"Everyone stopped at the door.

"'Pay the man this much,' said Janet.

"'But that's a lot less than we decided.'

"'It is, Mr. Weaver.' And she just stood there. 'Would you like something to eat now?'

"At a loss, Travis followed her. At home, the mountains were full of Chinese workers from the railroad work. Many labored for him during the construction of the house. He'd broken bread with them for years while supplying the railroad with various things. Chinese food appealed to him. Oh, but the meal they had—he described it later. He'd never eaten such food: didn't even know it existed. He lost himself in the sauces and delicacies, small portion after small portion. Whenever he inquired about what a dish was, Janet simply replied, 'Best not ask, Mr. Weaver,' accompanied by a rare, brief smile.

"Travis wrote that night that it was the first time he'd seen her smile. He realized, aside from being educated, elegant, and mysterious, Janet Wilson was also beautiful. During the animated bargaining with the merchant, her long, graceful fingers had mesmerized him moving about, emphasizing her stance in the negotiations."

Enthralled with the story, Cassie visualized it all in her head: the crowded markets, the smells, the elegant woman, the befuddled man. "And?" Cassie asked.

Lily said, "Okay, just a little more for today.

"That night, he was invited with the Ostlers to dinner at a friend's. Twelve people with two eligible daughters attended. It was one of those endless nights that Travis had heard about but never experienced: civil society, or whatever the hell they called it, was the way he wrote it. The daughters were attractive, exceptionally well-mannered, and displayed their skill in getting a man interested.

Exhausted when he returned home, he made no entry in his diary until the next night.

"The following day, Janet took him to an auction house and a large warehouse of used English and American furniture. 'Fortunes are made and lost on a regular basis in California, Mr. Weaver. There's no need to order expensive custom furniture or brand-new china and silverware from New York or London. Why don't we start with something simple like the dining room? Its needs are relatively universal.' They were standing in the middle of a gigantic warehouse full of furniture. 'Why not start with the dining table and chairs? Look around, see what appeals to you.' She placed her hand on a lovely Chippendale-style table with intricately carved chairs. It was about twelve feet long. 'Would this work in your home?'

"Janet was very specific in her diary about this conversation:

"Travis was sheepish. 'Um, larger.'

"It surprised Janet. 'Larger? How much larger, Mr. Weaver?'

"'Um, twice as big.'

"An eyebrow was raised. 'Exactly how large is your house, Mr. Weaver?'

"'Um, large.'

"Frustration was mounting. Stern now. 'How many rooms are in your house?'

"'Um, thirty, maybe forty rooms. I'm not sure what counts as rooms.'

"They looked for a while but bought nothing. Janet was uncomfortable with how a simple task had expanded. 'We need to talk, Mr. Weaver.' And she again marched off to a nearby restaurant.

"This next part was from his diary.

"Janet expressed her frustration in no uncertain terms. 'Mr. Weaver, this is not my area of expertise. I have no idea what your house looks like. I have no idea of your tastes. You need a professional interior designer. The house must be seen, measured, evaluated. There's so much to consider. The list is endless, and I have neither the time nor expertise.'

"Travis felt a bond with this strange woman—comfortable around her most of the time. Strength and confidence radiated off of her. Grace and ease contrasted with her bartering image in fluent Cantonese, not being bullied by the merchant.

"'No. No, I need *you* to help me, Mrs. Wilson. I don't think I could sit in a room for over ten minutes with some pompous designer who I didn't know and didn't trust. Please. I can talk to the Ostlers, and you could come to see the house. I'll pay *you* to speak to some designers. With the train, it's less than a day's journey. You could be back in less than a week. I have plans for the house somewhere. You could see it yourself and bring them back and show them to whoever you want. I need *your* help, Mrs. Wilson. I trust you.'

"'That's simply not possible, Mr. Weaver!' Janet was utterly taken aback. 'I have work. I have a son. I couldn't possibly leave.'

"'Your son would love it. I'm not so sure about you. It's not in a bustling, vibrant city. It's remote. Your son would love being on my lake, playing with the dogs, riding a horse.'

"'You have a *lake*, Mr. Weaver?'

"'More like a pond, but big enough for a small boat. He could wade in it.'

"According to Travis, the battle went on for a while.

"It was settled that night. She could go for a week. The Ostlers almost insisted. Twenty-six-year-old Janet Wilson was going to see the American wilderness that she'd read about and heard about for years. Her diary entry that night couldn't hide the excitement, the anticipation. She also wrote that night—'I estimate him to be ten to fifteen years my senior. I stumbled today and grabbed his arm for balance. It felt like grasping a steel pole. An approximation of age is difficult. His face is strong, lined, and tanned from the outdoors, but he is much more fit than city men.'"

Lily winked at Cassie. "Sounds like my brother, doesn't it? I'm winded. That's it for today. I have work to do."

"You're joking. You can't stop now." Absorbed in the story, Cassie's frustration showed. "Give me your paper, and I can read it."

"Nope. I tell it much better. When I'm finished, I'll give you the actual diaries to read."

Chapter Sixteen

Friday, at one o'clock, Cassie was again talking to Cliff by the unfinished pool outside the spa office. Over the past few days, she'd found herself making excuses to see him and soften the divide between them by asking his counsel about various items on her agenda, trying to learn about the construction work. The coordination of the new work was a mystery to Cassie, but it was her responsibility to keep track even though it was Cliff's domain. He was always easy to spot, running around in his cute orange vest.

Tank was quickly by her side, now a fixture in her life like the man in front of her. She reached down and scratched behind his ear.

While they were talking, Cassie saw him look up over her shoulder. There was a man by the construction door to the lobby wearing a camel-hair topcoat with a silk scarf and perfectly combed hair. Highly polished shoes stood out against the rough concrete. Not unusual around the hotel with the type of guests it drew, just out of place in the construction area.

"He must be looking for you," said Cliff.

Cassie turned, her mouth fell open, and couldn't help uttering a soft "Oh, hell."

Cassie looked back at Cliff and offered a quick, "Excuse me."

Herschel. Here.

She walked up to him. "Herschel, what are you doing here?"

"The office in New York told me, and then I tracked this place down. Can we go somewhere and talk?"

Not sure she wanted to be alone with him in her office, Cassie chose a remote table in the nearly empty dining room.

Herschel's lament started. "I made a colossal mistake, Cassie. I'd forgotten how wonderful you are and had to come out here and tell you face to face. I knew after a few weeks she wasn't right for me. It only took that long to realize how badly I screwed up, how much I missed you. Is there any chance of you taking me back? I'll do anything you want."

His sincerity touched Cassie, as did his effort coming all the way out to California. Not dismissing him immediately, she needed to think about this. Talk about a shock. The suddenness of it all confused her. Today of all days, especially with the party tonight.

Stall.

Not betraying any feelings, neutral mask in place despite the tension, Cassie said, "Herschel, this is all very sudden, all very confusing. I'm swamped right now, and we have a big party tonight. Why don't you settle in, relax, and we'll talk later? I'll get you a room. We'll have time after the party."

*

"What the hell am I going to do?" boomed into Vivien's ear.

As soon as she'd gotten Herschel into a room, Cassie bolted for her office, locked the door, sat for a few minutes, and called up her friend.

"Well, let's start by calming down. You say he just got there? Showered you with his new-found feelings and groveled for forgiveness? Please tell me you didn't commit to anything."

"No, I'm in panic mode. All I could do was stall. On top of everything else, we have an important party tonight. I put him in a room and said we'd talk later."

The coldness was evident in Vivien's voice. "Well, if it were me, it would be a very short conversation." Her tone softened. "But we're not talking about me, we're talking about you, so let's take it a step at a time.

"What feelings do you still have for him? Be honest. This isn't the time for vacillating, dear. By the time your night is over, you're either going to be free of him or bound to him. What did you feel right after you talked and before you called me?"

"Well, I sat at my desk for a while before I called. Seeing him here was quite a shock. I mean coming all this way to apologize—I don't know what to think. He seemed so sincere. But then, everything he did to me played in slow motion through my head. You know how hurt I was."

Vivien had her way of simplifying situations and tried to be tactful. "I'm sure Jaws felt bad after grabbing half the children in Massachusetts off the beach and eating them, but do you think he decided to retire after that? No, that's who Mr. Jaws is. That's his nature."

Well, maybe it was directness she was good at. This really wasn't the time to be tactful.

"Cassie, I understand a man who thinks he's in love and suddenly finds himself captured by another woman and breaks it off with number one. This happens every day. That's not what Herschel did to you. He played both sides, stringing you along while he was seeing and screwing number two for a *long* time. And now it's confirmed, he did it to give himself a career boost. The greedy bastard wasn't happy with the prospects of a future with you. He saw a flashier, more prosperous life with her and made his decision. Could you ever trust him not to do it again?"

Cassie sighed but said nothing.

"Me babbling at you is not going to help. The best advice I can give you is to allow facts and logic to be part of your choice, not just your emotions. Examine it. Is this still the man you see spending your life with?"

They talked for a bit more before Cassie hung up, slumped in her chair, and pondered the situation.

*

The festivities were underway. Even though it was closed for the night, a large sign outside the Mall said PRIVATE PARTY. This was only for the local businesses and hotel staff. Cassie and Herschel sat at one of the small tables scattered around the large open space of the second Mall building, the one with the lounge area overlooking the lake. She'd picked one as far away from the action as possible, feeling awkward about how she'd introduce Herschel to anyone who stopped by—she opted to say "friend from New York."

They had rolled the portable booths and stands to the sides against the permanent shops. A band was set up in front of the windows overlooking the lake to one side of the massive fireplace. Several makeshift bars served drinks; tables overflowed with food and snacks. The place was packed.

She'd asked that they put off talk about their relationship until later.

Herschel sat for a moment, legs crossed, and surveyed the room. The attire ran from dressed up to Levi's with plaid flannel shirts. Footwear went from high heels to cowboy boots. "God, this really is hillbilly heaven, isn't it?" said Herschel. "Whatever made you consider taking this job?"

Not a good start as far as Cassie was concerned. She understood where he was coming from; she'd been there. Sophisticated, cosmopolitan New York had no problem minimizing the rest of the world. She surprised herself as she jumped to their—and now realized, her own—defense.

"I haven't met a bad person since I've been here," she said. "See those people out there? Their lives aren't governed by ego, or greed, or an unbending desire to get to the top." Mild anger about what he'd done to her surfaced. "They're not thinking about who they can kick on the way up the corporate ladder. You're looking at an actual community—people who support and help each other. I was only here for a week before I realized that much. The manners around here shame New York, and, believe it or not, I admire them. Being here, in this new environment, has made me see a lot of my own shortcomings."

After she'd said it, she was shocked to realize it was true. It had never entered her mind before, was never given a thought. She didn't feel like she was alone, like she might in a bar or restaurant or social function back home.

"Wow, okay. Sorry. I've only been to places like this on vacation. I meant nothing by it. It was just another of my flip remarks. The whole town, the whole area, is stunningly beautiful. I'll go get us a couple of drinks."

While he was gone, Cassie surveyed the crowd. Dan and Rita were locked in conversation at a table with Ann and Jim Walker and several other people. Glimpsed through the throng of bodies, she watched Cliff as he finished one dance with a lovely blond his own age and was at it again with Ethel. The two of them should have been in a Fred Astaire movie. Cassie remembered what a wonderful dancer he was.

The night labored on. She danced with Herschel, danced with Dan, spoke with people she knew, and met new ones. Food was consumed along the way. It was all very relaxed and casual, everyone smiling and happy, not afraid to have a good time.

Periodically, she scanned the room to see where Cliff was: mostly on the dance floor with attractive women. Yes, she admitted, he was probably the catch of Manor Valley. Unfortunately, she wasn't in the market.

Why hasn't he asked me to dance?

Herschel was engaged in conversation with two guys at the bar. Cassie noticed Cliff sitting alone, looking exhausted from all the dancing. She took the opportunity to go over and say hi. She'd keep it light since he still seemed distant after their words earlier in the week.

"So, Fred Astaire, can I ride Old Molly when I want? Take her out on the trails? What do I have to do?"

Lots of dancing and a few drinks seemed to make him more receptive to her than over the past few days. Cliff straightened in his chair, swiveling his body to face her. A palm came up by his smiling face, the smile she was used to before this week's faux pas.

"No. It's too dangerous to go out by yourself right now. That was only your first ride." He paused to sip his beer. "If you're serious, I have an idea."

"I'm listening."

"Okay. Talk to Lily. She used to give lessons and do barrel racing all through high school and summers during college. Ask her if she'll give you a few lessons. She'll tell you when you're ready. I warn you, it will be more than a few. Riding well isn't easy—it just looks that way." To reinforce his logic, he added, "Ask Harry, the maitre d' in the dining room. Lily taught him and his partner."

"Harry in the dining room rides?" Eyes wide, Cassie showed her surprise. Older, around Dan's age, Harry was as elegant as they came. With short salt-and-pepper hair, a deep voice that seemed to have been cultivated for years, regal was a poor word to describe him. He had Denzel Washington's looks and James Earl Jones's Darth Vader voice. She knew that Dan had talked him into moving to the valley years ago after he parted ways with the management of Dan's favorite high-end restaurant in New York.

Cliff leaned over confidentially. "When Harry and his partner Clayton arrived here, they were somewhat unnerved and wary, not knowing what to expect. They were the first Black people in the valley. On top of that, they're gay.

"They wanted to fit in and be a part of the community right away. One day, they drove up to the stables and asked the first person they saw, which happened to be Lily, who was all of sixteen, about lessons. To this day, they go on and on about how welcome she made them feel. How she introduced them around and made them feel at home. To them, Lily is the queen of the valley. They dote on her."

Back to the point, he added, "Lily won't take any money from you since business is good, and you're the new Queen Kong around here." He leaned back in his chair, using his hand to push his hair back. "Buy her something or take her into Sacramento for a spa day."

People were drifting back to his table, and Herschel was standing in the distance looking for her. Time to get back.

She sat with Herschel for a bit and found herself preoccupied and determined to learn about this riding stuff. Every day she thought about how invigorating and peaceful that first ride had been.

"Excuse me for a moment," she said to Herschel. "I have to ask somebody something."

From one end of the room, Herschel watched Cassie talking to Lily. From the other end, Cliff watched the same discussion with a smile on his face.

Dan, tired from his own share of dancing, drifted over and plopped himself down beside Cliff. They were alone, so he confided in Cliff his apprehension about the old boyfriend showing up so unexpectedly.

Cliff sipped his beer and said, "No matter what happens, Uncle Dan, she won't go back on her word. She's not the type."

*

Later, back in the hotel bar tucked away in a quiet corner, Cassie was distracted while Herschel pleaded his case. While he talked, she made comparisons: uncomfortable and unexpected comparisons with Cliff. Things that previously flitted across her mind but never fully surfaced. Herschel talked about how perfect they were together in terms of social circles and combined income, hardly anything about her personally. Cassie wanted to hear some passion, some emotion, some curiosity about what *she* wanted in life. She was being offered a corporate merger.

On reflection, Cassie wasn't disappointed with Herschel. In their time together, she had embraced the corporate merger right along with him. She realized Vivien had been right. The feelings weren't there anymore. And, until now, she hadn't been aware of the beehive of new feelings that recently played with her: feelings about the challenging new job, about all the new people, about new experiences like horseback riding or quietly sitting by the fireplace in the Mall with a cup of coffee. Even some feelings about Fred Astaire twirling around the dance floor with all the women, which were quickly shunted aside.

Cassie gave Herschel the bad news before she said goodbye and drove home alone.

Chapter Seventeen

In bed, his hands stroked her body. Naked skin squirmed under the caress as his fingers glided softly over her thighs. Behind her, his mouth buried itself in Cassie's neck. She spun and pulled him on top of her. "Yes," she whispered. It was a blur of sensuality, a frenzied attack by both of them. She was on top of him now, taking in the muscled body below her. Both sweating, not getting enough. It was time. It had been so long. Cassie was moaning, ready.

The alarm went off.

Jesus! It was Saturday, why the hell was the alarm on? Cassie looked around to make sure she was alone. The sheets were all bunched at the bottom of the bed, and she was sweating. What the hell was all *that* about? Terrorist, shifty character, drunk, and now sex fiend.

What is my life coming to?

Up and somewhat organized, she swore not to go into the office on a Saturday. But thoughts of work and the uncomfortable encounter with Herschel caused the stress to rise again, and she was unable to relax in the cottage. The dream hadn't helped. Rita was right, she had to develop some activities outside of work, or she'd fall apart. She grabbed her coat and scarf, drove down to the Mall, parked her car, and set out on a walk along the lakefront. A half hour out and a half hour back at a good clip left her relaxed as she sat by the big Mall fireplace with a cup of coffee, ignored by the milling crowd of shoppers, lost in the fall view around the lake. As she went to her car, a place called the Sports Shop across the road drew her attention. She marched across the street.

*

Sunday morning, she was jogging down the hill, past the allotments, and along the lake in her new outfit. She hadn't jogged since college. At the gym in New York, she used to pick a nature video to put on the treadmill screen and picture herself jogging through the woods or along a beach. Now she was actually doing it! She felt free and happy.

On the way back, she slowed to a walk before climbing the hill by the allotments toward home. The narrow dirt road opposite the greenhouse led back to the stables, hidden behind the trees. She walked back to see Old Molly.

One worker recognized her from the party; he knew she was the new manager. "Can I help you?"

Cassie introduced herself and asked where Molly was. Asked him if he had any carrots. He ducked into a building and returned with two carrots.

"Over there, the stall with the open door is Molly's. If it's not busy, we leave it open so she can come and go. She's gentle with everybody, especially the kids. She's afraid of cars and won't go past the parking lot or out to the road. Have a look around, she's here somewhere."

Molly was over by the riding ring, supervising some dressage practice. As Cassie approached, Molly lifted her head from the fence and turned to her. She tried to smile, but the lower lip wasn't up for it, so Cassie got a lot of happy teeth.

She broke the carrots in pieces and put them on her palm like Cliff had taught her. Molly chewed while Cassie stroked her head.

"Why do they call you Old Molly?" she asked. "From now on, you'll be Queen Molly."

Molly had never heard 'Queen' before but felt like royalty nonetheless.

On her way back past the allotments heading home, Cassie noticed the repaired fence. Did Mr. Deer have a wife and kids? Would they starve with snow and winter coming? Maybe she should knock it down again.

*

She steamed through Monday and Tuesday. No more nagging tension in her neck and shoulders after starting her jogging routine for an hour at lunchtime. Tomorrow was her first lesson with Lily.

Cassie headed for the dining room. She'd been surprised by Cliff's revelation about Harry, the maitre d' from New York and now a horseman. In her short weeks at the hotel, she'd spoken to him only briefly on several occasions. He'd always been pleasant and somewhat formal. His bearing and command as he walked around the dining room intimidated her a little, she admitted to herself. On the few occasions she'd been in the dining room when he was on duty, she found herself sitting up straighter and pulling her shoulders back when he approached. She'd never met his partner, Clayton. Never gave it a second thought until Cliff mentioned it.

Time to get to know Harry better.

It was late afternoon, and the room was almost empty. She knew from the staff rotation that he had just come on for the evening shift.

"Good afternoon, Harry. Could you sit with me for a few minutes?"

"Of course, Cassie. Coffee?"

"Yes, thank you."

A nod from Harry and someone started to move on the other side of the room as they sat at a small table away from the few guests. He held her chair out for her.

"Harry, I'm sorry I haven't spent more time talking to you. As you can imagine, there's a lot I have to learn to get up to speed around here. I did learn early on that two people I'd never have to worry about are you and Ethel. Let's just call the two of you old school and leave it at that. By that I mean reliant, efficient, dependable problem solvers who don't need me over their shoulders. This is actually a social visit."

"That's very kind of you, Cassie. I was wondering why you hadn't taken advantage of the dining room more often."

She smiled as she reached for her coffee cup, not wanting to be scrutinized by him in case she held it wrong. Was he looking at her as if she had a baseball cap backwards on her head? She kept her arms off the table. "I just found out you're from New York. I think you can relate to my experience that the transition to Manor Valley is quite a jump. How did you feel about it when you arrived?"

He actually laughed out loud. "How long do you have?" he managed. "What have you heard about my background so far? It might help to keep my story to a few hours." Another nod and he summoned the dessert cart.

"I know about the restaurant in New York. How Dan conned you into coming here, just like me. I know you have a partner, Clayton, who I haven't met yet. And I know you ride—that's one of the main reasons I'm here talking to you. Cliff took me on my first ride recently, and I'm taking my first lesson with Lily tomorrow."

He seemed to relax in his chair, crossed his legs to the side and even put an elbow on the table as he sipped his coffee. *God, maybe I should reprimand* him.

"Clayton and I ride at least three times a week. Because of my shift changes, we get to go in the mornings sometimes, sometimes in the evening. The changes in the landscape depending on the sun are wonderful. Gray skies, rain, cold—it makes no difference. Don't get either of us started on Lily. Wonderful young lady. We're gay, Black, and from another section of the planet, and she helped us settle into this new environment, showed us around, introduced us to everyone. She'll turn you into a rider in no time.

"As far as the adjustment goes, come to me anytime. I'm sure our perspectives are the same. Believe me, it *is* an adjustment. I can only tell you how it is for us, but we would never move back to New York. We love to visit but could never live there after being here this long."

They chatted a little longer. Cassie knew he had work to do and decided to leave him to it. She was thrilled she'd taken the time to break the ice with him.

"If you need anything, you know where to find me," she said. "I'll meet Clayton soon?"

"You will. When you're all trained up, we'll ride together— maybe have you over for dinner, and we can compare stories about Manor Valley surprises for us easterners."

Chapter Eighteen

Lily said Old Molly wasn't the horse to learn on—too gentle. Molly watched from the side of the riding ring while Cassie rode through her first lesson. Molly tried to smile and get Cassie's attention, but it didn't work again—just a mouth full of big, stained teeth. Toothpaste companies wouldn't be signing her up for photoshoots. She knew humans always waved to each other with their front hooves. Molly tried that, but couldn't get her leg high enough. Cassie was totally focused on Lily's instructions and the lively horse under her. She finally noticed Molly with her head over the gate on her third turn around the ring. She waved. "Hi, Molly! How am I doing?"

Lily had Cassie up on Molly's son, appropriately named Sonny, five years old and spirited. A new rider had to learn how to control eleven hundred pounds of nervous energy under her, and that idiot son of hers fit the bill. Molly watched as Lily taught Cassie the basics. She approved. Lily was a good teacher. Sonny was a good-looking quarter horse. She thought he must have gotten his looks from his father. The hour flew by.

When the lesson finished up by the gate, Molly's son caught Cassie off guard with her back turned when she dismounted. He smacked her with his head, throwing her off balance. Cassie stumbled and caught herself on the top rail of the riding ring. Molly leaned across the low fence and bit Sonny in the ass. He'd been a pain in the same place since he was a kid, hanging out with those other young hooligans in the south paddock.

The two women walked back toward the barn. "A little different from Old Molly?" asked Lily.

"Wow, I can see how something this big can get away from you. That was exciting."

"You don't have to worry when you're in the riding ring, but if you're out on a trail, never let him get his head and neck stretched all the way out. He'll be off, and it'll be hell slowing him down," said

Lily. "Do you want to do it again later in the week? Business is quiet now before it picks up in a few weeks. Do you have the time?"

"Sign me up!" With her renewed energy, Cassie could make up for it by working late.

Cassie gave Molly her carrots and a big thank you for looking out for her. Leo, the stable manager, came up to her. He was ruggedly handsome and spoke in a soft voice. "You looked terrific for your first lesson, Cassie. You had a good seat out there." He gave her a pat on the shoulder.

"Thank you, Leo." She knew it was a compliment, and satisfaction ran through her. She'd forgive the uninvited touching, understanding that many of the men out here were still not enlightened about the appropriate conduct employed during interpersonal communications. Cassie had no idea what 'good seat' meant, but it sounded dangerously close to Cliff's comment about her butt on the way to Auburn. She'd have to check with Lily, who was getting into her car.

"It means you were sitting correctly in the saddle." Lily laughed. "No need to file a complaint with human resources, especially since you *are* the human resources department. And Leo is one of the nicest men in the valley."

As Lily drove away, Cassie looked around at the complex. She'd been too distracted and nervous the day of her first ride, ditto for today's first lesson. She'd never been to a stable before and assumed it would be all worn, ramshackle buildings with chipped paint, broken fences, and mud and manure all over. However, it was, after all, a hotel concession and therefore the hotel's responsibility. This place was pristine. More in line with an elaborate English estate than her vision of a working stable open to the public. Maybe the horses had toilets in their barns? Her mind briefly grappled with imagining the size of a toilet a horse would need and quickly cast *that* thought aside.

In the car heading toward the hotel, Cassie reviewed her lesson. There was so much to it—walk, canter, trot, gallop. A horse could even go backward. She knew some cars had four speeds, but a horse?

In the office, she logged onto Amazon and searched out horse books and videos. She chose a few and hit purchase. It was her first time using Amazon in the valley. How long would things take to arrive? Two weeks? Two months? She went looking for Justin.

His glasses were halfway down his nose. Justin peered over them like a schoolteacher. "Cassie, we're twenty minutes from a freeway and an hour from the capital of California. If you want overnight delivery, you can get overnight delivery."

*

She checked her schedule and spent the afternoon with the accountant in the office next to Dan's. Rose had been with them for ages. She was a friend of Rita's and lived in one of the neighboring valleys with her husband. Both daughters were off at college.

Cassie understood numbers, knew their worth in running a business, and knew they could point out danger signals as well as health. The usual profit and loss statements, balance sheets, and cash flow statements gave a broad overview, but Cassie occasionally liked to look at the actual ledgers, the real nitty-gritty, and see exactly what was purchased, by whom, and for what purpose. It was tedious work, but today she was energized after her lesson. Focused.

She spent some time rolling through the ledger before looking up at Rose. "Wow, this is all so different than the items I'm used to back East. I'm going to need you as an interpreter. Evidently, we have our own landscape department?"

The various items were a puzzle to her—fertilizer, irrigation parts, equipment expenditures, even gas for vehicles. In New York, she didn't even know if they had hose bibs on the outside of the hotels.

All the things that went into maintenance for the Mall and boat concessions were equally confusing. Payroll alone, with all the part-time younger workers, required its own part-time worker.

Wine expenditures shocked her. She rolled her eyes at Rose. "Why doesn't Dan just buy a winery?"

"Actually," said Rose, "we are heavily invested in a couple of them."

Cassie rolled her eyes again. Enough for today. She'd ask Cliff to explain the ins and outs of landscaping later.

A text from Justin came in. He wanted to discuss staff scheduling for the coming busy season. She remembered Ethel telling her he

was in charge of that volatile item, jockeying all the part-time staff
for damn near the whole valley.

Chapter Nineteen

Cliff thought she looked terrific as she approached across the pool construction area. He'd seen her jogging along the lake and knew about the lessons. It showed. Unlike her haggard appearance of the past few weeks, Cassie was radiant now. He thought back to the Fall Party and the boyfriend showing up unexpectedly. *I wonder how that went?* He seemed like a decent guy, a snappy up-to-date dresser like her. They looked like a nice couple when they sat together at the party. They'd do well together back in New York.

It had been a tough few weeks for her, adjusting, settling in. He thought back to the horse ride and how she'd snapped at him. To give her credit, when Rita explained, she had apologized and it seemed sincere.

She smiled as she approached. At least he hadn't done anything wrong this week.

"Looks like Cassie Bryant from New York, age thirty-one, is settling in. I've seen you jogging. You look like a new breath of fresh air around here. How was your lesson with Lily?"

Cassie beamed at the comment. "Some equestrian people from the Olympics are already calling, Mr. Walker. You're going to have to pick up your game if you want to keep up with me. I can even make a horse go backward."

Cliff shook his head and smiled.

Their professional relationship was comfortable. He enjoyed it when Cassie would bring coffee to his office, where they'd sit while Cliff patiently explained things about the new buildings, scheduling, the timeline for completion. Early spring was still the target.

A professional trust was building between them. Today he answered her questions about various people in the hotel and how best to handle them, allowing her to get a different viewpoint. "Carmen, the head of housekeeping, is a trove of information. I think she's the most observant and hardest worker here. Let her know you recognize that."

Cliff enjoyed his time with Cassie, but felt her friendliness was just that. He sensed that she wanted things to remain professional and did his part to stay the course. Now and then, he'd noticed some edginess surface, probably from being unsettled and insecure in the new job and strange living environment. In any event, she had no time for a personal life. At least her long hours were broken up by her jogging and riding lessons. Cliff thought the diversions balanced her, made her happy.

"Now, landscaping, Mr. Walker. Explain, please."

"Yes, all the green stuff around the hotel, and the Mall, and the stables, and the rest of the valley. I've seen it."

She squinted at him over her coffee cup. "Are you going to be difficult today, Mr. Walker?"

His shoulders slumped in resignation. "It's no small operation around here. They have their own warehouse way at the back of the stable area. Is this going to take long?"

A stern, raised eyebrow accented the squint.

"Okay, okay. Spit it out. Give me some questions."

"That's better. Landscaping sounds like an outside activity or outside operation, or whatever it is you're in charge of. Is it your responsibility?"

Cliff folded his arms across his chest and smiled. "Nice try. No, you can't blame me every time a leaf turns brown or a rose drops on the ground. Since it's a hotel department, it's all yours." She was trying to find her way, so he explained better. "Luckily, it's run by Juan Hernandez. He's on top of everything. You should find him and introduce yourself. His son works with him. They have a crew that varies from about three to six or seven depending on the season."

Cassie looked down at her notes. "Thank you. Now, something simple. What's irrigation about around here and why is it so expensive?"

Oh, God. It'll be a late dinner for me tonight.

Chapter Twenty

Cassie wrapped things up in the office around seven Thursday night. Physical diversions were going well with riding and jogging, but she needed a mental distraction. She drove over to the Mall and entered Lily's shop. It closed at eight.

"Time for a drink after you lock up?"

"I'd love to," said Lily.

Cassie went over to the restaurant, bought two beers, and was seated in the relaxing area, taking in the view, when Lily came up. Many of the merchants stayed on for a drink after work when the front doors were locked.

They gossiped for a while before Lily sipped her beer and said, "Okay, let me guess. You want to hear more of the story."

"Yes, please. When you left off last time, Janet Wilson was going to Manor Valley to see Travis's house, and wife shopping wasn't going well for him."

Lily warmed to the subject. This was her favorite part of the tale.

"Janet recognized the house immediately. It was right out of Georgian England, a neoclassical design that architect Robert Adam would have been proud of. Janet hid her surprise well, but the house wasn't all that grabbed her attention. She was transfixed by the surroundings. Capability Brown, the famous English landscape designer from the time, couldn't have done better on the landscaping around the lake.

"Janet Wilson had seen flat, endless oceans for weeks at a time on her voyages from England to India and on to Hong Kong, and again from China to America. When you read her diaries, you'll cringe at her description of a typhoon just a few days out of Hong Kong on her way to San Francisco. You'll feel the terror of her not being able to do anything, except cling to her son and pray.

"Along with the endless oceans, in her youth she'd glimpsed the gentle, sparse rolling hills in the countryside outside London. But this—Manor Valley—this she'd never seen before. The majesty, the ruggedness, the rawness of it all: imposing mountains, dense forest with trees of every description, the wild surroundings put at ease by the placid lake. 'The primitive grace of it all,' was how she summed it up.

"The entire experience consumed her. It was autumn, and hundreds of the small, recently planted sapling trees around the lake were shedding their meager bounty of colorful leaves—colors from her childhood, colors from happier days. She watched the awe on her son's face and thought that's how she must have looked at his age.

"Janet, Travis, and Adrian, her son, were standing outside the front door after settling in. She could smell the pines and fir, and feel the crisp, clean air carried on a breeze caress her face. She thought she could smell the water while listening to the distant sounds of the forest.

"'Duss, pony. Duss, pony.' Little Adrian tugged on Mr. Weaver's jacket and pointed.

"Having little experience with children, Travis looked imploringly at Janet.

"She gathered the boy to her. 'I'm sorry, Mr. Weaver. 'Duss' means ducks.'

"Travis leaned down and said to Adrian, 'Well, let's walk down and see them.'

"When he stood, Janet gave him a rare smile. 'I thought you said it was a pond, Mr. Weaver?'

"Dark was creeping in when they returned. When they were halfway up the sweeping exterior stairs, they caught sight of a large buck deer creeping along the front of the house. It stopped thirty feet from them. He raised his head and held his ground, fixing them in his eyes. Dim light bounced off his massive antlers. Both Adrian and Janet were transfixed as the animal stared at them. Finally, two of Travis's dogs chased him off.

"In bed that night, Janet Wilson allowed herself a selfish moment—a rare moment thinking of herself and not her son. After a lengthy description of what she'd seen, what she'd felt that first day, she wrote of her epiphany—a sudden revelation that she belonged here in Manor Valley. Her soul belonged here, she wrote. The unflinching eyes of the magnificent stag that afternoon, as if transmitting a message, had bored it into her mind.

"Tomorrow Janet would be bold. She would ask Mr. Weaver if the position of housekeeper had been filled."

Lily cut off her story again. "More next time. I have to get home. I'm beat."

On her drive home, Cassie felt goose bumps all over. When she passed the greenhouse, she slowed and looked at the allotment plots, remembering her experience with the large stag her first day in Manor Valley. His message to her was probably different than the one to Janet years ago. His message was probably "Get out! Get out now while you still can!"

*

The Monday before Thanksgiving, Cassie's stress meter swung into the red zone. Saturday, she'd had her first fall off a horse. It had shaken her, but, like the proverbial riding a bike, Lily had mad e her get back up and continue. Sunday, she ached and limped around as she tried to pack for her trip home, all the while preoccupied with things she had to do at work. Guilt at letting the team down by leaving surfaced periodically. To compound it all, Herschel had called, pleading his case again. She'd lied and told him she wasn't coming home for the holiday.

The plan was to catch the afternoon flight to New York tomorrow, Tuesday. Her plans were scrambled when the airline bumped her to a red-eye flight at night and threw in a connection in Chicago to boot.

At her desk, she rubbed her head, the pressure of another twelve-hour day looming. Justin completed the staff's scheduling for the holiday, but she felt it her responsibility to review it. Cassie knew she was a micromanager and needed to work on fixing it. The tendency had grown worse recently with all the things on her plate. On top of everything else, the boss wanted her to review the hotel's management agreement with the chain before giving the lawyers final approval.

No time for a run. Around two o'clock, Cassie took two aspirins to ward off a headache, frustration from the icing being layered on her pressure cake. Fatigue and hopelessness were also creeping onto the table.

Only two years. Only two years.

Cliff stuck his head in the door. "Just wanted to give you an update. The marble tiles for the bathrooms will be six to eight weeks late. The supplier—"

"That's a major setback," Cassie snapped. "Everything is going to be two months late? Can't anybody get things right?" Her voice rose, control lost. Normal, composed hotel calm evaporated like water spilled on a hot New York summer sidewalk. Now of all times, a devastating blow to the completion schedule. "Do we deal with anybody besides incompetents? Did the tile company leave someone without work experience in charge?"

Cliff tried to explain, but she shut him down again. More words were spoken so coldly you could skate on them. "No. No. I don't want any excuses. I want—"

Cliff abruptly turned and walked out the door.

Long seconds passed as Cassie stood there with her mouth open. The ramifications of the outburst descended on her. She flopped back in her chair and held her head in her hands.

Some self-control regained, she dialed the supplier for an explanation, vowing to check her emotions. Someone had to fix this. Dan would flip when he found out.

The voice on the other end explained. "Didn't Cliff tell you? The shipment arrived from Italy, was offloaded in New York, and the tractor-trailer went off an icy bridge in the Midwest. They lost the whole shipment. We sorted it out yesterday. Cliff is always calling for updates. He's on top of it. The minute we found out, I called him. The new order will be here in six to eight weeks. Sorry, Cassie. One of those things nobody can do anything about. Cliff is having us ship the exterior pool stone tiles early, so the installers can just do them first and then move back to the bathrooms. He's going to do some tenting or something outside in case it snows or freezes. He'll stay on schedule that way. He's a clever, organized guy. We love dealing with him." He laughed. "And you guys always pay on time."

Oh, God, thought Cassie, as her appalling outburst etched itself deeper in her brain. He had been on top of it. He had been tracking it. God, everything had been going so smoothly. *One hiccup and I lost it.* Lost it badly.

Another apology rehearsed, she dialed Cliff's cell.

No answer.

This one was bad. She had to fix it now. Forgetting her coat, Cassie rushed down to his office. He wasn't there. She stopped and asked one of the workers.

"He and Tank just drove off."

Unable to focus, reprimanding herself again for her conduct, Cassie made her way back to her office. She sat at her desk, trying to regroup, struggling to pull it together, searching for some direction.

A vehicle is a mysterious collection of thousands of assorted parts, she thought. At any time, one could break, fall off, wear out, or just disappear. Hell, maybe they forgot to put it on in the first place, but you didn't jump all over the mechanic and unleash a Greta Thunberg–style rant on his incompetence: lambast him like he was responsible for all of General Motor's problems. The blame for World War II was probably still lying around somewhere. Why didn't she lay that on him too?

Back to business. She had to call Dan, make sure he was kept up to speed.

"There's a problem with the bathroom tiles."

"Cliff already called and explained it all. Nothing to be done about it."

Cassie wound down a notch. Unfamiliar with the construction business, she said, "You seem calm. Does this happen often?"

"Cassie, this level of construction can be a nightmare with all the different materials and all the different subcontractors. Stuff comes from all over the world. Hotel *management* is a repetitive process: systems are in place, minor mistakes are addressed and corrected. Construction is the opposite: everything is new, dependent on a list of architects, suppliers, and contractors too long to think about. It can be a nightmare at times. That's why Cliff is the project manager. He's good at it, stays calm through it all, jumps right on a solution. This won't be the last problem, I promise you."

Cassie offered her confession. "I snapped at him when he told me. Lashed out like it was his fault. There is no excuse for it."

"Well, guess what, Cassie? That's normal too. He said nothing about that on the phone, but it's water off a duck's back to him. Like I said, he stays calm and gets on with it. Don't ever be fooled by that easy-going manner of his."

Cassie sighed and slumped in her chair. *He didn't even say anything to Dan about my screaming at him.*

"Don't worry about it," Dan continued. "We'll be passing each other in the sky tomorrow. I'll talk with you when you get back. Have a pleasant trip home. You've earned it. I know you're under a lot of pressure." He searched for a few words of encouragement. "Trust me, it's not always like this."

After hanging up, she sat in silence for a long time and tried to sort out what was making her like this: an angry, mixed-up person she didn't recognize. All she wanted was for people to accept her in this new place, give her some recognition for her good work. Was all this pressure and tension coming from being out of her element? Had she taken Satan's silver and was now over her head? Were this hotel and this valley going to be the ruin of her both personally and professionally? Was she destined to join Homeless Harold on the High Line walkway, tattered shawl over her head and around her shoulders, hands in fingerless gloves pulling her cart behind her? The responsibilities here, the nuances of such a high level of service, were far removed from the modest chain of small business hotels back East. And that was just the hotel, not the added weight of the hotel's part in seeing to the well-being of the valley.

Cassie took each item in turn, evaluating and dismissing them. The job was *not* too much for her. It was a variation on what she could do well: organize things, identify problems, and solve them. Manor Valley was simply an assortment of different functions and problems she wasn't familiar with this early on. Doubt was the issue. She *would* resolve it. Once she settled in, organized it all in her mind, and understood how everything worked, it would become routine. Homesickness was waning, and she'd only been here a month. Being alone in an unfamiliar environment, however, was a separate issue. In the first few weeks, she'd met people, and things were becoming more comfortable, more relaxing. The realization hit that she liked Manor Valley: the hotel, the place, the people. She vowed to lessen the pressure on herself, let people help her, stop micromanaging every little thing. Justin was a godsend, as was Cliff. She had the Weavers and a new friend in Lily. Time to quit feeling sorry for herself and get on with it.

*

All she got was voice mail. Cassie realized she didn't even know where Cliff lived. She wouldn't leave a message or text. It wasn't right for this level of abuse. On the way to Reno on Tuesday, he still wasn't picking up. On the plane, they made the announcement to turn off cell phones.

Chapter Twenty-One

From Newark, she took a cab home. Staring out the window through the light rain, she noticed the years of dirt and recent graffiti on various buildings. Gone for only a month, she'd barely registered it growing up. The city just was what it was, and she'd had nothing to compare it to. The constant highs and lows of noise caught her attention next, another thing she'd previously thought normal. *My God, where did all these cars come from?*

Exhausted on arrival, she spent time with her parents before begging off and going to bed. She'd regale them tomorrow about life in Manor Valley.

Noon in New York was nine a.m. in Manor Valley. Voice mail or text? Cassie opted for text. She could compose it, not stumble through it.

Thanksgiving is a time to be thankful, and I'm thankful for you. You've been nothing but protective and helpful to me since that first day, my many mistakes forgiven and kept private.

Who has someone like that?

I couldn't leave a message or text before. It would be an inadequate way to express regret for my appalling conduct. It's no excuse, but this new job has been overwhelming at times. You're always there, close by, offering help. Unfortunately, you're also a convenient target when I slip. Sad, but I have no one else to vent on.

When we first met, you saved my reputation with the company, made my disaster seem like a small problem.

You took upon yourself Rita's concern about my isolation in work, forced me to experience one of the best days of my life on the trails.

You donate hours of your time to help me learn about Manor Valley; I don't just mean work.

Selfish again, writing this helps me enjoy Thanksgiving.

I'm thankful for you.

Please forgive me—again.

*

Helping her mother in the kitchen settled and distracted Cassie. There would be seven for dinner, a typical East Coast Thanksgiving meal of turkey and stuffing, mashed potatoes and gravy, vegetables, and pumpkin pie. Aunts and uncles, along with Mom and Dad, wanted to hear about Cassie's adventures in the mountains of California.

Rising to the occasion, she mesmerized them with her description of the valley, the small town, and the hotel. Enthralled with it all, they bombarded her with questions—wildlife, fishing, business questions from the men, elaboration on the hotel's décor and the village shops from the women.

At the end, they offered comments and advice.

Her father jumped right in. "Ha! You on a horse? I'd pay to see that. You were scared to get on a merry-go-round horse when you were a kid."

Helpful, Dad.

Mom was next. "Jogging? Oh, honey. Well, dress warm and watch out for traffic. Be careful of muggers."

Traffic? Muggers? In Manor Valley? Thanks for the input, Mom.

Parents—what could one do?

Friday, she shopped in Manhattan. A stiff breeze, light rain, and the cold had Cassie rushing between stores along with everyone else. Shoulder to shoulder, shopping bags banging against other combatants, everyone was out for Black Friday. The holiday street and store decorations were up. She found no comfort on the packed subway home. As the rails screeched into her station, Cassie wondered what Christmas shopping was like in Sacramento or San Francisco.

At dinner with her parents, Cassie knew it was time to drop the holiday bomb. She'd been worrying about her parent's reaction for several days. "Unlike hotels here, the holidays are a busy time for the hotel in Manor Valley. I honestly have no idea what's ahead this month. I don't think I can take the time to come home at Christmas. Why don't you come out and stay at the hotel? We can be together, and it's all on me. You'll really enjoy yourselves, I promise."

Ed and Nancy exchanged silent glances. A slight pause ensued before Mom said, "Well, that might be fun. Dad and I haven't taken a trip in years. What do you think, Ed?"

"If that's the only way we can be with our baby for the holidays, I'm up for it. Never been to California."

It was settled.

Saturday was a catch-up dinner with Vivien. She'd explain her latest faux pas and suffer the humiliation of Vivien's delight.

"Well, welcome back, Miss Saturday Night Live." Accompanied by a big hug from Vivien. "I've missed you, honey. I canceled a formal soiree to be here. I knew it would be more fun."

Cassie related her shopping adventures and let Vivien get her reaction out of the way.

"You actually went out among the great unwashed on Black Friday? Ran around in that rain? Oh, honey, I'd have sent you a car and driver, or at least lent you my personal shopper."

Finally, Cassie got it out: the stress in the office before she flew home, Herschel's visit, her offensive outburst with Cliff, all the details up to her apology text message. "And the look on his face before he spun around and left my office. It made me feel like I was the one who suggested to Hitler that he invade Czechoslovakia."

"Oh my, that's not funny," said Vivien. "The text was a good idea. Has he responded to it?"

"No, he's so confusing. Very competent at what he does, all of which I still haven't figured out. He's protective of me. Like you, he doesn't talk about my mistakes or screw-ups. I'm starting to like him. I don't want him thinking ill of me."

Cassie explained about the comparisons with Herschel, about her unexpected feelings when she danced with Cliff. She explained how he was always there for her, helping her, guiding her, getting her to experience different things.

Vivien turned serious. "You've got to fix this, Cassie. Don't let him feel minimized in your life. Don't take him for granted. The text sounded sweet, but you really have to let him know that outburst wasn't the normal you." Vivien waved for another bottle of wine. It could be a long evening. "It sounds like some of *those* feelings are sneaking up on you. Let's talk more about this Cliff person for a bit."

*

Monday, Cassie was back in the office. It had been a good but busy weekend at the hotel; everything ran smoothly while she was gone, and everyone was happy. Rested, she dove in, trying to focus on work. The holidays were here, and things were gearing up.

On the flight back, she'd been consumed with thoughts about Cliff, worried that he'd never responded to her text. Had she destroyed every bridge? The text had been the catalyst. That, and the final night she and Herschel talked—the night when those comparisons filled her head. She'd named it the Herschel-Text syndrome. She couldn't destroy the thing she had with Cliff, whatever that thing was. She refused to let her mind drift that far— into romance. He probably thought of her as 'that psycho from New York.' She'd been feeling the need for someone like Cliff in her life, and not just her work life.

At ten o'clock, the genie appeared at her office door. All smiles, like nothing ever happened. "Have a good holiday, Jefe?"

Tentative. "I did, thank you. Did you get my text?"

"Got it. It was very nice. Caring and thoughtful." The smile went up a notch. "Who wrote it for you? If you still want to kill me, let me know. I don't want to be buried in this orange vest."

She knew by his smug look to ignore the comments. Everything normal. Relief tingled from her hands to her toes. Days of tension drained away. Perplexed for a moment, she looked at the man who could generate this range of feelings in her. Cassie wanted to elaborate more on her apology but decided against it.

Is he really this nice, this forgiving?

"Tomorrow we go pick up the lobby Christmas tree," he said. "The manager is the final say. You're back, so you must still be the manager. I'll pick you up at ten. Wear stout shoes, warm socks, and an old coat. Do you even own an old coat?" As he turned to leave, he laughed at his latest foray into humor.

She was ahead of him. At home, she'd bought riding boots *and* Sorels for the snow. Soon she'd leave her shoes in the office and change there. She'd seen the Christmas tree lot, set up Friday when she was away, at the entrance to town. How hard could picking a tree be?

Chapter Twenty-Two

Cliff saw her standing at the entrance when he drove up in a flatbed truck. She just stood there looking at the vehicle until he waved his arm and called, "Are you coming?"

He watched as Princess McPerfect moved down the steps. At least she wasn't bringing her scepter with her today. Rita had been nagging at him again about making her feel at home, getting her away from the office more. He hoped today's excursion would go over better than her first ride with Old Molly. The Countess of Funville was going to get another new experience in Manor Valley.

She fumbled into the passenger door. "Where's your pickup?" A chain saw took up space on the floor between them. Cassie watched the Hallmark channel, so she knew some people in the hinterlands actually cut down their own Christmas trees. "You've got to be kidding, right? Why can't we just stop at the tree stand down the street?"

"Ms. Bryant, *your* lobby is three stories high. The biggest tree at the stand is only ten, maybe twelve, feet high. My sister's flower arrangements on that big table are almost that high. Well, maybe not that high, but you get the idea." The floor gearbox ground loudly as he slipped it into gear. "Hope you've had your shots. We're going into the woods. Don't worry, there's a snake bite kit in the glove compartment."

Oh, how he loved watching those blue eyes expand into saucers.

They drove deep into the forest for about fifteen minutes before turning on a dirt road for another mile. A hastily hand-painted sign announced THE TREE FARM. Obviously, some marketing genius didn't want to confuse anyone.

On one side of the road were large, roped piles of trees being loaded on trucks bound for San Francisco and the rest of the Bay Area. On their side, several trucks the size of Cliff's flatbed were parked next to large logging equipment.

A man called out, "Pick it and cut it, Cliff. We'll haul it out and load it."

He noticed the bewildered look on Cassie's face. "It's slower now," he said. "We're about a week late getting the hotel tree, but Dan said it was okay. He wanted to wait for you to get back and enjoy the experience. Last week they were swamped out here. This is where people get large trees for their hotels, corporate lobbies, shopping centers, etcetera." He reached in for the chain saw, threw a backpack over one shoulder, and tossed Cassie a pair of gloves. "Let's go." At the front of the truck, Cliff raised a hand and turned to her. Knowing her apprehension of the wilderness, he asked, "Did you bring your dragonglass dagger? There might be some White Walkers hiding in the Christmas trees."

They hiked up the mild slope. Cassie pointed. "These look like they were planted, not like that dense forest back there."

"You're right. They're spaced far apart so they don't lose the branches on the bottoms of the trees. The sun can reach all around them for even growth. We want one about twenty feet high."

Paths meandered through the mini forest for the logging equipment. They marched into the maze for about ten minutes. "Your choice, Jefe."

Cliff watched as she gazed around. She looked like she didn't know where to start.

Cliff took a thermos of coffee from his backpack as she turned and said, "I'm going to need some help here."

He squatted and sat on a newly cut stump and poured out two cups. He wanted her to have fun, loosen up. "That's why the coffee. You don't have to rush this. Enjoy it. We have time." Cliff handed her a cup as she stood beside him. He gave her a small spool of yellow marker tape. "Go mark five or six, and I'll help you decide."

An hour later, he thought he was with a teenager buying a prom dress: I like this one because—; I like that one because—. Finally, she committed. Cliff fired up the chain saw before she changed her mind.

"Wait!" Cassie unconsciously slipped her arm around him.

Her political correctness training must not cover a situation like this, thought Cliff.

"Am I making the right decision?" she pleaded.

Cliff had a life to lead sometime before Christmas. "Yeah. We're good to go."

Their eyes met, and Cassie smiled. He noticed she kept her arm around him for longer than expected and said nothing. Was that a small blush when she released him? Being here with her, watching her run around in her new unmarked Sorel boots and NYU baseball cap made his day. He could tell she was enjoying herself, stress and tensions left in the hotel lobby.

"Stand over there," he instructed.

Cliff lined up the fall of the tree. The owner left him alone, unlike some people. He knew Cliff wouldn't ruin four other trees when he felled it.

*

Spellbound, Cassie watched, lost in the noise of the chain cutting through the base. A notch on one side to direct the fall and a deep cut on the other, then the slow decent as it crashed between several other trees, barely touching them.

After squaring off the base, Cliff poured two more cups of coffee. "Relax and enjoy it all for a minute before they load it."

Cassie sat on the stump and Cliff sat on his haunches beside her. After a few blissful minutes of silence and enjoyment in another new setting, she felt she had to make Cliff understand that she was not the woman who had unleashed on him about the tile fiasco. For some reason, she needed him to understand that normally she was a caring and composed person, not the raging bull elephant, tusks thrashing about, bent on destroying everything in its path.

"Cliff, I want to apologize again about my blowup before Thanksgiving. I'm not like that. This new job, being away from home, plopped down in this new environment, it's all a bit frightening for me. Sometimes I wonder if it's all too much. The responsibility is oppressing, and sometimes I doubt if I'm up to it. Can you understand that?"

For Cassie, it was a surprising admission of vulnerability to make to a relative stranger. She looked straight ahead, not wanting to meet his eyes as she waited for a reply.

"Really? Maybe you should try my hat on. Yes, my degree is in Project Management, but Dan and my dad just dumped this massive job on me. All my work is normally much smaller stuff, basically being a carpenter slash general contractor on residential or small commercial things, along with all the maintenance at the hotel and the Mall. I know exactly how you feel." He raised one hand to make his point. "Does 'over your head' cover it? One thing I have noticed is that you keep it all to yourself. You shouldn't be afraid to ask for help—that's why Dan, Justin, and myself are here. You're not supposed to know everything. Just figure out how to get it done, however you can, just like me."

"Then you don't think I'm some psycho imported from New York to make your life miserable?"

Cliff smiled. "Well, I wouldn't go that far. Psycho is a bit strong. You're just a little wacky, like my sister or my mother. You're a woman. All women are a little wacky. Although, I will say you're not hard to look at. Together, we'll just have to figure out how to get this damned hotel built, opened, and running."

Cassie watched him grin as he took another sip from his steaming coffee and look out over the forest. She couldn't suppress her own smile. Great. In a few short months, she'd graduated from ecoterrorist to shifty character, and now all the way up to 'just a little wacky' and 'not hard to look at.' She shook her head and looked skyward, longing for her next evaluation.

On the way back to the hotel Cassie felt light and happy. At least today, he didn't try any of his amusing stunts like stable bonding. Earlier, she feared he might have her do tree petting, stroking and whispering to them to make sure she picked the right one. A bond was forming with the man beside her. What kind of bond, she wasn't sure, but it both confused and delighted her. He was right; they were in this together, for better or worse. She glanced at his hands on the steering wheel—strong and rough, tanned from his work. She briefly wondered how they'd feel on her body. The thought jolted her, and her gaze was quickly fixed front, concentrating on the road.

Chapter Twenty-Three

Riding lessons resumed on Wednesday. Old Molly and Lily were happy with Cassie's progress. Molly had given her son, Sonny, a good talking to; he performed better after the good manners speech. She'd been singing that song for years, for all the good it did.

As they walked back to the barn, Cassie asked Lily, "Can you come to dinner at the hotel Friday night? I feel like dressing up a bit and enjoying a night out with some pleasant female company. We can take a real break."

"In the dining room? Oh, yeah! I'm not missing that." Lily paused. "Oh, I almost forgot. My brother is having a small party Saturday night at his house. I'm supposed to ask you to come. I think he's nervous about asking you himself. Please come."

"Sure. I'd love to," said Cassie.

"Ever been to his house?"

"No. I have no idea where it is."

Lily laughed. "Boy, are you in for a treat." She laughed again. "Wait 'til you see what he's done with the place."

*

The next day, Cassie thought it was an invasion. She'd finished jogging and sat on a bench in front of the hotel next to the water to cool off before pestering Ethel for some lunch.

They swooped in over the mountaintop behind the hotel. Not a band of silent ninjas—this was a raging Mongol horde. The alternating high and low, loud and soft honking put the residents on notice that they were back. The grand V-formation of the migrating geese flew a long, graceful surveillance loop over the lake. They lowered their altitude and completed a graceful slow glide across the water's surface before coming to rest by a marshy area on the far side of the lake. Cassie thought there were hundreds of them, all in a perfectly disciplined formation. Words like breathtaking and magnificent stamped themselves on her retinas as she sat frozen during the five-minute spectacle. The initial terror from their noise changed to awe. She berated herself for not capturing it on her phone camera.

Cassie wanted to see them up close but didn't know how to get to that part of the lake. Her phone came out, and she dialed Cliff. She gasped into the phone. "Where are you right now?"

"Is this a dirty phone call?"

Be nice to the idiot, you want something.

"Did you just see those geese? They were geese, right? I've never seen anything so beautiful. How do I get to the other side of the lake and see them?"

"I'm in the back, outside one of the new wings. I'll meet you in front in ten minutes."

She knew she was acting like seven-year-old beside him in the truck but couldn't help it. "Did you see them? Did you see them? They're magnificent. Why are they here? I saw something like that on National Geographic once, but it was *nothing* compared to seeing it live. Where are they from? Where are they going?"

"Well, let's make an expert out of you so you can dazzle your friends when you go home at Christmas. They're Canadian geese, probably from Alaska or Canada, resting on their way to Southern California or Mexico. They're late this year. The marshy water is shallow in that corner of the lake, so there's plenty of food for them. They'll rest for a day or two. All that honking you hear are geese telling the ones in front of them to keep up their speed and maintain their height in the formation for wind resistance. Basically, they're all tailgating behind the bird in front of them. When the leader gets tired of cutting the wind, he drops back where it's easier to fly, and another bird replaces him. In formation, they can fly seventy percent farther than a bird by himself. They go about six hundred miles a day at forty miles an hour—up to seventy miles an hour with a tailwind. They mate for life. If one is injured, family members will stay with them until they're better and can continue."

They parked at the end of a dirt track and continued on foot through the woods for about ten minutes. As they neared the lake, Cliff grabbed one of her arms and held her back. One goose was standing on the shore by himself, honking at them and flapping his wings.

"This is far enough," said Cliff. "That guy is a guard. They post them as lookouts for danger. You don't want him after you. Sit here."

Cliff reached into his backpack and pulled out the same thermos from when they had cut the Christmas tree. He poured two cups of coffee, and they sat on a big fallen tree trunk, keeping a wary eye on the guard goose. Cassie completely focused on this new nature experience.

After a few minutes of blissful silence, Cliff turned to her. "I'll get the shotgun out of the truck, and you can pop one off for dinner."

Coming out of her reverie, Cassie almost jumped. "WHAT? Are you crazy? First, you want me to assassinate some poor deer, and now one of these beautiful birds?" She snarled at him. "You probably hunt puppies and kittens too. Look at those lovely things. They don't walk around carrying guns."

She could see him thinking for a moment. "You're right. I see your point," he said. "I understand you want to be fair. I'll get my hunting knife for you instead. You can wade out into the water, go one-on-one, toe-to-toe, mano a mano with one of the big ones. Get some bloody scratches from those strong flapping wings and bite marks from those deadly beaks while you slit his throat. Have that first hunter's initiation blood on your hands and cheeks, knowing it was a fair fight."

"How old did you say you were?" A pointed finger came up. "You're a very sick man, Cliff Walker. Do you enjoy making fun of me?"

"Well, it beats the hell out of Monopoly."

A calm, questioning frown crossed Cassie's face. *Is it too late in life to send him to the vice-principal's office?*

Cliff smiled and patted her knee. "Don't worry. They know they're safe in this valley. Local hunters would never poach one of them." His voice softened. "They are beautiful, aren't they?"

They sat in silence a little longer, drinking their coffee. The geese settled. Cassie and Cliff listened to the wind whispering through the trees and the gentle lapping of water against the bank. They smelled the marshy scents stirred up by the geese mixed with the pines.

Cassie reached over and put her hand on his knee. "Thank you so much for bringing me here. I'll never forget this."

Both enjoyed the intimacy for a few moments before Cliff looked up at the sky. "We'd better get back. There's a storm coming."

"How do you know that?"

"Trick knee, I can feel it in my joints. Mountain men have that gift." He acted it out, pretending to rub a sore knee. "Or they can check the weather forecast in the morning." He pointed up and laughed. "Or just look up and see all those black clouds coming in."

Cassie shook off the intimacy and once again marveled at his ability to amuse himself.

It was quiet on the way back in the truck—another wonderful experience with you-know-who. Cassie recalled the pleasure of putting her arm around him a few days before, while cutting the lobby tree. How comforting it was. It happened again today when he took her hand and helped her down the small slope to the geese after she slipped.

"Thank you for the geese lesson. But I won't be showing off my woodsman knowledge with my friends back East, because I'm staying here for Christmas. My parents are coming out here." She kept her eyes straight ahead, not wanting to see his reaction. "I'd like you to meet them."

In bed that night, Cassie thought, *Meet the parents?* What was going on here? Yes, she enjoyed being with him. Something was developing with Cliff, and she wasn't sure she wanted to fight it.

Chapter Twenty-Four

It was a well-deserved girls' night out, if out for Cassie was the hotel dining room.

A light rain was falling, and Cassie gave thanks for her assigned parking spot in the underground garage. She ascended the stairs to the lobby. Once again, she paused at Lily's fall display on the center table. Dinner plate dahlias in deep burgundy, gray-blue eucalyptus branches, and rich, warm oranges from flowers she didn't recognize shot out from a grand golden metal vase.

"I'll be changing it to a holiday arrangement next week," said Lily, as she came up beside her.

Cassie shook her head in amazement. "You have such a talent."

Justin came out of the dining room, scribbling on a piece of paper. He looked harried. Cassie knew the hotel was fully booked this weekend, and his time was crushed filling the guests' demands. He pulled up abruptly and almost ran into the two ladies. Surprised, he fumbled with the required pushing back hair and straightening glasses. This time he even checked his tie. In front of him was Cassie, hair up, wearing a lovely green dress with earrings and a tasteful necklace to match.

"A guest who checked in late wanted to know if he could get reservations for dinner. Harry the magician helped me out." He then added, "You look terrific, Jefe."

Cassie almost laughed as he finally recognized Lily standing beside her in a long-sleeve violet dress cut at the knees, with her beautiful brunette hair flowing over her shoulders. He couldn't keep his eyes from drifting over this version of the woman who changed the flowers in the lobby. He left decorum in one of his pockets and blurted out, "I've never seen you in a dress before!"

Lily blushed. Cassie stifled a grin.

"Justin, could you show Lily to our table? We should have one at the back. Let's save the window tables for the paying customers. I need to check something at the desk."

Cassie had nothing to check at the desk; she just wanted to give them a moment alone.

When she entered the dining room, Harry whisked her to their table and held out her chair. "Your first dinner with us I believe, Cassie? Are the riding lessons going well?"

"Yes, thank you for asking, Harry. Soon I'll be able to go out with you and Clayton, if we ever get a day off."

"I look forward to it but, alas, you're right—the busy season is upon us."

"Any suggestions for the main course tonight?" asked Cassie.

Harry leaned over the two ladies. "The veal cordon bleu. Ethel came in tonight since we're so busy. She's outdone herself again."

"Looks like Justin is a fan," Cassie teased Lily as they settled in with a cocktail.

"He's so nice. Do you really think he likes me?"

"Lily, his manner and body language just then were about as subtle as a tsunami. You better make a move soon. Guys like that don't stay on the market long. He's educated, has a good job, isn't going anywhere, and, let's be honest, he's handsome. Show some interest before he gives up." Something registered with Cassie, something she'd thought out in the lobby. "You know, I just thought of something. He may be nervous about pursuing you because he knows you're family with Dan. Maybe he's worried that the boss will disapprove."

"That's nonsense," said Lily.

"I agree, but..."

Cassie thought on it a moment more, considering how she might help. "Justin's been working long hours lately. On top of his regular job, I'm having him help me with much of the new stuff. Things settle around here about eight o'clock. Can I invite him to Cliff's party tomorrow after work?"

"Of course!" Lily perked up. "I'd like to see Justin out of his native environment. I have no idea what he does in his time off."

Both women enjoyed watching the show around them, silent staff delivering impeccable service to all the diners, the piano player discreetly off to the side by the entrance to the bar. Candles flickering from all the tables illuminated smartly clad men with expensively dressed women.

"I saw the geese come in yesterday," said Cassie. "It was thrilling. I had your brother take me to the other side of the lake to watch them. He wanted me to wade in the water and kill one for dinner with a butcher knife. Your brother is seriously warped."

"We all live in hope. If you haven't figured out when to ignore him by now, your future is hopeless, just like the rest of us."

They started with salads and white wine.

Harry, noting a lull in the conversation, discreetly approached. "May I select a red to go with the mains for you and Miss Walker?"

Lily turned to the maitre d'. "Ha! *Miss Walker?* Try that on somewhere else, Harry."

Harry smiled and acted appalled. "Oh, Miss Walker! We're not at the stables now. One mustn't talk like that in the dining room."

Lily smiled as he glided away. "Isn't he a pleasure to watch moving around the room?"

Cassie quizzed Lily on holiday events in the valley. She needed a heads-up, and even Justin hadn't been here last season. Eventually, she probed Lily about her love life. Too busy with work, not much available, etcetera. She sounded like she made as much effort as her brother, or herself, for that matter.

"Now," said Cassie, "I have to hear the end of the Janet Wilson story, and no more stopping before you finish. I have enough tension in my life. We ended when Janet went to bed, and she would ask Travis the next day if he had filled his housekeeper position."

"Good," said Lily as she glanced around the dining room. "This is the perfect setting to finish the story."

Cassie took a sip of her wine and settled in happily to listen.

"Well, the next day, Travis assigned a woman to take Adrian on a walk by the lake and then to the stables, where one of the men would take him on a pony ride. They'd have no distractions going through the house. Janet refused to do anything until he found the plans, so she could take notes and make references on the plans. Travis wrote that it frustrated him because the entire morning was taken up by questions about staff quarters, kitchen requirements, how and when they arranged deliveries, servant flow in the house, where was the firewood kept, what type of candles did he use? He'd barely given any of this a thought. Building the place had been his passion. All he wanted was to get it decorated and furnished so he could live in it properly. Why did women have to make it so complicated?

"They took a brief break at lunchtime; Travis was exhausted. Janet was concerned about Adrian. Travis told her that the men would cook him meat over a campfire and tell him Wild West stories. She'd be lucky if he ever wanted to come back.

"In the afternoon, Janet beat him down with questions while she made notes and referenced them to the house plans.

"At the end of the day, Travis found some relief as they sat at a small table set up in a room off the kitchen. Dinner had been prepared for them, and Adrian was safely tucked in bed.

"It was time."

Lily teased Cassie as the waiter refilled their wine. Neither had room for dessert. "Maybe we should stop now."

"Don't even think about it."

"Janet asked, 'Mr. Weaver, have you filled your position for a housekeeper? If not, I would like to be considered. I have experience and think I would do a good job for you.'

"Travis's mouth fell open. Across from him sat this worldly, educated, sophisticated, and beautiful woman. Intelligent and strong-willed, she spoke two languages fluently and never had to say a word—she could bully him with a look and melt him with a smile. And now she wanted to move here to the wilderness and be his housekeeper? He'd become more and more attracted to her every time he was around her. It never dawned on him she would want to sacrifice life in San Francisco, never dreamed she would consider a place like Manor Valley.

"Janet misinterpreted the look on his face; she was mortified. 'I apologize, Mr. Weaver. I've overstepped. I did not mean to make you feel uncomfortable.'

"Feelings surfaced and surged through Travis as he questioned her. 'You could live here? Wouldn't you miss the society of the city?'

"'I would not miss San Francisco. My son and I live a quiet existence. And, yes, I love it here. I've seen nothing so beautiful in my life. My son thinks he's in a fairy tale. The house is large, but I could manage it well for you, Mr. Weaver.'

"Travis was in shock. He could hardly control himself. 'No, Janet, I could not have you as a housekeeper. I don't think I could bear to have you here in that capacity. Forgive me, but I think I've fallen in love with you. I could only dream of having you as mistress of the whole place, the whole valley. I never allowed myself to wish you'd like it here. I want you to be my wife.'

"That's an abbreviated version, but you get the idea," said Lily.

Cassie just nodded eagerly and Lily picked up the story again.

"Janet trembled and tears formed. She was disoriented and filled with despair. The only word she'd heard was *mistress*. She knew what that meant. The deception of her son's father in Hong Kong, long suppressed, resurfaced. The mind-numbing pain when he had cast her aside after becoming pregnant. She'd been wary of rich, handsome men ever since, and here it was again. She was being seduced.

"Janet mustered her strength. Tears ran down her cheeks. 'I've heard those lies before, Mr. Weaver. I will not be used again.' Defiantly, she held his eyes. She was not ashamed and would not lower them. 'I've never had a husband, Mr. Weaver. My son was born out of wedlock. When I was twenty, I was seduced by a man who hurled the same type of promises at me. No, Mr. Weaver, I'm not a piece of furniture. I am not up for auction. I will not allow it to happen again. Please take us to the train tomorrow.'

"He rushed to her side and knelt on the floor beside her. 'No, you don't understand. I don't want you to be *my* mistress. I want you to be *the* mistress of everything here. What I fervently desire is to be your husband. I'll marry you tomorrow if you will allow me. I know this is sudden, but I think you could grow to love me as I do you. I couldn't bear to live here with you as housekeeper. Please, at least say you'll think about it. I want you to be the shining star of Manor Valley. I want you to be *my* shining star.'

"Janet almost fainted as the realization of his proposal sunk in. Her most important question came first. 'And how would you feel having an illegitimate bastard son around?'

"'He would only bring me joy. People who have lived lives like ours all have pasts. We're not perfect. This is not England.'

"She needed time to process this. 'May I think about it, Mr. Weaver?'

"In her room that night, Janet outlined her rationale in her diary. She knew her market value hovered around zero: older, no money to speak of, and a child out of wedlock. She never allowed herself to think she would be happily married someday; the thought was too painful. In the short time spent with Travis, he'd also grown on her.

She found him easy to be around, easy to talk to. No pompous airs like wealthy city men. She wrote about her fears. Never would she have dared to think about being with a man like Travis Weaver.

"Her demands the next day bordered on ridiculous. Travis wrote that the only thing she could negotiate for was furniture in Chinatown. Janet wanted her own horse; she'd missed riding for years. He had a stable full of them. Janet wanted recognition for her son. He would adopt him gladly. Janet wanted control over her savings for her son's future. He'd match her money and put it in a private account for her. Travis fought her on her requested personal allowance. It was so modest, it took him an hour to convince her it had to be at least double."

Lily summed it up. "Janet also wanted a piano. Duh? They married the next day in Auburn. Rarely out of each other's sight, they had three daughters. They honeymooned in Chicago, where they purchased many things for the house."

Lily left the clincher for last. "Have you ever looked at that painting in the lobby?"

Confused, Cassie said, "Which one? There are quite a few. It's a big lobby."

"At the end of their first year of marriage," Lily said, "the Weavers threw themselves a party. Their first daughter was two months old. Look for the painting of the woman in the stunning, green, form-fitting Chinese dress, floor-length with long sleeves and a high mandarin collar. Pay attention to the details of the colorful embroidery on the dress, perfectly captured by the artist. Green is the Chinese color for harmony, wealth, fertility, and hope. That's Janet beside Travis. They were a beautiful couple."

Cassie couldn't wait. She jumped up and almost ran into the lobby.

And there it was. Cassie had only glimpsed it in passing. Travis was handsome, but she, *she* was the painting. Chestnut hair piled on top of her head, piercing green eyes that matched the exotic dress. The erect ramrod posture from years ago broadcast how regal she was. Cassie knew that no one smiled in the old portraits, but Janet's serene face, barely hinting at a smile, couldn't hide her joy. Not the background, not the husband—the artist had captured *her*, preserved her, for years to come.

After that lovely story, she knew she'd be tied to the picture, knew she'd be exchanging words with Janet whenever she passed it. Janet would become her muse, help her solve modern problems in Manor Valley.

She wondered at this woman who had traveled the world and knew she belonged in Manor Valley the minute she entered it. The words were still vivid in her mind: 'My soul belongs here.'

Lily came up behind her. "Isn't it beautiful? Now, you're the new mistress of the Manor Valley house. You can write your own story."

Chapter Twenty-Five

It took five minutes. Going up the hill past the allotments, Cassie only had to drive slightly past her own driveway on the right to where a small road branched off to the left and dropped down an incline, which led to a widely spaced enclave of homes near the water. She could have walked. A numbered sign signaled Cliff's driveway. The house was nestled in the trees right next to the water. Single story with a steeply pitched roof and natural wood siding, it melted into its surroundings. Cassie was impressed until... .

She entered the house and was greeted by stark, white primed walls in the large open floor plan. No baseboards, no door casings, no artwork. A massive leather sofa, entirely out of place, took up a large portion of the living area. Flanking it sat a worn recliner—no problem telling who usually sat there. A stained and scratched TV tray to the side looked like it helped support the chair. A small portable card table for four with duct tape holding on the edge trim defined the dining area. Guarding it were four beaten-up plastic folding chairs, the kind used by the hotel for outside parties. Bizarre carpets were scattered in random spots. It looked like a gym due to its lack of other furnishings. The highlight and salvation of the room was a lovely fireplace of rounded river rock in a far corner. Beside it was an uninterrupted floor-to-ceiling windowed wall with a magnificent view of the lake. From above, large beams supported a sloped natural-wood ceiling. An exotic hardwood floor added warmth to the room. Cassie immediately thought of the hotel years ago, when it was Travis's house, and Janet had first seen it: floors, ceilings, and walls, a strong skeleton and not much else.

She gravitated toward Dan and Rita, who were talking to Cliff's parents.

Introductions were made to other guests.

"Have you seen Lily?" Cassie asked.

Rita pointed. "Try the kitchen. It's tucked around the side over there."

Curious, Cassie wanted to see more of Cliff's castle. "And the bathroom?"

Another point. "Down the hallway."

Necessities done, Cassie stalled in the hall outside the bathroom. No one could see her. She'd just have a peek at the other rooms. The stark white walls assaulted her again as she noticed that the only door with a handle was the bathroom. The first two rooms were bedrooms—empty. At the end of the hall—it had to be the master bedroom—Cassie braced herself. The door swung open to a large room with a small bed, side table, and dresser salvaged from God knows where. A sliding glass door opened to a large deck with a beautiful view of the lake. Fearfully, she ventured farther into the master bathroom. A shock—it was lovely. A large tub next to a window looked like it was suspended over the water. One side wall housed a spacious shower, the other, two sinks with modern fixtures. Furniture aside, it looked like the only completed room in the place, except for the missing door handle.

She noted on her return to the kitchen that the house was spotless. Perhaps he was salvageable after all.

Cassie found Lily in the kitchen with Ethel. Every surface was covered with hors d'oeuvres, platters of sliced turkey and ham, buns, and bread. Large bowls held enticing salads.

"Where's Cliff?" asked Cassie.

"The idiot had to run back to the hotel to get a large folding table for the food. I told him some chairs for people to sit on might be nice," said Lily. "Justin is waiting for him by the service door."

"Well, he must have been distracted by preparing all this wonderful food. It looks like he's handy in the kitchen."

Ethel laughed, and Lily looked up from her work. "He who? Do you mean my brother? That oven over there, when we went to heat up some of the snacks, we saw he was using it as a wine rack. He's married to the microwave. Tank is more domestic than he is. On the rare occasion he dreams up a function like this, he dumps it on Ethel or me. Says he doesn't have the strength, says he has sudden attacks of leprosy or scurvy or Ebola, or whatever the latest world health news is talking about."

Lily pointed to a large platter of prawns artfully set atop a bed of ice on a table off to the side. "There's a textbook example. Poor Cliff was exhausted after driving to Auburn to get them. He comes back and bats his baby blues at Ethel, hands her the bag, and she has to get the ice and platter and arrange them. We can't wait for him to find a woman to sort him out."

Cassie got into the flow. "Um, the walls. Is he color-blind? And the carpets?"

"Primer white. He's never gotten around to painting. That monstrous sofa? Pirated from the lobby of the hotel during the last remodel. The carpets? From the same place. He just cut sections randomly out of the patterned lobby carpet. The environmentalists love the hotel. It doesn't fill the dumps. Just call Cliff, and it ends up back here. *House Beautiful* is coming to photograph it next week. It's been this way for three years since his last girlfriend left." Lily wasn't through venting, a wooden fork pointed at Ethel. "And all she does is encourage and pamper him. He tells Ethel about his brilliant idea, and she gives him a shopping list to bring back to her. It's all too much for her little Cliff."

"Now, now," piped up Ethel. "Don't be talking about my Cliff like that. He does the best he can. Has a heart of gold, that boy."

Lily said, "What do they say in those old movies? Ethel, you're such a *sap*."

The Great Organizer finally returned with the table and chairs, and things got underway.

Justin arrived around eight. He came up to Lily, Cassie, and Ethel and lauded the ladies on the work with the food. Mr. Happy Go Lucky approached.

"How was the soccer game?" he asked Justin.

"We lost to Rocklin, two to one."

Cliff said, "Before you leave, let's get your rowing shell off the deck and into the garage. The weather's changing."

"Say when, and I'm ready," Justin replied. "Excuse me, I want to say hi to Dan and Rita and your folks."

Lily and Cassie looked at each other with questioning glances.

Cassie was the first to ask Cliff. "Soccer? Rowing shell? How well do you know Justin?"

"We're mates. Hit it off as soon as he arrived in Manor Valley. He plays soccer down in Colfax on Saturday mornings. Likes to row to keep in shape, so I let him keep his shell here. He's an active guy. Even sneaks away on some Wednesday nights to do ballroom dancing at the community center in Auburn." Cliff shrugged his shoulders. "Excuse me, ladies, I have guests to attend to."

As he sauntered off, Lily said, "At least he's not going to turn on the TV. That's progress." Perplexed, she looked at Cassie. "Soccer, rowing, dancing? Our meek, quiet Justin? How does he keep those glasses from falling off his nose?"

"Wow, evidently, there's more to that man than either of us thought. No wonder he likes working a little late on Saturdays. It frees up his mornings to play soccer."

New eyes evaluated Justin as he returned, brushing his hair back and pushing the glasses up his nose.

Lily turned to him. Time to make a move. "Justin, do you ride horses?"

"I'm from Oklahoma. Of course I ride. Just haven't had the time."

"If you're interested, let me know. I can ride out and show you the trails."

Cassie smiled as Justin tried to hide his excitement.

"Of course," he stammered. "Sure, sure. I'd really like that!"

*

Mingling continued and Lily searched out her brother. If she could make a move, so could someone else.

"Have you thought about asking Cassie out, Cliff?"

"Way above my pay grade, sis. Anyhow, she'll be going back to New York in a couple of years to some big job and rich boyfriend."

"Two years is a long time."

"Why? Did she say something?" Cliff asked. "Why would she be interested in going out with *me*?"

"No, you idiot. You're right. She probably just likes hanging out with Tank."

Lily shook her head in exasperation and started walking away.

Cliff said, "I've been thinking—"

Lily shot back over her shoulder, "Stop bragging, brother dear."

A short time later, across the room, Cassie spotted her host standing by himself, lingering over the platter of prawns. It looked like he'd eaten enough of them to feed a harem of seals.

"Thank you for having me." She pointed to the dwindling tray of prawns. "May anyone else have some or is this a personal snack?"

He stepped to the side and motioned to the platter while chomping on another one, looking as guilty as a Nazi retiree in Buenos Aires. "Sure, sure. Help yourself."

"I'm impressed by your home." Not wanting to comment on the décor, Cassie added, "It's very clean. It must take a lot of work to keep it like this."

"Don't be," said Cliff. "I have a deal with one of the maids from the hotel who lives in the valley. She comes once a week. Even does the laundry."

Cassie tried to imagine bachelor heaven after a week: empty containers of take-out food stacked beside his lounge chair, piles of dirty dishes and bottles in the kitchen, muddy construction clothes lying beside the laundry basket because he missed. The poor maid must be a treasure.

Chapter Twenty-Six

Winter wasn't for everyone. In New York City, a love affair with snow lasted fifteen minutes: until you had to venture out in it, until you stepped into the six inches of slush at the corner crosswalk where the drain was plugged, until you got your second shower of the day from an Amazon delivery van hitting the pothole full of freezing water and hurling it in your direction. The city would strain and scream from canceled trains, motionless airports, and crippling traffic—swearing and complaining the prevalent form of communication. The upside was that muggings and stabbings dropped off.

Cassie woke to snow on Sunday morning, another new experience in Manor Valley. It filtered through the trees, slowly spreading its grip on the ground as she watched through the bedroom sliding glass door, arms folded behind her head on the pillow. No acoustics, completely silent, her usual orchestra of squirrels and birds were quietly tucked in their nests—peaceful. Certainly not New York, where there would be a symphony of horns and at least one fender bender outside her window, with a heated discussion going on in multiple languages. This was more like the magazine pictures of European mountain villages in winter, or scenes from a Hallmark Christmas movie. Until now, she'd always thought them a scam, photoshopped or film edited to fool the unsuspecting. But this—this was beautiful, and it was real.

Excited, Cassie dressed in her new parka and Sorel boots. She wanted to see this winter show near the lake, sitting by the fireplace in the Mall with a coffee and warm croissant from the bakery.

Her Honda SUV had no trouble; it came with snow tires and had all-wheel drive.

Ten thirty, and the Mall was a beehive. Cassie watched Cliff outside with workers setting up holiday-colored lights among new artisan stalls. They must have been set up Friday or yesterday; she hadn't been by to notice. People labored outside all the stores on the street—up on ladders, emptying boxes, finishing up lights and decorations.

She stood off to the side until Cliff noticed her and said, "Oh, hi Jefe. Go ahead in. I'll take a break in a minute and find you."

Inside, she stopped by Lily's shop on the way to the back, wanting to thank her again for the lovely company Friday night at dinner. Lily was rushing around, checking and replacing stock.

"Yesterday was busy, and today we'll be slammed. People will drive up from Sacramento to shop and see the snow. The mountains farther up get much higher amounts of snow than here. People know they'll be able to enjoy this and still make it home." Lily straightened from some boxes, shook her ponytail from her face, put her hands on her hips, and said to Cassie, "Now you see why I was so spun up yesterday at Cliff's party. I snuck away from here about three, left it to the girls, and rushed over to help Ethel with my brother's little gala."

"Well, I'll leave you to it," said Cassie. "I'm going to relax in the lounge area and enjoy the snow. It's not beautiful like this in New York."

It was early, and Cassie had no trouble finding a soft leather chair right next to the window. She angled it to take in the already blazing fireplace along with the view outside over the lake. Strings of tiny white lights swooped up and down from the rafters above. Mini trees with colored lights smiled at her through the windows of the shops. Bows and garlands hung from doorways and merchant stands. Soft seasonal music stuttered through the sounds of happy store and stall owners milling about with early shoppers. Cassie knew how vital this month was to many of the area artisans.

The smells tempted her to buy many treats at the bakery, but she limited herself to just one croissant. She smiled as she critiqued the large Christmas tree in the center of the place, impressed by the Manor Valley's Toy Drive plastic box set on a pedestal beside it, already half full of coins and paper money. Happy with herself, she judged the hotel's tree was prettier. The Weaver family down through the years had collected old ornaments from around the world. In the library, Justin had unearthed photographs from Christmases long ago. He and some of the younger staff took several nights to decorate the tree, the task eased by a supply of food and drinks to create a party atmosphere.

Cassie felt like a kid again. Why was snow so different for the young? It came down gracefully over the lake, melting away as it hit the water. Evidently, this was the time of year that everyone paid attention to the weather forecasts. Lily had told her that it would not be pretty higher up in the mountains; an army of snow-removal equipment would be fighting to keep the freeway open over the High Sierras through the strong winds of a significant storm. Here in Manor Valley, the snow was serene and peaceful, lifting everyone's spirits with its embrace.

Cliff interrupted her daydream. "Not bad, huh? In New York, you probably have an app for something like this, so you can watch it on your phone... underground... on the subway... right before someone dips their hand into your shopping bag... and steals your niece's favorite toy the day before Christmas."

Cassie turned and gave him a hundred-watt smile, now used to, expecting, and even enjoying his forays into sick humor at her expense. She watched as he sat on the edge of a coffee table close to her, comfortable with his usual casualness. She reached over and brushed something off of his shoulder, oblivious to any thought about invading his personal space like she would have been conscious of in New York.

Her curiosity had to be satisfied. "Who organizes all this stuff—the new outside stalls, the decorations inside, the tree lot next door. Is this the hotel's responsibility?"

"Everything in here is organized and done by the tenants—the same for all the storeowners on the street. We have nothing to do with it. Outside is a different story. Since the hotel owns the building, we manage everything out there." The smile on his face told her more humor was coming. "As Senior Executive Vice President and Managing Director of Outside Activities, I supervise it all, unless you'd like to micromanage me some more." Pleased with his wit, he sipped his coffee.

Cassie parried back. "Senior Executive Vice President and Managing Director of Outside Activities? Did you fit all that on your business cards? Do you even have any business cards?"

"Nah, I'd just lose them."

"Well, maybe I'll knit it on a sweater for you, so people will know."

Cliff gave additional details, educating the boss some more. "It's a small street out there. Traffic this month is a consideration. Cars and trucks will be lined up for Christmas trees. Since we lease the space—the same people rent it at Halloween and for spring or summer events—we make sure on weekends that they have a guy in an orange vest directing the flow." He proudly pointed a finger at himself. "We, meaning Lily and I, review all the applicants for the outside stalls to make sure there isn't any conflict with what's sold inside: not too many sellers of scarves and woolen hats, only one or two selling Christmas cards and calendars, things like that."

Cliff raised a palm. "Excuse me a minute." He went over to the coffee stand for a refill, stayed for a minute for what Cassie could see was a laugh, and returned. She noticed it was no charge. God, he had the whole town conned. Between this place and Ethel, why would he bother buying food?

Class resumed. "People don't come up here for Black Friday Weekend. They flood the malls in Sacramento, shopping for different things. This is our first big weekend. It's even busy during the week, and when the kids get out of school, it's a zoo." He waved his arm over her head since she was facing the lake. "You'll notice in here and outside, Alice and Henry, who run the bakery, have set up several more small coffee stands. Otherwise, the line at their shop would wind all over the place in here. Coffee's big in weather like this. On weekend afternoons and evenings, we have Christmas carolers all dressed up in Victorian costumes, singing by the entrance. You should come to see them. Now, Cassie Bryant from New York City, age thirty-one, aren't you glad I'm here to take this monkey off your back?"

She remembered Vivien's caution not to minimize him, take him for granted. Maybe show a smidgeon of interest, of gratitude. She put down her cup and leaned slightly forward. "Cliff, remember my text. This is all still foreign to me, and you are my shepherd through it. No one has helped me more, been kinder to me, than you. I'm beginning to see that you're just as busy as me, but you handle the stress better. I'll be better after I settle in. I *do not* do outbursts like I did on you about the tile. There's no way I can show my appreciation." Nervous, Cassie got up to leave but wanted to give a jab back to lighten the mood. "You still have to seek some professional help with that sense of humor, but I find it growing on me."

On the way out, she remembered his comment about 'woolen hats.' She had the scarf from her first visit to the Mall. A stop at one of the stalls outside yielded two lovely woolen caps for winter.

*

In her small, cozy living room that afternoon, Cassie lit her first fire. Dan had pointed out the paper, the lighter, and the wood, and explained how to start the kindling. She'd put off doing it until now, never having any experience. Proud of her work, she brought her book and a drink over to the sofa, unfolded the wool throw blanket, and prepared to settle in. But first, a call to Vivien.

"You were right. My tirade on Cliff about the tile fiasco is forgotten. He thought my text was very nice and then asked me who wrote it. Like you said, it was water off a duck's back. Speaking of ducks, the other day..."

Cassie gave an animated account of the geese, followed by her tree-cutting excursion. Cliff figured prominently in both. Fifteen minutes later, she wrapped it up with the first snow in Manor Valley. Somewhere she fit in how comfortable, dry, and warm her new Sorel boots were.

"Oh, Cassie. Boots like that are so unfashionable. Next time just stay in the truck and watch. Haven't you learned anything from me?"

"Vivien!"

"Fine. Another practical suggestion shunned. And they have you running a major hotel?"

Talk returned to Cliff—his disaster of a house, how nice he was, all the help he volunteered, and how she liked having him near. She added the now funny story of how he wanted her to wade into the lake and cut some poor goose's throat.

There were a lot of Cliff references, so Vivien said, "Cassie, you obviously need help. You still know nothing about men. I go through more of them in a month than you have since college. A nunnery might be a good option to end your misery. Are you still using a Wi-Fi connection to help your sex life?" She paused for a second. "I'm canceling my trip to Paris. I don't like the family condo there anyhow. Book me a suite for the holidays. You do have suites, don't you? One room can be so confining." Vivien bubbled with her new plans. "I'll be spending Christmas with you and that Cliff person! Your folks and I have so much to tell him about our little Cassie growing up in New York. Which airport will the limo pick me up at? Oh, and don't go overboard. I'll only need two or three minions assigned to me. And, if it's snowing when I arrive, do *not* have staff lined up on the stone stairs outside like in those old movies. You know I'm all about consideration."

Cassie alternated between reading and watching the snow through the window before tiring and leaning her head back on a sofa pillow. She remembered the interior of Cliff's house. The hodge-podge of mixed furniture couldn't hide the warmth of the home. Today it would be cozy and inviting. Like his truck, he loved his home. Give him the basics, and he was content. Never striving to be at the top, he simply wanted to be present for his friends. Active in town charities, helpful to anyone at the hotel, warming everyone's day with humor and kindness, he sought neither recognition nor payment. And his reward? Love from all around him, a modest home, his dog, his truck, and contentment in a job he loved.

Cassie almost laughed as she pictured him at home tonight, ending his day in that awful recliner watching his satellite TV with Tank, eating something from the microwave unless he stopped and stole some food from the hotel kitchen. God, they'd probably roast him a turkey if he asked.

Later in bed, Cassie tossed around, trying to find a comfortable position. He was moving furniture around in her head again. It was all surfacing, romantic notions she thought she had control over, feelings she thought could be dismissed.

Everyone loved him. He should have been a con man in a carnival. *Now I'm under the spell too.* Maybe she could have some revenge. She could have Cliff pick up Vivien—two foreign objects trapped in a truck for an hour and a half. Would either even understand what the other was talking about? She'd like to see the look on Viv's face when he met her with the cardboard sign saying VIVIEN VAN HOUTEN FROM NEW YORK CITY, AGE 31, and then watched him throw her Louis Vuitton luggage on top of the snow and tools in the back of his truck. She'd like to see the look on *his* face when Viv swanned up to him at arrivals, her three-thousand-dollar Chanel topcoat flapping as she walked, handed him her four-thousand-dollar Louis Vuitton tote bag, brushed up her sleeve from the tote strap, and said, "Bring the limo around, please" and "Can one get a latte for the ride?" *I could hide microphones and cameras in the truck and make a fortune on YouTube.*

Sure, women were nurturers by nature, but really? That house? Easy going and undemanding Cliff. Christmas wouldn't be a problem for him—just buy him a train set, and give him the cute little village to go with it. *God, he's not even close to my carefully crafted ideal of a man, and I'm falling for him.* He'd worn her down without even trying. She wouldn't have to worry about the parents; they'd both fall all over him.

So confusing and unexpected, these feelings. These weren't high school sweetheart feelings. These weren't Herschel feelings. These were tempting, sensual, erotic feelings for a man who shouldn't be able to generate them in me. *I love being around him. When would we dance again? Would he hold me close?* When work got her tense, she loved finding him, seeing that smile—reassurance that life wasn't so bad. She couldn't wait to go out on the trails with him again. His warped sense of humor was growing on her. She couldn't help but laugh. Half her time at his party, she was watching him move around the room, mesmerizing the rest of them.

No, don't even think about home and children.

It was Anger's time to weigh in. Cassie smacked her pillow and flipped to her other side. The future loomed bleakly. *I'm such a fool,* she thought. *How did I let it get this far?* No solution would be cresting the horizon to save her. He damned sure wasn't moving to New York. What was to be done? And she didn't even know how he felt about her. Sure, she knew he liked her, at least when she was civil to him. *Does he even think about me romantically, after the way I've treated him?*

Cassie wallowed in a quagmire of conflicting emotions, a flexing field of sensations and feelings. It was dawning on her that having a single driving passion—in her case, work—usually meant she ended up sitting next to loneliness most of the time.

How do I resolve this mess? Pursue it? Pass on it? Try to let it go for now?

She did not need this in her life right now!

But, there it was.

Chapter Twenty-Seven

Everything was up and running for the holidays. Cassie charged into week two of December relaxed, comfortable that things were under control. Justin had taken care of the lobby tree decorations before she'd even thought about it, and the Senior Executive Vice President and Managing Director of Outside Activities had everything on schedule. After seeing the Mall and the shops downtown, how wonderful they looked and the business that was pouring in, Cassie was afraid to ask Cliff what else he did to make things run so well. Dan had told her several times about her micromanaging, and it was starting to sink in. Who could ask for two people as organized as Justin and Cliff?

Over the weekend, she had fretted about the New Year's Eve package the hotel offered each year. The East Coast hotels offered nothing like this. She'd completely missed it and only just heard about it by a passing remark from Lily. She cornered Justin in the lobby first thing Monday and discovered that it had already been sorted.

"Sorry, Jefe." Even Justin was calling her that in private; it was now Cliff and his little joke. "Invitation went out to a select mailing list in September, before you arrived. I assumed you knew about it. We offer a package that includes two or three nights' stay and New Year's dinner in the dining room, followed by a dance in the lobby rotunda. I followed the format from years past, which included a caveat to reserve early."

Visions of December overtime nights dampened her spirits. "What else has to be done to bring it all together? Who organizes all this?"

"Harry, Ethel, and I formed a committee. Honestly, Harry and Ethel just told me what to do since I wasn't here last year either. We booked up within three weeks, which was also before you took the job. Harry does all the seating, Ethel does the menu, and all I had to do was book the small orchestra and arrange decorations. I'm sure they would have consulted with you, but, like I said, it was before you arrived.

"Dan always has two tables for six or eight reserved. I'm working that night; you're off duty. Staff isn't a problem because Dan insists on triple time." He pushed his hair back, thinking if he missed anything. "Don't worry, your parents and friend will be at one of Dan's tables."

What was it Cliff said at the Mall—another monkey off my back?

Cassie detoured on her way back to her office, happy and relieved at how well things were functioning. New Year's Eve, and she'd been so preoccupied she hadn't even thought about it. Was Janet smiling at her as she passed the portrait? A comical smile that said, "Get on top of it, young lady." She lightly tapped the massive gilt frame as had become her habit.

In Cliff's office, she waited in front of a banquet table stacked with plans while he finished up on the phone. After he hung up, not having thought about it in detail, Cassie said, "Are you coming to the hotel New Year's dinner and dance?"

"Whoa, boss! Are you fraternizing with the help? Hitting on an employee? Did you just ask me out on a date?" He jumped up and grabbed what looked like, based on its cover, some technical manual. He pretended to leaf through it, looking for a page. "Let me check this human resources manual. I don't even want to think about all the political correctness laws you just violated. Dan should send you on a refresher course."

"Are you through? You're not an employee, you're an independent contractor," said Cassie. Although the ramifications of her question now spun up in her head. "I simply asked if you were coming."

She hadn't seen the stricken, sad act before. Cliff looked down and sheepishly ran his fingers over some papers. "Oh, sorry. I thought you were asking me to be your date. No, it will probably be just Tank and me alone... by ourselves... on New Year's. Ethel may have some leftover crumbs, so I don't starve." The theatrical closer could have earned him an Oscar. A palm came up. "No, no. Please don't worry about me. I should be fine. I'll probably do some catch-up paperwork."

Big decisions sometimes had to be made on the fly. Cassie knew she'd come down here because she didn't want to be by herself—

meaning without him—on New Year's. And he looked so sad. She never imagined Cliff Walker being alone on such a big night. She almost wanted to go over and hug him but knew he'd pick up the damned book again and search for the 'invading personal space' violation.

The hell with it. I'm doing this.

"Yes, I'm asking you to please be my date on New Year's."

"Me?"

"Yes—don't push it."

Serious now. "Thank you. I would love to go with you. It's very nice of you to ask."

Back in her office, delighted and surprised that she'd asked him to be her date, Cassie refocused onto items for next year. The holidays seemed to be under control. It was the first time she didn't feel pressured since she'd arrived in Manor Valley.

Two folders held her immediate priorities for the coming year: the hotel website and a blog that focused on new activities, inside and outside, to promote the hotel and Manor Valley. She now knew the greatest advertisement for the hotel was the valley itself. She'd seen how autumn worked with the changing colors, Halloween, horse shows, hiking, and riding, and the Mall. At this point, the holidays needed nothing else. What could be added for other seasons?

A little more work and the website ideas should be ready to ship off to a professional. Cassie wanted to be sure the new blog link would be easy for the users to find and click on. It would be a quarterly blog so she and Justin could stay on top of it. More ideas were written down. They'd be bounced off Cliff, Justin, Dan, and Lily to see if they were feasible. She'd also press them for additional ideas. Her list grew: outside or inside yoga classes with occasional prominent-name guest instructors to augment the new spa; half-price spa promotions to generate new business from Sacramento and beyond—not just hotel guests; a slow paddlewheel barge for lunches on a cruise around the lake; fly fishing lessons; double Frequent Stayer Points for a while when the new wings opened. Fireworks and swimming lessons for kids were a no-no due to liability.

One of her favorites, which she'd ask Lily and Leo about, was a high-end overnight horseback-riding adventure deep into the woods in a remote neighboring valley complete with luxurious tent accommodations and chef-prepared meals.

Seeing Justin's rowing shell on Cliff's deck gave her another idea: a two- or three-day rowing regatta on the lake like they did with universities back East. It could be a big draw for the valley. Justin would enjoy exploring that, checking on colleges and universities around the state, even private clubs. Entry fees? Prizes? Accommodations? Cassie had no idea, but it was worth checking into, another draw for the expanded hotel and the valley businesses.

She caught herself, remembering this was not New York City, where you could invite every rock band in Europe on the same night, and it wouldn't faze the inhabitants. This was a small town. Granted, their livelihood depended on the hotel, but how high was their tolerance level for some of these ideas? Was a regatta full of college kids too much? She'd have to discuss this with Dan, see how these things were handled.

Possible half-day tours in the area for guests were another option to explore. Were there any lumber mills that did tours? A horticultural walking tour around the lake? Trips to artisan studios in neighboring valleys? She'd heard there were weavers, glass blowers, sculptors, and painters in the area.

Her concentration was broken when Leslie came through her door. Leslie was Dan's secretary when he was in town and also worked for the resident manager and assistant manager. Justin raved about her. Cassie liked working with her, although she'd used her only sporadically so far, still not having her feet firmly on the ground. That was changing now that things were sorting themselves out.

"Dan wants to see you. Something about a new office for you?" she said.

Cassie was comfortable in her temporary office of over two months but knew that would have to change. The hotel had booked several Christmas parties for smaller companies from as far away as Sacramento. Her half of a partitioned banquet room would need to be rejoined with the other half to accommodate one of the parties. She knew the old manager's office was hers when she was ready, more organized. What did new office mean?

If his past history of disappearing to California was any indication, Dan was back now until at least mid-January. Something was off when Cassie entered his office. The lovely built-in bookcases were still full of his collection of old leather-bound classics and newer ones on business and other areas of interest. But all the knickknacks had been removed, the desk was bare, and his old high-back leather chair was missing, replaced by a more utilitarian version. She could hear Dan, Cliff, and another employee talking in the small private study next door, accessed from his office or the hallway.

"Shove the desk under the window. I like the view," said Dan. "And when you bring the bookcases up, put them along the back wall. Leslie will sort out the books and the boxes later."

"You wanted to see me, sir?"

"Cassie! Come in. I put my foot down with Cliff about your office. He said you'd be happy if he blocked off a parking spot in the garage with some plastic, and he'd give you a portable heater to keep warm. Even had a good idea about a desk from crates with an old door on top." He looked at Cassie and threw up his hands. "He's a creative dynamo, don't you think?"

She looked confused. Maybe it was the thought of being in the garage in winter with the gently scented air of gasoline.

"Come back into my office and sit down in this chair." Dan guided her by her elbow back to his desk, and then he and Cliff stood on the other side.

"Looks like she was born to be there, doesn't it, Cliff?"

"Sorry, Uncle Dan. I still think the employees would be happier with her in the garage."

Still the blank look from Cassie.

Dan said, "This is your new office, Cassie. I'll be next door in the study when I'm here. Cliff suggested giving Justin Rita's old office across the hall. She quit on me a few months ago, said I could work myself into the ground by myself if I wanted to. You can both use the old manager's office as a meeting room or a special projects room where you can lay a lot of stuff out. Cliff knows you two should be near each other. I don't need anything that big. Like I said, I'll be cutting back soon too. I always thought that little study was comfortable. I used to go in there to think when I was alone." He swept his hand in front of him. "I thought you might want my old desk."

Finally, Cassie spoke. "I can't take your office, Dan. This is too much. Let *me* have the study."

"You wouldn't be able to fit all your stuff in there. No, I've made an executive decision. Here you'll stay. This large, old partner's desk used to have chairs on both sides of it. It's big, and when you have meetings with staff, they can sit opposite you, and you can get work done. That's why I always kept that extra chair over there." He pointed to the corner.

"Do you know why you can't say no?" said Dan, enjoying himself as he nudged Cliff in the side. "Well, Lily told me you were fascinated by the story about Travis and Janet. This is the same desk they used together, all those years ago. He'd be on one side running his empire, and Janet would be on the other running the house and him."

Dumbfounded, Cassie ran her hand along the desk. *Janet sat here?*

"Cliff will bring some boxes to your old office. You can fill them, and they'll bring them up here."

Cassie got up, walked slowly around the desk, and silently hugged Dan. She then turned to Cliff, a bit of accusation in her voice. "The garage? I was thinking the boiler room."

Palms lifted toward his smiling face. "Hey, just trying to look out for you. Feels kinda stuffy up here to me." And he turned and went about his business.

Alone now, Dan had Cassie sit behind the desk—his old place, and Travis Weaver's long before him. He pulled up a chair and sat opposite. "Since Rita abandoned me, she's been teaching Justin about what she used to do: community activities, charities, and I don't know what else. She really did put in her share of hours around here. Now, with the new wings almost done, you and Justin are going to be busy. It's your show now. You should think about bringing someone else on to help the two of you. And, it's your call, but you may want to give Justin a raise and some sort of title or recognition. I'm sure you've seen how that man works." He slapped the desk and got up. "Me? I'm gone for the day."

*

Cassie was good at staying on top of her personal life—what there was of it. The holidays would be a challenge. Both Vivien and the parents would be here, and they would have to be attended to. The

164

hotel was fully booked. They were prepared, but minor problems always arose. It was the third week of December, Christmas shopping needed to be done now, and she was not the gift card type. She shook her head and smiled, picturing Cliff walking into a store to buy beer. A stand of gift cards from all the big companies beside the cash register would catch his attention. "Oh, yeah, Christmas. Almost forgot. Give me fifteen of these too." Men had it so easy.

She called Lily. "I need help. Is there any way you could take time out of your day or evening to take me shopping in Sacramento? I've never been there."

"That's actually a great idea. I want to get a jump on it too. Tuesday. Meet me at the Mall around three, and we'll drive down, shop, and grab some dinner."

Her list wasn't long. A fancy Cuisinart for Rita, since Cassie noticed the old one was small and failing. She was still thinking about Dan. Some little things for Vivien and her parents, since they couldn't carry anything large on the plane. Lily she'd have to think about too. The main gift, the one she was excited about, wasn't a problem—a monster, state-of-the-art TV for Cliff. Something was needed to cover up those white walls. She knew better than to screw with a man's recliner, but she might add a giant metal trash can to go beside the chair so he wouldn't have to strain himself walking to the kitchen. He could simply chuck his microwave cartons into the bin, and never miss a play of the game. She'd bounced the idea off of Lily, who'd cautioned her. "Be careful, he'll be over the moon. You'll have to have sex with him."

Chapter Twenty-Eight

The hotel was booked solid for the holidays, and the hectic time would kick off next week.

Justin stuck his head into Cassie's new office. "A bunch of us are going to the pub tonight. Lily says we have to let off steam and enjoy ourselves before next week. She says the week before Christmas is a zoo in town. Tonight is like a big valley holiday office party. You should come."

Cassie sighed. She knew she needed a break. On top of everything else, both Vivien and her parents would arrive the coming week. She hadn't been sleeping well—perhaps a few drinks would help, and she'd yet to set foot inside 'the Pub.' It was probably named by the same marketing genius who came up with the Tree Farm. It was the only bar in town and also served as an alternate eating establishment for the locals. Opposite the lake, it was tucked back off the road against a hill coming into town. Until halfway through the last century, before they built the Mall, it was the only place in the area to get a drink. The building was an attractive mishmash of Tudor design, like pictures of English village pubs in movies and books, but without the thatched roof.

Grateful for the diversion and a chance to relax, she said, "Count on me. What time?"

She arrived at seven, thinking she might be early, but the parking lot was already packed. A light mist had settled on the valley, and the glow of Christmas lights through the mullioned windows made the place look warm and inviting.

Lily waved as she passed through the foyer. "I got here early and grabbed a table. The girls are covering the last hour at the shop."

Lily went to the bar for two bottles of wine so she wouldn't have to keep running back and forth, fighting the crowd.

Cassie sat and swept her eyes over the place. God, it was an English pub. Elaborate draft beer handles lined up on the other side of a varnished wood bar, complete with polished brass rail and even a foot bar. A jukebox played music beside a spacious parquet dance floor. Decorations hung haphazardly everywhere among drooping strings of small white Christmas lights broadcasting holiday cheer.

How come I haven't been in here before?

A short time later, Justin and Cliff arrived, along with young people from the hotel and the Mall. Leo, the stable manager, waved to her from the bar. She greeted people she recognized from the Fall Party. Their table for eight filled; Cliff sat across from her, next to Justin.

"Are Ethel or the Weavers coming?" asked Cassie.

"Not their scene," said Cliff. "It'll be a little rowdy and noisy later." He moved his hand in an up and down gesture in front of her chest. "That's not an expensive blouse, is it? Somebody will probably throw up on it before two a.m."

Cassie ignored him, and Lily gave him an admonishing, "Cliff!"

At least Cassie had one champion in the room.

Burgers were ordered. "Thank goodness you didn't order a salad," said Cliff. "They take forever." He leaned over and whispered to Cassie, "When you order a salad, a child will pedal down to the allotments and bring back fresh lettuce and tomatoes in a wicker basket on his restored seventies bicycle."

Cassie smiled and patted his cheek, not wanting to encourage him.

Someone turned the jukebox up, and the dancing started. Cassie expected country music, but it was all a surprising mix of '70s and '80s rock and soul, well balanced between slow and fast. Pent-up energy from dancing workers flowed off the crowded parquet floor. Two girls came and hauled Cliff and Justin out to dance.

Cassie watched Cliff from her seat while talking with the remaining group.

Will he ask me to dance tonight?

Finally, he did.

A few drinks and she felt herself loosening up, the week's tension peeling off her. Cassie was thankful he picked a slow one. Close to him, it felt infinitely better than the last time at the final managers' meetings party. Was it that long ago? Why was it different in his arms now? She surrendered to the slow movement around the floor, pulling herself closer to him. Suddenly, the song registered; the Manhattans were singing "Shining Star." Her body quivered for a second, and she reflexively tightened her grip on him.

"Are you okay?"

"Yes, sorry." They went back into quiet mode, and Cassie rested her head on his shoulder, close, intimate.

She found herself in the middle of a bizarre déjà vu. She remembered Janet Weaver's story from years ago of seeing the big stag on her first day in Manor Valley, silently telling her she belonged here. The recollection crushed up against her vision of the stag on her first day at Cliff's allotment shed, staring at her in the morning mist. The lovely proposal to Janet from Travis came next. "I want you to be the shining star of Manor Valley. I want you to be *my* shining star," was what he'd said to Janet. And now, here she was dancing with Cliff while the Manhattans sang about being someone's shining star. God, was it the same stag, appearing again after all those years? Was she meant to be *his* shining star? What the hell was going on?

Returning to the table, Cassie pounded down the half glass of wine in front of her and refilled it, still trying to sort out the sudden symbolism of both the stag and shining star. She wondered why Cliff looked confused until she realized she'd been staring at him strangely.

Cassie returned her focus to the group. Leo joined them as everyone exchanged funny stories about life at the Mall and the hotel.

"Your turn, Leo. Tell us something funny about the stables."

"Well, let me see," he said as he ran his hand over the day's stubble on his chin. "Okay. A couple of months ago, one of the guests from the hotel came out with his girlfriend and rented horses to go up in the hills. The guy had attitude. I asked the usual question—do you have any experience riding?" He looked at Lily, who nodded back, knowing the importance of the question. "Showing off, the man said he had lots. The girlfriend had none, so I put her on Old Molly, and I put the guy on Sonny." Leo looked around the table. "For those of you who don't ride around here, Sonny is, well, somewhat spirited, but not a problem for an experienced rider.

"As soon as they started out, I could see the guy was over his head. I didn't want to embarrass him, and I figured Old Molly would keep her kid in line.

"Anyway, when they got back, I could see Sonny had run the guy ragged. He was not happy, and Sonny looked pissed. I watched him get off the horse by the parking lot and walk to his car. He probably wanted some water or something to drink. He handed the reins to his girlfriend, who was doing everything she could to suppress a smile after being on the trails with John Wayne. There was a loud bang. When the guy closed his door and turned around, Sonny had taken his rear hoof and smashed out one of the car's taillights.

"I watched the whole thing. I almost threw up laughing."

The banter continued for a while before Justin and Lily dragged everyone back out to the dance floor again for a fast song.

At the end of the night, Cassie was floating. It had been a welcome, much-needed, fun break from the holiday crunch, a natural stress reliever. Cliff told her to leave her car and drove her home.

After a quiet ride, they stopped at her door.

"See you tomorrow," he said.

Would you like to come in? almost crossed her lips.

In bed, she wondered how large a barrier she'd created with Cliff in her unmistaken quest for professionalism. Had she made it insurmountable for him? Tonight had been the same as the Mall party. He was always proper and attentive to her, but she noticed how he was a little bit more free and loose with the other women at the table and on the dance floor—cautious with her. Was he even interested? What could she do?

Chapter Twenty-Nine

The next day Cassie felt great. The night out had done her good. She ran around checking with all the department heads to make sure supplies were in: laundry, housekeeping, and kitchen staff at the level they'd need. Justin looked like he might have fudged sleep time on a school night with someone, but he was on top of it. Everything was running smoothly.

The night before, Lily had told her she could go out on the trails by herself for the first time, but on Molly, not Sonny. To be safe, she or Cliff should go with her the first time with Sonny. Lily cautioned her to go on the lake trail, not up in the hills because of the snow.

And, damned if she wasn't going to do just that this afternoon.

Leo, the stable manager, leaned against the barn's side across the expansive central yard, drinking coffee and talking to another man with his back to Cassie as she walked up to Molly's stall. The stranger was tall, fitted out in weathered cowboy boots, worn Levi's, and jacket. He wore a thick wool scarf wrapped around his neck, and his cowboy hat with gray hair below was weathered to match the rest of his outfit. From the back, he reminded her of an old ranch hand from a movie.

She was opening Molly's door when she heard Leo say, "See you tomorrow, Dan."

As the man turned, Cassie gasped and said, "Dan!"

He ambled over to her. "Cassie. Wish I knew you were riding today. I'd have gone out with you."

Mr. GQ from New York surprised her again. "You ride?" she said.

Dan laughed. "Who do you think taught Lily and Cliff to ride when they were kids?"

Oh my God, thought Cassie. Recovering from the shock of seeing the boss dressed like this, she realized that it was one o'clock and she wasn't in the office on a workday. "I'm taking Molly out for the first time by myself. Lily has been giving me lessons. I'll make up the time by staying late."

This time Dan laughed out loud. "You still don't get life out here, Cassie. In your head, out on those trails by yourself, you'll get more work done in an hour than you would in three hours with all the interruptions in the office." He reached into his pocket and pulled out a piece of paper and a pen. "See? Now that I'm old, I carry these with me to write notes so I don't forget the ideas that pop into my head out there. My advice? Go out more during the week. You'll be more relaxed and productive." He smiled at her and put a hand on her shoulder. "Enjoy it. Just think, when you get back to New York you can rent a horse in Central Park for a fortune and lose yourself in the view of all those lovely skyscrapers." He turned to walk away and said over his shoulder, "By the way, Lily says you're doing great on Sonny." She heard him chuckle. "Don't forget the stable bonding with Old Molly when you get back."

Is there anything this man doesn't know?

The saddle went on, the bit placed in Molly's mouth—no help needed. Janet Weaver would have nothing on her; Cassie was going out to survey her domain. Next would be a rifle holster for the saddle if she wanted to hunt when she went out. Janet must have had one of those, right?

This was her first time on the lake trail. Molly and Cassie leisurely walked across the main road and past the allotments. As they approached the hotel, she smiled with pride. It was a gray day, and she could see the Christmas lights shining around all the windows and on various decorations outside the entry. In front of her, just off the walking path, was a large snowman someone had enjoyed making yesterday. It was still there, still with the carrot for a nose, still with the colorful scarf wrapped around its neck—beautiful. After one day in New York, the scarf would be gone, a cigarette would be sticking out below the nose, and some anti-Christmas protest sign would be hung around its neck, or someone would have spray-painted it.

People bustled in and out of the Mall, danced around the outside stalls, and muscled trees onto their cars at the tree lot. At the far end of the lake, tucked in a small copse of trees, a bench next to the water was perfect for a quiet break. She dismounted and unhooked her small pack from the saddle horn. A light breeze hummed through the branches around her as she sat on the bench and unwound her scarf. She unscrewed her new thermos; today, it was tea, not coffee. Ethel was converting her; it was English Breakfast from Fortnum & Mason in London, brought in among other blends for the dining room guests and room service.

Molly deserved a break too. She wolfed down the carrots Cassie fed her while she talked to her and stroked her neck.

Molly's ears twitched as she sorted sounds carried on the breeze. *Cassie is doing much better,* thought Molly—*not the lead weight like her first time out.* She moved well in the saddle now; definite progress after suffering through those lessons on that nitwit son of hers. *Yes,* she thought, *this is what life is all about, two women taking a nice break and having a gossip.*

Cassie sighed as she took in all the beauty around her. Dan and Cliff had been right. The peace of riding out alone did free up your mind, give you time to think. The valley was her second home now, and she realized she couldn't have asked for more. People were the most significant part of it—Dan, Rita, Ethel, Justin, Lily, Leo, and of course, *him.* In her wildest expectations, she couldn't have imagined this a few short months ago.

She thought back to the week after Thanksgiving when she met with Dan and confessed to her stress, her micromanaging, how she snapped at Cliff about the tile, and how she was questioning her decision about the job. He'd been easygoing and reminded her of their talk when she managed her first hotel. A hotel was like a well-run ship, he'd said. Competent officers ran their departments. Her job was to tap the rudder once in a while to keep it on course. The micromanaging was from fear of the unknown. Let Justin and Cliff do their jobs. She was lucky to have both of them, as well as Ethel, Harry, and the rest of the department heads. They'd keep her informed and discuss any problems.

He explained how her job now was planning and forward-thinking. Everything didn't have to be done this week. There was no rush on the website or advertising and promotions for the new hotel. "Hell," he'd said, "the damned thing won't even be finished for five or seven months." Cassie knew the pep talk was basically—lighten up on yourself.

In a few short weeks, she had learned to take herself less seriously and was enjoying the job and the valley more and more, like last night at the Pub, like right now. She looked around at Molly and the lake. Hell, now she even knew what 'outside activities' were and was enjoying some of them. *Things are going to work out,* she thought.

She sipped her tea and lost herself in the view for a few minutes. In the distance, a lone kayaker braving the cold weather in orange gear gave perspective to the lake's size. *Maybe I'll try that next,* she thought—but not in this weather. Two squirrels chased each other in the tree above her before stilling and looking at her inquisitively. Loosened snow from their antics in the branches drifted down in front of her.

She'd known it would return: the déjà vu experience of the stag and "Shining Star," and here it was again, trampling through her head, reminding her of him. She knew she was weakening, failing to banish Cliff from her thoughts. Home alone at night, he occupied her mind, as he did periodically during her days. The physical attraction had grown along with the desire to be with him at work and socially. She was comfortable and happy around him. Felt secure. He was part of her life now.

Thoughts from the night before intruded. Yes, she'd conveyed her wish to keep things professional only too well by her conduct, by her attitude. No wonder he dare not make a move. Her mind drifted again to what *he* might think of *her. Does he even think about me, romantically? Is he attracted to me?*

Cassie wanted to go forward, see if anything was there, but how?

Molly moved close, scratched her hoof in the dirt, and put her chin on Cassie's shoulder, bringing her back to the present. It was time to get back.

Chapter Thirty

Vivien Van Houten landed on the twenty-second. Porters were summoned. Holiday-grade tips dispensed, she settled into Cassie's Honda for the scenic trip back over the mountains to Manor Valley, California.

"My, this is cute—small, but cute. Is it allowed to go on the freeway?"

"Viv, you have a car this size in your garage, along with several others."

"You must mean the Volvo, dear? It's just for luggage. You know me, Little Miss Understated."

Cassie rolled her eyes back in her head. She wanted to show Vivien Lake Tahoe, but time was short today. She'd get a bigger car and take her up with her parents during the week. Maybe Cliff could be conned into driving one of those fancy vans the hotel used to ferry guests around. Give him a taste of his own medicine, three or four hours on the road with her parents and Vivien. She could get the flu again at the last minute.

The road was clear, the snow-covered trees and mountains a delight. Both ladies were impressed by the sheer quantity of snow. It was an early winter, and the snowbanks at the sides of the freeway over the summit were already four feet high. They had a lovely catch up, sometimes serious, sometimes funny, before Vivien would have to go into her act again at the hotel.

They pulled up to the entry and were swarmed with attention. Before leaving, Cassie had alerted everyone to Vivien's name and the level of pampering required. With her social connections, this woman could generate serious bookings back home, and Cassie wanted to impress her friend, show off the hotel, and shower her with old-world service.

Brian, the doorman, was on his game as he opened Vivien's door and offered his arm. "Please, Ms. Van Houten, we're all so excited about having you with us."

Fingers were snapped and luggage unloaded while Cassie and Vivien ascended the stairs. Vivien leaned toward her. "Excellent, Cassie. The 'Ms. Van Houten' was a nice touch." Formal act resumed, she added, "Let's see how you do inside."

Vivien swanned across the lobby toward reception, taking everything in as she went. She stalled at the center table, entranced by Lily's holiday arrangement, an explosion of white and gold. White amaranths, white French tulips, and white Icelandic roses pushed out from birch branches with heavy sugar sparkles, magnolia leaves dusted with soft gold, and pine boughs. Pomegranates were stacked around a fat, wide golden urn.

A cheery person slid up beside her. "Beautiful, isn't it? Let's not waste your time with check-in, Ms. Van Houten. Please, follow me."

"I want to check messages. I'll be up in a minute," said Cassie.

The woman whisked Vivien up to the best suite in the hotel. Flowers, champagne, chocolates, it was all there. Soft classical music played on the sound system. Luggage followed shortly behind.

"Will you need help unpacking, Ms. Van Houten? I can summon one of the maids. The towel warmer has been turned on if you need to relax after your long journey. Room service will be instantaneous if you're hungry. Should I open the champagne?"

All of the young staff paid attention when Luke returned to the lobby with a forty-dollar tip for delivering the bags.

Cassie gave Vivien time to digest the suite—a *large* living room and a *large* bedroom and the spacious modern bath. The closet was the size of one of Cassie's New York hotel rooms. Vivien found herself distracted between the Georgian décor and the magnificent views of the lake and snow-covered forest.

When Cassie came in, Vivien was sipping some champagne, looking out the window. All decorum disappeared. She turned to her friend, holding out another full glass. "You've got to be kidding me with this place!"

*

Vivien's first-night dinner would, of course, be in the hotel dining room. Cassie's parents wouldn't arrive until the next day, so it would be Vivien, Cassie, Cliff, Lily, and Justin. Poor Justin deserved a break. The following two weeks would be crushing, and Cassie wanted him to have an enjoyable night out with Lily.

Cassie stood by the door, tapping her foot. "Let's go, Viv. Give the mirror a break. We're late."

It was a show night. The audience might not be Broadway, but Vivien Van Houten would not be rushed out of wardrobe and makeup. "Keep your wig on—I'm coming." She came out of the bathroom, adjusting the dress over her ample bosom. "I almost fell asleep in the tub. Whatever that aromatherapy bath oil is, send me a case. As a matter of fact, box this whole place up and ship it."

They went down in the elevator, and Cassie let Vivien swan across the lobby in front of her. It was busy. Men gawked, and their well-to-do wives couldn't hide their envy at Vivien's outfit. It was a stunning lamé weave of silver metallic fibers woven through a delicate light-gray fabric flowing over her impressive body—very Christmassy, and very expensive. Cassie took it all in and suppressed a laugh. Between the clothes and the jewelry, Vivien was walking around in the net worth of Somalia. Cassie stalled when one elderly couple came up to Vivien. They exchanged words, and introductions were made. Cassie excused herself and went to wait with Cliff, standing by the dining room entrance, his eyes also glued to her friend.

As she stood beside him, Cliff whispered, "Whoa. I see she wore her bingo dress. Where did she find all the tinsel to make that thing?" For which he received a gentle elbow in his side.

"How can she keep her head up with all those diamonds around her neck?"

Another elbow, not as gentle.

Cassie was nervous. She wanted Vivien to like Cliff. She knew the scrutiny from her friend during dinner would be subtle but thorough.

Vivien joined them and said to Cassie, "A business associate of my father. Charming people. When they return to New York and tell my parents they saw me here, father will be on the phone wondering why I'm not in Paris where I'm supposed to be."

She turned to Cassie's companion and put on her brightest smile. "Oh, let me guess. You're that Cliff person! Aren't you adorable? Cassie's told me so much about you."

Cliff snorted. "From Cassie?" He smiled and raised his arms in surrender. "Please don't call security."

Vivien ignored the restraining hand Cassie put on her arm. "You look just like your picture." As expected, Vivien noticed his confused look. "You know, the framed one on Cassie's bedside table?"

"Vivien!" Cassie was turning red. "I do *not* have a picture of Cliff on my bedside table."

Vivien turned back to Cliff. "She tried to hide it in a drawer when I came into the bedroom. Have you been in her bedroom?"

Now Cliff was turning red.

Vivien's hand went to her breast. A look of contrition blanketed her face. "Oh, I hope I'm not being indiscreet." With that, she whisked past them and flowed into the dining room.

Harry, the maître d', was on her instantly. "Ms. Van Houten. An honor. Please, follow me."

Cassie caught up with her. "What the hell was that picture stuff all about?"

"I told you, dear, I'm here to help." She leaned over and lowered her voice. "Let me handle this, Sister Cassandra. You'll be in the sack with him before I leave. They'll need a crowbar to pry him off you."

As Cliff held out her chair, Vivien patted his bicep. "You must do all the *manly* things around here. I'm so happy my Cassie has someone like you to see to her more pressing needs."

Vivien naturally had the head of the table. Cliff and Cassie flanked her. After introductions were made, Vivien spoke to Lily.

"Your flower arrangement in the lobby is breathtaking, Lily. Such a talent. I want to take it back with me and show the management of my building what a floral display should look like in a lobby. Last time I looked, I think they had a dead corsage on a side table."

Vivien balanced her demanding nature with a complimentary side. Nothing went unnoticed. When necessary, she was the epitome of manners. A person doing their job well should be acknowledged, no matter what the job. The dining room staff adored her. Whether it was wine poured by the sommelier or water refilled by a trainee, Vivien took the time to turn her head, make eye contact, smile, and offer a 'thank you so much.' People were not there to be ignored.

The dining room was full, and Cassie thought she might receive complaints the next day from the other guests with all the attention staff directed toward her friend.

Partially through the meal, a young girl silently approached and filled Vivien's water glass.

"Thank you so much, dear. You're such a treasure."

There was a lull in the conversation when the girl left. Vivien asked, "Do you know her? She's so small and quiet, like a mouse. Very efficient. I've been watching her glide between tables. That young lady is sharp. She watches everything. There's not an empty water glass in the room."

Cliff explained. "Her name is Gail Norman. She's quiet and shy and lives with her mother and younger brother in the next valley. She's worked here since she was a freshman in high school, earning money for college. Never misses a summer or holiday season. Now she is in college. Comes up from Sacramento to work weekends. She started in the kitchen with Ethel. This job is important to her. There's no extra money at home, and she helps out. She should be ready to be a waiter this summer."

"Interesting," said Vivien, as she tracked the girl's silent journey through the room.

Cassie felt bad. She didn't know any of that.

Vivien quizzed everyone about what they did in Manor Valley. Eventually, the conversation turned to horses. Cassie knew Viv was a conversational magician from hearing stories about her fundraising events, schmoozing people out of their money. Western or English? Dressage, steeplechase, even barrel racing were touched upon. Funny stories were exchanged. Cassie was surprised her friend knew so much about horses. Vivien perked up when Lily suggested the three ladies go for a ride the next week after the Christmas rush was over. She was down for that.

Finally, Cassie got a word in. "Vivien, you never told me you rode!"

"Well, I lost my virginity in a stable at fifteen. I never told you that, either."

Everyone laughed; they were all under the spell.

As they prepared to leave, Cassie noticed Vivien subtly reach into her purse. As they reached the door, Harry stood smiling with his hands folded in front of him. His resonant voice said, "Please, Ms.

Van Houten, tell me we've met your expectations. Staff would be shattered if we hadn't measured up."

Vivien shook his hand with both of hers, discreetly slipping in a wad of bills. "Such a pleasure, Harry." Names were one of Vivien's things; she never forgot one. "Thank you so much. You'll see to everyone?"

"Of course, Ms. Van Houten. And thank *you*." Two professionals wrapping up a mutually beneficial evening.

Ignoring the group as they filtered into the lobby, Vivien glided over to the near corner of the dining room, where the water girl stood, scanning the room, meekly holding her pitcher. The young girl's mouth opened in awe as Vivien approached with a big smile. Another discreet handshake.

"I've been watching you, young lady. Extremely professional. You'll do well at anything you do in life. Next time I come back, you'll be headwaiter. I'll be asking for you."

In the lobby, Cassie asked, "What did you give her?"

"A hundred dollars."

"God, Vivien!"

Vivien looked down her nose. "I know how you people operate. If I left it up to you thieves, the poor girl would probably end up with two dollars at the end of the night." That dispensed with, she turned to Lily and Justin. "We'll see each other soon. I'm making it an early night. It's been a long day."

Lily and Justin made for the bar, leaving Vivien with Cliff and Cassie.

Vivien asked Cliff, "I trust there have been no major issues with my Cassie's conduct since she's been here in Manor Valley? She can be so passionate about work and other things. Quite vocal. Believe me, I know. I had the bedroom next to her one summer, and I can tell you—"

"Yes, yes, Vivien. He doesn't need a history lesson. Why don't you go up and get some sleep? I think the altitude is getting to you."

"An excellent idea." She squeezed Cliff's arm as she started toward the elevator, finishing over her shoulder, "But he would be a delightful Yuletide diversion for you."

Neither knew what to say as they walked across the lobby to the garage elevator, Cassie somewhat embarrassed, and Cliff sifting through Vivien's last bit of information. His hand rested lightly on the small of her back.

"So, roommates, huh?" Cliff said with a grin.

She wouldn't meet his eyes. "Don't you start."

As they passed the painting of Janet and Travis, Cassie looked up and mumbled, "What are you laughing at?"

"Excuse me?" said Cliff.

Cassie flipped her hand toward the picture. "Nothing. I was talking to her."

Before her so-called girlfriend screwed it up, Cassie was almost at the point of asking him home for a drink, but he'd probably go into the bedroom, see if his picture was there, and check to see if the room was soundproof.

*

At breakfast the next morning, after berating Vivien for her meddling, Cassie had to ask. "What did you think of Cliff?"

"Ping pong," said Vivien, as she focused on cutting her eggs Benedict.

"Pardon me?"

"Ping pong. That's what the two of you were doing last night. He'd look at you—you'd look at him. Back and forth all night. I felt like the white stripes on the green table sitting between the two of you. I like him. Good-looking, funny, seems sharp, has a responsible job—why's he interested in you?" Vivien turned serious. "How heavily are you into this guy? And don't lie."

"I like him. He's grown on me, but I don't know what to do now. I'm not even sure he's interested in me, you know, in a romantic way."

"Oh, trust me," said Viv. "He's interested. He couldn't take his eyes off you. You've got some sorting out to do, young lady. Lucky, I'm here to help."

"Yeah, right. After your efforts last night, Match.com won't be requiring *your* services."

"Are you crazy? After I planted the seed, he's still thinking about passionate you, moaning and groaning in that bedroom when we lived together. You've got to step up, take the initiative before it's too late, let him know how you feel. At least you'll know. Close the deal. Show some New York City pride and aggression."

Cassie just shook her head. She gathered her things and was off to pick up her parents. "Justin is taking you on a tour today?"

"Looking forward to it. Drive safely."

Chapter Thirty-One

The weather report was grim as Cassie got onto the freeway from the Manor Valley exit to pick up her parents. There was nothing to be done about it. Plane reservations had been made before Cliff offered his advice: in winter, pick up people at the Sacramento airport, not Reno. The weather could be drastically different. The freeway's high point in the Sierra Nevada Mountains between Reno and Manor Valley was seventy-two hundred feet at Donner Summit. You could be sunbathing in Sacramento while, less than a hundred miles away, there was a blizzard in the mountains.

Driving out of the valley, Cassie had time to focus on the night before. She was thrilled with Vivien's approval of Cliff, even more thrilled about how the lovely dinner party went with Cliff beside her. He'd looked terrific dressed up, had been attentive toward her, and seemed more interested than she had previously thought.

Perhaps there was hope after all. She'd make an effort to show more interest herself: chip away at the walls she'd erected in the name of professionalism. It was a firm fact now. No more denial, she liked being around him. How, though? How was she going to move forward—close the deal, as Vivien had put it? The big question lurked in the back of her mind; how far forward did he want to move, if at all?

It started to drizzle. Precipitation chased her up the mountains' west side, changing to light flurries at the summit before the road dropped down toward Reno. At the airport, rain mixed with snow and intensified.

"I'll drive. You navigate," said her father. "You don't have experience in the snow, and your mother and I would like to continue living, at least 'til Christmas."

Cassie didn't argue.

They couldn't believe the change as they climbed back up into the mountains and passed Truckee. Not a whiteout, but heavy snow.

Slush already covered the roadway, and they were still fifteen hundred feet below the summit.

"Jeez," said Cassie, "I wanted a white Christmas, but this is ridiculous!"

"Thank God, this SUV is four-wheel drive," said Dad. "Look." He pointed to the portable yellow flashing sign the Highway Patrol had just turned on at the side of the road—CHAIN CONTROL AHEAD blinked at them.

They were the last group over the summit before chain control was enforced. It seemed like a car ahead of them was spinning out every half mile or so, unable to grab traction on the steep inclines. Visibility was minimal. Cassie thought the blizzard was some kind of beast bent on their destruction. Everyone crept along at ten miles an hour in a single-file lane. Snow depth rapidly built on the road. As the altitude dropped on the western slopes, things improved. The temperature rose. It wasn't sticking to the freeway by the time they exited for Manor Valley.

Both parents gasped as they entered the valley and the vista opened before them. Light snow allowed them to see it all. Pristine white covered the trees and buildings. Christmas lights twinkled as they drove past the Mall and the town shops; smiling people rushed in and out, arms full of packages, as if all this weather was normal.

Check-in completed, the parents finally made it to their room.

"Rest and take a nap before dinner," said Cassie. "We'll eat early. I know you're exhausted. You've had a long day."

She'd made reservations for five thirty—eight thirty on her parents' time—a quiet dinner for just her, the parents, and Vivien.

*

Cassie and her parents sat early in the dining room. It gave her a little alone time with her folks before Vivien came down. Tense earlier, she was now relaxed. It had been two days away from the office. Phone calls to Justin helped, but now that she had a chance to see for herself that everything was smooth, her mood rose.

The parents expressed their surprise over the valley, the hotel, and now the dining room. Both of them basked in pride over their daughter's new job.

"Dad and I were talking, honey," said her mom. "We're surprised at how good you look. You seem a touch more vibrant. Life around here seems to agree with you. And now you're doing jogging and riding on top of all the work. We were worried if you'd be out of your element here, but now we're relieved that you're fitting in so nicely."

If you only knew, thought Cassie.

"It was a little rocky to start with, but it's all good now. The hotel and how it's run is a lot different than the ones back East. Sorting it all out took some time. I don't know if I could have done it without Dan and all the great people who work here. And I've made some friends during my free time. Obviously, the lifestyle is different, but it's growing on me. I like it here a lot more than I thought I would."

"And men? Have you met anyone?"

Cassie knew it was coming. "Let's not get ahead of ourselves, Mom. I've only been here a few months."

Thankfully, Dad reached over and held her hand before the *grandchildren* came up. "Mom's right, we were worried about our little girl. You know we miss you, but it's easier knowing you're happy, finding your way, enjoying it. We're so relieved. Frankly, we could feel the stress in your voice that first month when you called."

Vivien arrived, and Cassie recounted the not-so-fun-filled trip from the airport.

"And I missed all that excitement when I arrived yesterday?" Vivien said to Ed and Nancy. She turned to Cassie. "Can you and I go back tomorrow and do it again?"

"Not a chance. I had no idea it would be so terrifying. At least, on the rare occasion a storm like that hits New York, you know you'll find shelter in a subway station within two blocks. It seemed like it took forever for us to get through it. Katie at the desk just told me the freeway is closed now. Luckily, most of our holiday guests are coming from the west and don't have to drive through the high mountains."

Vivien reviewed her day. "Well, it was beautiful around here. Justin drove me around, and we lunched at the Mall. We stopped in to see Lily at her shop. Those two seem to have a thing going on. Tomorrow is Christmas Eve, but tonight, Justin told me that a group of them were going to the Pub. Isn't that one of the cutest buildings you've ever seen? We should go."

The long, tense day was showing on Cassie's parents. Dad said, "You two young ones should go. Mom and I are going to collapse soon after this fabulous meal."

Cassie knew she wasn't keeping Viv away from the Pub. Fair point—she was on vacation and deserved to enjoy herself. She could use a little wind-down herself after the airport trip and getting her mom and dad settled. Hopefully, Cliff would be there. Maybe it was time to start sorting things out between them, and not on a business level.

"Okay, Viv, looks like we're going to the Pub." She cast her eye over her friend. She was done up in another of her pricey outfits. The dining room staff had acted like there was no one else in the room. Water was never a problem. Little Gail Norman, holding her pitcher, swelled with pride when Vivien first entered the room, marched over, and had a short conversation with her. Other members of staff noticed and appreciated the attention to the quiet girl. "You should run up and change into something less... less, well, something more casual." One of Cliff's comments popped into her head. "You'll probably have a glass of beer all over you by midnight."

Chapter Thirty-Two

The locals were out in force, Santa hats all over the place. Women wore belts of blinking lights or bells. Men laughed in hilariously bad Christmas sweaters; one had a mare and her foal outlined in small colored lights with snow-covered trees behind them. Cassie figured he must have a battery attached to his belt under the sweater. Every other song on the jukebox was a holiday tune.

As they squeezed past a group of revelers in the entry, Cassie spotted Leo seated at the bar. She ushered Vivien over. "Hi, Leo, happy holidays. This is my friend Vivien from New York. She's visiting for the week." Cassie turned to Vivien. "Leo runs the stables and all the equestrian events and training here in the valley."

Cassie watched Vivien zero in on Leo as he politely stood to greet them. Tonight, he belonged up on a billboard for handsome outdoorsmen—fit, still tanned even at this time of year. Elegant lines from being out in the sun ran from the sides of penetrating hazel eyes, a tell that he smiled a lot. Cassie noted that this Leo was not Leo from the stables. A pricey salmon-colored shirt made his tan pop. Beige slacks, in fabric well above mid-range, stopped at the perfect length over brightly shined light-brown loafers. It took Cassie by surprise. Was soft-spoken, easy-going Leo from the stables another Manor Valley surprise? She calculated that he was a few years older than Vivien or herself.

Cassie noticed the look between them lasted that extra few seconds. Vivien, tall herself, always said her ideal man was one who stood eye to eye with her when she was wearing four-inch heels. Well, well, lookie here. She'd left her four-inch heels at the hotel when she dressed down for the pub, but Cassie knew her friend was measuring him.

"A pleasure, Vivien. I hope you're enjoying your stay. Please, sit." Leo nudged the man next to him, engrossed with something on the TV over the bar. "Glen, a lady needs a seat."

Glen, who worked for Leo at the stables, got up and turned. "Oh, hi, Cassie. Please, take a seat. Don't see you here often."

"Thanks, Glen. I didn't know this place existed until last week. Remember, I'm kind of new to the valley."

"Let me get you a drink, ladies," said Leo. "Cassie, after a December in the hotel gearing up for the holidays, I'll understand if you want a couple of double shots."

Glen moved down the bar to some other friends and engrossed himself again in the TV, while Leo stood and talked to the ladies.

"Let's not start with horse talk, please," he said. "I need a break." He shifted the conversation to them. "Tell me something funny about the hotel or New York."

"First off, Leo, I have to say you're dressed for the hotel dining room," said Cassie. "I love the shirt."

"Thank you." A modest smile took the compliment. "I just drove back from Sacramento. A big Christmas party with the relatives. I had no idea how many nieces and nephews I have."

"Do you have children?" asked Vivien.

Crafty, Van Houten, thought Cassie. *Already filling the information bank.*

"No, haven't found the right woman yet."

Their banter continued. Laughs were exchanged. Cassie noticed that he had a great laugh and could give as good as he got from Vivien, which was saying something. She mentally shook her head at the contrast between now and the watchful, soft-smiling man of few words at the stables.

After about fifteen minutes, Leo excused himself for a bathroom break.

Vivien grabbed Cassie's arm. "Please tell me he can pole dance too. What's in the water supply around here? Why are there gorgeous men like Cliff, Justin, and Leo running around unclaimed? Thank you, Cassie!"

"What for?"

"My Christmas present." Vivien glanced toward the restrooms. "He is coming back, isn't he?" She checked that no one was close and said to Cassie, "Quick, give me some background. I like to be prepared when I seduce a man."

"Settle down, Viv. Honestly, I don't know anything about Leo. I only ever see a shy man of few words at the stables going about his business. This is a big surprise for me tonight, too. It's the first time I've talked to the man away from the stables. Cliff or Lily would know more about him."

"Well, that's not good. I need help here."

Cassie sighed and threw up her hands. "What do you want me to do? Hold him down for you? Tie him up?"

"No, no, nothing so drastic, at least not for now, anyhow. When he gets back, just tactfully highlight some of my good qualities. I'll take it from there."

"Wow, that'll take about thirty seconds."

Leo returned, made sure the ladies' drinks were okay, and resumed the conversation. It didn't take long before Cassie realized she was the third wheel. As she scanned the room, she noticed Cliff, Justin, and Lily across the room at a table. They were just settling in, taking off their coats.

"Excuse me," she said to Vivien and Leo.

The seat across from Cliff was open, so she grabbed it. "My girlfriend's abandoned me for Leo. Can I join you?"

"You don't have to ask," he said.

Some catch-up gossip exchanged, Lily took Justin out to the dance floor, leaving the two of them alone. They were in a corner, so noise from the music didn't overwhelm the conversation.

Cliff reached into his pocket and pulled out his phone. "I was touched the other night when Vivien told me you had a picture of me on your bedside table. You should have told me. I'd have signed it."

The warning look he got didn't deter him. He fidgeted with his phone while he continued with mock seriousness. "I carry your picture with me always. I couldn't abandon it for hours at a time on some bedside table like some people." He lifted the phone close to her face so she could bask in the details of the photo he took while she was sleeping that first night in his allotment shack.

Cassie's eyes expanded as she saw herself sound asleep, hair disheveled, patches of dirt visible, curled up in his sleeping bag, a happy child exhausted after a long day of playing. *Oh God.*

"Look, our first date," he said, as he gently rested his hand on hers. "You're doing so much better now. Remember back in New York when it was passing out instead of going to sleep? Waking up versus coming to? Manor Valley has been good for you."

Her first reaction was to decorate him with her drink, but on reflection, she thought it cute, touching even. It seemed so long ago. He had always guarded her Manor Valley disaster secret, never spoke of it. Months of exciting memories with the wonderful buffoon seated across from her flashed through Cassie's head. Used to his humor, she even smiled at the alcohol reference. If he ever showed that picture to anyone, she'd accuse him of photoshopping it and have him fired. Maybe throw in a sexual harassment charge.

A quick glance at the dance floor told her Lily and Justin were staying on for another slow dance. She had time. It was time. Get this sorted. Hands folded in her lap to hide the shaking, she silently locked eyes with him for a few moments while a hurricane of conflicting feelings blew all of her carefully crafted scenarios off the windowsill. Under her long-sleeved red blouse, she felt the mounting tension create goosebumps on her arms. The best way to get his attention, she reasoned, was the sledgehammer approach.

"Could you walk outside with me for a few minutes? I want to get some fresh air."

"Sure."

They were alone at the corner of the building. Cassie wrapped her arms around herself but didn't feel cold. She turned and faced him.

"Do you find me attractive?"

Taken by surprise, Cliff squirmed around and mumbled, "Well, um, I ..."

Cassie was calm, nervous, but calm. It was time to sort this out. "Please, don't embarrass me. It's a simple question."

He stopped squirming and held her eyes, silent for a few moments, while he gathered his thoughts. "Yes. Yes, I find you very attractive."

"In a romantic sense?"

Cassie could see he was nervous. It seemed like ages before he said, "Yes."

She'd been over this several times recently in her head and pushed on. "I know about your past girlfriends. How they left because life in the valley wasn't for them."

He nodded but didn't speak, so Cassie rushed on.

"I'm booked into this hotel for a two-year commitment. Two years is a long time. Neither of us know what could happen in that time. I'm definitely attracted to you in all kinds of ways. Is it possible for us to see each other romantically? Enjoy each other's company? Spend time together in the here and now and not worry about the future? See what happens?"

Cassie's eyes didn't waver from his. He stood there, looking stunned. Was he still conscious? Finally, he smiled, not the usual impish smile, and spoke.

"I can think of nothing I'd like more. I think you're beautiful. I love being around you. I ... I, well..."

Cassie was in heaven. Seeing that he was more anxious than she was, she decided to have a go at him for once. "Were you *ever* going to make a move on me?"

He stood frozen, like the proverbial deer in the headlights. How appropriate for Manor Valley. Finally, she leaned in, took his cheeks in her hands, and pulled him close. "God," she said and kissed him, deeply, passionately. She lost herself in it. Her tongue explored his mouth as she ran her fingers through his hair. Flashes were going off in her head, and not from the blinking lights on the building.

Finally, she released him and backed up a bit. "*That's* how you make a move. Aren't you supposed to be the man around here?"

Better than she thought, and that was saying something. Time to take charge. He seemed to be in shock. "You're going to have to romance me—put some effort into this. I expect to be wooed, courted." When she saw the confusion on his face, she added, "You can buy a book on it, maybe Google it. Now, can you take me in for a slow dance?"

Coats thrown in the booth, they made their way to the floor. They talked softly as they swayed together to the music and agreed to take it slow. Both confessed that they were nervous but thrilled. They both needed time to digest these sudden, joint declarations. They'd agreed to keep it between themselves for a while, take it nice and easy.

Back at the table, they sat for a while with Lily and Justin, enjoying the night. In time, Cassie whispered to Cliff, "I'm exhausted after another long day, two trips to Reno, and our wonderful talk. You stay. I'm calling it a night." She discreetly placed her hand on his. "Please, see that Vivien gets back safe. Invite Leo and her over to the table so you can keep an eye on her. I appreciate it."

She slipped out quietly and smiled as she glanced at Vivien at the bar, Marie Antoinette hanging out with the peasants at Versailles.

*

Cassie tossed and turned and repeatedly pounded her pillow into shape in a futile effort to ease up on all the happiness and get some rest. Nervousness about how their relationship would develop, and the thought of soon having him in this same bed didn't help her to relax. She marveled at how quickly both their feelings came out. She was no longer confused about how he felt—stronger than she'd even hoped for. She knew this was different than the few relationships she'd had before: more sensual, more intimate, not the cooler evaluations of compatibility, job category, status, and other connecting advantages of many couples in New York. Being around Cliff was visceral, electric, his easy manner a wonderful counterpoint and calming effect on her sometimes too serious episodes. *Eyes aren't supposed to look at you like that,* she thought. Hands weren't supposed to feel like that. Simple comments weren't supposed to warm, comfort, and make you smile like that. God, what were Manor Valley and that man doing to her?

Chapter Thirty-Three

The next morning, a very high-spirited Cassie took the elevator up from the garage. Still coming down from the wonderfully surprising previous night, she was early. Sleep evaded her; delightful hopes and dreams about finally breaking the ice—hell, exploding the iceberg—with Cliff permeated her mind. She'd made the first move; it was up to him to make a move now. Coffee and a bun from Ethel, and she'd lock herself in her office for a bit, get some paperwork done, check how things were running before breakfast with Vivien and her parents. Her mom had texted that ten would be suitable for breakfast. She and Dad wanted to go for a walk first.

When she'd parked her car, Cassie had noticed Leo exiting the elevator and head in the opposite direction toward his car—wearing the same clothes from last night. Someone had some explaining to do, but it could wait until she roused her friend for food.

Later, she tapped on the door before inserting her master key. At home, she had a key to Vivien's flat; no need to stand on ceremony here.

"Good morning, dear," said Cassie. "Care to explain?"

A groggy Vivien pulled her pillow over her head. A muffled, "Explain what?" escaped.

"Why did I see Leo slinking out of the garage earlier?"

"Leo?" Vivien surfaced, turned over, and stuffed the pillow behind her head. "God, I hope he didn't pass out in the hall after he dropped me off."

"Nice try." Cassie stood with her arms folded, waiting for the confession.

"Okay, okay. His hands should be a national treasure."

"Excuse me?" said Cassie.

"Oh, sorry, I forgot about your delicate little ears." She squirmed into a sitting position. "I found out all about him in one night, and you're lucky to remember his name after months out here. He's from somewhere nearby—Marysville, I think he said. He grew up on his parents' farm, had a big education somewhere in high tech stuff, and worked for a start-up company in Silicon Valley. It got sold to some big outfit, and he pocketed a ton of cash and stock options. He realized he wasn't cut out for urban life, so he moved back to this area. Evidently, your Dan knows his family. Leo bought the stable concession and has been, according to him, in heaven ever since."

Cassie was shocked; she had no idea. "You found out all this last night between your other *activities*?"

"I did. The only thing you had right was that he is shy. At least until that bedroom door closes." Viv gave it a few seconds. "How about you? What was going on with you and Cliff last night? Don't look away. I was watching. I can multitask, you know."

Cassie's head rose a notch; pride lit up her eyes. "Well, I'm no longer the timid girl who left New York in the covered wagon to move out West a few months ago. Last night, I did it! I took your advice and, as you so vulgarly put it, closed the deal." Cassie beamed, crossed the room, and sat on the side of the bed. "I came right out and asked him how he felt and told him how I felt. Short version, we care for each other. We're going to give it a try." She reached out and took Vivien's hand. "We want to keep it quiet for now. Start slowly. Please don't say anything."

"That's cute. But did you get laid?"

Cassie smiled, got up, and said, "Your middle name should be Contemptible. Breakfast downstairs in half an hour."

"I need some more beauty sleep. You go ahead. This is going to be a lounge around and do nothing day for me. See you at dinner."

*

Refreshed from their morning walk, her parents wanted to see more of the valley, so Cassie opted to start with breakfast at the Mall. It was the twenty-fourth, and everybody was gearing up for the final big day, bustling about getting shops and stalls ready before the rush. The building and all the activity impressed Ed and Nancy Bryant, as they settled into a window table overlooking the lake in a nearly full restaurant. Fully recovered from their flight after a good night's rest, they bombarded Cassie with questions. Her description of the valley and the hotel on her two visits home now seemed grossly inadequate.

Why was a waitress actually smiling, they wanted to know? In New York, it meant she was probably on drugs. Why did all these people seem so happy and well mannered?

Her phone beeped, a text from Cliff.

Going to Sacramento. Christmas shopping. I'll call later.

She smiled. The idiot waited until the twenty-fourth to do his shopping?

A minute later, Cassie was surprised as their food arrived, and Cliff sauntered up to their table.

"Just stopped in on the way out of town to get some coffee, texted you, and then saw you over here."

Well, thought Cassie, *I guess it's meet-the-parents time.* Nervous about this moment, she now thought it for the best. Get it over with. Her new ad-lib approach to life with this man seemed to be working well.

Introductions made, Cassie explained that Cliff was in charge of the new construction and other activities in the valley. She invited him to sit.

"A pleasure, Mr. and Mrs. Bryant. I think it was a wise decision you made to send your daughter out here for rehab. Look how well she's doing. Drug and alcohol addiction are tough things to crack, and our facility is one of the best in the country. I'm her counselor."

Oh, God. Cassie looked across at her parents. Mom's eyes were wide and Dad, catching on right away, already liked him.

"Don't you have somewhere to be? Sacramento?" said Cassie.

He brushed her off with a wave of his hand. "Yeah, but that can wait." He turned to the parents. "Is Cassie taking you on a tour? What do you think of the hotel?"

A fellow construction guy, Ed jumped right in. "That's the plan for today. Maybe in the next week, you can show me around the new wings. I'd love to see the work."

"Sure." Cliff leaned across the table and adopted a confidential tone. "Sometimes the new hotel manager can be a bit... difficult, but I'm sure I can get her okay. If not, she spends most of her time riding horses, so I can sneak you in."

They sat and talked for a while before Cliff looked at his watch and subtly squeezed Cassie's knee under the table. "Got to go. Sacramento traffic is probably going to be a mess. I'll see you both at Dan's tomorrow."

Parents aren't dumb. Mom had noticed her daughter light up when the man came up to the table. "That was Cliff, right? The outside activities guy you told us about?"

"Yes, he is."

Cassie tap-danced around her mother's interrogation for the remainder of breakfast while Dad took in the view of the lake and all the activity in the Mall.

*

Early afternoon, tour completed, the parents wanted a nap. Cassie checked in with Justin and was reviewing some things in her office when Cliff appeared in the doorway around five. Having just lapsed into a daydream about him, she looked up distractedly at his outline framed by the doorjamb and a shimmering aura of light. *God, he has an aura?* A second passed before she realized he was backlit by the lights in the hallway. Aura? She had to get a grip.

Big grin on his face, he approached and set down some flowers on her desk along with a coffee mug. "I couldn't wait." Pointing to it, he said, "That's not a Christmas present. It's because I'm already so good at that wooing, courting, and romancing stuff."

The flowers were lovely. He'd even put them in a vase. "Thank you," she said, as she lifted the mug. It said, ALL I WANT FOR CHRISTMAS IS YOU. Cassie gave him a suspicious glance as she pulled out the tissue paper in the cup. In it was a lovely thin gold chain with a heart on it.

Because she'd had few relationships in her life, because she'd received few gifts from men, Cassie was surprised and impressed by the level of thoughtfulness and his idiotic comment about his new romantic skill set. She could only offer another soft, "Thank you." Slowly rounding her desk, she pulled him into her arms and gave him a long kiss. "You've come a long way since I thought you were the mountain nightmare my first day in the Valley." She smiled and patted his cheek.

Everyone would be with families that night, so the two of them sat together in the office and talked for a while over coffee. Cassie, of course, used her new mug.

Chapter Thirty-Four

They were expected at Dan and Rita's for Christmas dinner at four. Every year, the Weavers alternated with the Walkers, and this year it was their turn. Rested from a quiet night and leisurely morning, Cassie, her parents, and Vivien arrived on time. Everything at the hotel was organized, so Justin was freed up to join at Lily's request.

The dining room grew into the living area, with the table expanded to handle the group. Cassie's people, the Weavers, the Walkers, plus Justin, Ethel, and her husband, brought the group to thirteen.

The tree, visible across the living room, was surrounded by gifts. The Weavers' dogs, holiday bows on their collars, meandered through the crowd greeting everyone and sniffing all the packages.

Cocktails finished, people sat for the feast. Dan sat at the head, flanked by Vivien on one side and Cassie on the other. Rita sat at the other end, and everyone else filled in. Not fast enough to grab the seat next to Cassie, Cliff sat himself beside Vivien.

Seasonal toasts completed, the table broke into different conversations.

Cassie scanned the table and noticed an empty seat. "Who's missing?" she asked Dan.

"Leo. He'll be here later for dessert. He's having dinner at his folks' but promised to stop by. We set a place in case he comes early."

Vivien perked up. Cassie thought she might bolt for the ladies' room to check her makeup.

Cassie said to Dan, "I spent some time talking to him at the Pub the other night. He's more interesting than I originally thought. How long have you known Leo?" She thought a small fishing expedition for Vivien might help fill in any information blanks.

"I've known his family for years. Giving him the stables concession when the last man retired was one of the smartest things

I've done. Leo always upsets me by spending his own money, keeping that place looking pristine repairing and painting the fences and buildings. Won't let me reimburse him." He raised a finger like he'd remembered something. "When you have your ideas ready for the website and any of that other social media stuff, take it to Leo. That's his hobby since he moved back to the area. He's a tech genius, does websites for his friends. If he can't do what you want, he'll know who can."

Cassie and Vivien exchanged raised eyebrows.

Vivien and Dan had a delightful time talking about her job running the charity, her father's company, and who knew who in New York. Ethel was in heaven being out in company, not being allowed to bring anything or do anything for the meal. As they finished up, everyone moved dishes to the kitchen, puttered around cleaning up, all ignoring Rita's objections. She announced that dessert would be buffet style while people opened gifts and urged everyone to help themselves.

All moved to the living room so everyone could sit. Dining chairs were brought over and crammed in among the sofa and other chairs. This time Cliff managed to squirm in next to Cassie. Still a kid at Christmas, antsy and happy, he nudged her and whispered, "I always score big around here. See that big one over there? When I came in, I saw it had my name on it."

She thought he might start rocking back and forth in anticipation. Maybe she should have gotten him the train set. She'd keep an eye on him, make sure he didn't eat too much sugar.

Leo arrived just in time, fumbling gifts for Dan and Rita as he came through the door. He greeted everyone before heading to the dessert table and pouring himself some wine on the way back while everyone started unwrapping things.

There were gifts for everyone, but Cassie was only worried about one. That morning, Dan had helped Cassie muscle Cliff's present from her cottage.

She glanced at Cliff next to her. God, he wasn't kidding. It looked like he was getting two presents for every one that anyone else got. Cassie smiled and gave a small shake of her head; he really did have them all conned.

Finally, saving it for last, he reached for the big box. As soon as he ripped the wrapping off, Cliff beamed. He turned to Justin and

Leo. "We have to get this up this week. Just in time for the playoffs." A warm smile. "Thank you, Cassie. It's perfect. Justin's eyes are failing, so this will be a big help."

Everyone laughed as Justin smiled and pushed his glasses up his nose, and Lily kissed him on the forehead.

Vivien was surprised as she received several small gifts, including one from Leo. Dan and Rita had something for everyone. When the room was full of wrapping paper and boxes, Cliff disappeared and returned with a big, heavy gift-wrapped box and placed it on the floor in front of Cassie. "This is from Dan, Rita, Lily, and I."

Expectant eyes watched as she unwrapped it, all nervous about how it would be received. It was Lily's idea, and everyone had agreed. Cassie opened the top, and Cliff came over and hoisted it out of the box and set it on a TV tray he'd gotten from Aunt Rita for the occasion.

"Oh!" said Cassie. "Oh my, I don't believe it!"

There was a collective sigh as Cassie gaped at a new Western saddle beautifully crafted with hand-tooled leather and silver decorations.

"I remembered how you commented on my show saddle," said Lily. "Now, you'll have the nicest one in the valley. You're ready."

Leo raised his glass from across the room where he was standing with Vivien. "Well done you, Cassie. You're definitely ready."

"But the weather? When can I go out again?"

Cliff said, "I'll take you out on Sonny for a ride sometime this week. We'll do the trails around the lake. They're flat and safe. Up in the hills, the snow isn't deep, but you always have to worry about what's under it near the edges of the trails. You'll have to be careful. On those long flat stretches by the lake, Sonny will want to let it out. Maybe you'll get to gallop for the first time."

Her father shook his head. "She was afraid of a merry-go-round horse when she was a kid."

*

Things broke up early, the tiring buildup and climax of another holiday season evaporating from everyone's shoulders. As her parents and Vivien said their goodbyes to everyone, Cliff carried the saddle to Cassie's cottage. Tucking it in a corner, he excused himself for a moment and went out to his truck and retrieved his other gift for her.

"I know you want to keep things low-key for now, so I waited to give you these for Christmas," he said.

Cassie unwrapped the box and pulled out a green, English Barbour oilskin jacket and a beige quilted vest. Surprised, she put them on and modeled them for him. In the pockets, he'd put a pair of lined leather riding gloves.

"Now you're ready to ride in this weather. The coat is waterproof, the vest is warm, and the gloves are a must if you want to keep those lovely hands."

She threw her arms around him. "Thank you so much. They're lovely. I was wondering what to wear when it got cold and wet." A kiss followed. "I have to take my parents and Vivien back to the hotel. Do you want me to stop by your house on the way back?"

"Oh yeah. I'd love that."

At the hotel, the parents were ready to call it a day. She knew Vivien would slink off with Leo somewhere, so she didn't feel guilty about going to Cliff's.

*

He was waiting for her with a fire and a glass of wine when she arrived. First, she had to help him carry his prize TV through the front door. "We'll leave it here. I'll get Justin or Leo to help me with it in the next few days. Things are on schedule with the construction, but this holiday week will be slow."

They sat on the sofa in front of the fireplace, the stark white walls and sparse furniture out of sight behind Cassie. "When are you going to work on this place again?" she asked.

"Well, I might have some incentive now. I may even let you help me paint."

Cassie patted his cheek. "No, you're not going to con me like you do with everyone else around here. I may *watch* you paint while I enjoy your new TV."

In time, they moved into the bedroom, two nervous adults finally arriving where they both wanted to be. Undressed, lying under the covers, Cassie lost herself in his lips as his hands explored her body, bringing up long lost and entirely new sensations inside her. They were slow with each other, each enjoying the treasure beside them. She squirmed about as his tongue worked its way from her ears to her mouth, down to her breasts, fighting the urge to dig her nails into his back as the tension rose.

Their lovemaking simmered for a long while. Finally, unable to contain herself any longer, Cassie exploded with gasping moans and muted cries. She clung to him tightly as he followed, feeling his rapid warm breath on her neck.

Sweating and exhausted, her head on his chest, Cliff stroked her hair. "Wow. I see what Vivien meant when you were roommates. You can be vocal. Should I have the place soundproofed?"

Cassie was too spent to offer anything but a quiet, "Well, you weren't exactly in quiet ninja mode yourself."

Cliff sighed. "I think that was almost as good as my new TV."

Cassie rolled up, smiled, and kissed his cheek. "Casanova and Don Juan could take lessons from you on how to talk to a woman. Maybe you should invest more time in reading your wooing, courting, and romancing book. Try and get past the introduction this time."

*

They slept a little, and Cassie slipped out around two in the morning and drove back to her place.

In her own bed, a BEST CHRISTMAS EVER banner ran across her mind, dwarfing the illuminated signs on the buildings of Times Square. How could this have happened in just a few weeks? Her life had made a big turn, and she reveled in it. On top of everything else, he was a warm, considerate lover. She didn't know if she was capable of keeping their relationship discreet and didn't know if she wanted to. Around him, she discovered she was a touchy person, loved the sensation of feeling his arms around her. His hand placed lightly on her arm was as sensual as hers running over his gorgeous cheeks.

Suddenly, she shifted in the bed. Apprehension snuck in an appearance. New feelings surfaced and attacked her joy. What would happen when the two years were up? No, she said and cast out those thoughts. Not now. She was not going to let anything interfere with these wonderful new experiences. This was all to be enjoyed to the fullest.

Chapter Thirty-Five

The twenty-sixth was a Sunday, downtime for everyone. Christmas guests were departing, and they had a relaxing day or two before the New Year's guests started to arrive. Cliff understood that Cassie had to spend time with her folks and Vivien.

Tuesday, she pampered Cliff into driving the small hotel transport van up to Tahoe and showing her parents and Vivien around. This time, they'd do the whole loop around the lake, taking in the casinos and sights on the Nevada side.

"I don't believe all this. I've never been to a ski resort." Cassie was in awe, holding Cliff's arm as the group walked around the small village at the Squaw Valley ski resort. On their first visit, it was fall, and there'd been no snow. Now, the place was packed with skiers in bright outfits taking breaks or getting ready to assault the slopes. Parents schooled children with silly caps on their small heads to carry their skis without killing people as they worked their way through the crowds toward the lifts.

"That's a joke, right?" said Cliff. "You don't ski? We'll be curing that this winter. Everybody in these mountains skis." He squeezed her arm. "I've got a lot of work to do with you, Cassie Bryant."

"Well, that makes two of us. I've found a studio in Auburn where we can take ballet lessons together."

Was that stark fear on his face?

As they worked their way to the casinos on the Nevada side for lunch, Cassie looked out her window, taking in the massive snow-covered mountains. Skiing? The idea of another new experience with Cliff excited her. She was no longer trapped in her limited New York comfort zone. A bystander, an observer all her life, Cassie now anticipated new things with him. She laughed at all she'd missed just watching people live life outside New York on TV or in magazines. Now, fear of the unknown was being replaced by curiosity, mainly due to him.

As they walked into the casino, she whispered to Cliff so no one else could hear. "A bunny hill. I've heard of bunny hills for beginning skiers. I'd start on a bunny hill, right?"

"Maybe for the first half hour. After that, we'll be way up there in break-a-leg territory."

Great, she thought. *First, it was shooting the stag, then strangling the goose, and now it's breaking-a-leg territory.* He was a magician at relaxing her.

*

Mid-week, Leo took Vivien on a horse ride around Manor Valley, and Cliff and Cassie tagged along. It would be her first day out on Sonny and her new saddle. Dan and Rita were having the parents over for lunch.

Old Molly, let loose to wander around as usual, stood at Sonny's stall door head-to-head with her son like they were whispering things to each other when Cassie and Vivien drove up. Wanting to take it easy for the holidays, Molly balked a little when she saw Cassie's friend, fearful that she might be put to work, but settled when she saw Leo take her over to Clara, her younger friend, and make the introductions. Molly figured the new girl must know how to ride since Clara was as spirited as her son.

From her trunk, Cassie took out a new horse blanket, a Christmas present for Molly. She walked over and showed it to Molly while talking to her. The horse stood still while Cassie put it on and made fussing sounds when she stood back to see how it looked.

While Cassie was doing this, Cliff took the new saddle from the car and got Sonny ready.

Everyone mounted up. Molly snorted them off and meandered back to her stall for some hay. She stopped, decided to parade about a bit and show off her new blanket, letting the young ones know who still mattered around here.

"The saddle looks great," said Cliff, as they neared the Pub an hour later. "How does it feel?"

"I'm in heaven. And I love my new Barbour jacket and gloves."

They rode around the side of the restaurant to an area with rails to tie up horses away from the parking lot, an area of the Pub Cassie hadn't noticed before.

Settled at a table for brunch, orders placed, Leo said, "I'm impressed with how you handle Sonny. He wanted to go a few times, and you had no problem controlling him. You're officially ready to roam the valley on your own, Cassie."

She blushed slightly at the compliment, as Vivien added, "Never thought I'd see the day. You're actually enjoying yourself, aren't you?"

"I am, and it's all the better with all of you."

Cliff patted her leg under the table. "Just think, in New York, you could be on a crowded subway holding onto a pole because there aren't any seats on your way to redeem a spa certificate you got for Christmas."

She gave him a scowl and turned to Vivien. "I almost forgot. Tomorrow, Lily, you, Mom, and I are going to Sacramento for a spa day. Cliff promised to show my dad around the new addition and take him to lunch."

"I'm up for that," said Vivien.

Cassie drifted from the conversation and thought about how wonderful and different the last few days had been. She and Cliff had committed to try things out, and she had cemented her resolve after their lovemaking, ecstatic at the possibilities, looking forward to time with him. The new saddle and her first time out on Sonny bound her closer to the valley. Her work made her feel like she was contributing to the well-being of everyone connected with it. Hers wasn't simply a challenging job; it was a responsibility, a responsibility she was learning to cherish.

Chapter Thirty-Six

New Year's at the Manor Valley Hotel lived up to its hype. The dining room was packed and decorated magically by Justin and his crew in banners, balloons, and other touches. In the three-story lobby rotunda, a half-circle walkway from the hotel entrance to the reception desk was tastefully set off along the far wall; the balance of the grand circular space was reserved for the band and dancing after dinner.

Dan and Rita's table for twelve filled out. Everyone got a kick out of the way Leo's eyes rarely strayed from Vivien since she'd walked into the room. He was mesmerized by the full wattage Vivien Van Houten. It took most of the attention away from the way Cassie and Cliff doted on each other, unable to succeed in hiding it.

Seated beside Cassie, Dan leaned in and said, "Well, are you glad you made the commitment to the job or is it as awful as you thought it would be?"

The question caught her off guard. She'd almost forgotten how she'd felt just months before when she'd agreed to this job in the middle of nowhere to advance her career. She reached over and held Dan's hand. "You said you wanted to expand my horizon on life outside of New York. You most certainly did, and I can't thank you enough. It was a rocky start, but I feel like I'm settling in, feel like I'm belonging. I'm impressed more every week with everything around here. I can't thank you enough. I'm confident we can get the new wings open by summer and make them a big success." She pointed to Cliff on her other side. "Despite sticking me with him."

Smiling at the answer, Dan returned his attention to the Walkers and Cassie's parents.

After dinner, they emerged to find the lobby transformed into an old-world ballroom. White Christmas lights took deep swoops around the lower perimeter of the rotunda above, drawing the eyes up. In the center, the large chandelier had been augmented by matching strings of white lights hanging down at varying lengths.

How Justin and his crew figured that out, Cassie had no idea. The band were done up in tuxedos or lovely black dresses for the women. Acoustics were perfect. Attentive waiters and waitresses with trays of champagne flutes wove in and out of the guests standing around the circle watching the dancers.

She spotted Justin keeping vigil over the proceedings. Unfortunately, he was working tonight and doing a brilliant job. He was looking longingly at Lily as she watched the dancers. Cassie drifted over to Lily. "He can watch everything from the dance floor just as well as the sidelines. It seems like he's focused on only one thing anyway." Cassie nodded over her shoulder, a signal that Lily should drag him out on the floor.

Several times, while dancing with Cliff around the beautiful space, Cassie's eyes drifted to the old painting of Janet and Travis, wondering how different this night would have been back in their day. The oversized lobby fireplace with a massive warm blaze caught her eye. It was decorated with garland and antique ornaments. A comment Janet had made to Travis in the story popped into her head, something like 'And where is the firewood kept, Mr. Weaver?' It had never dawned on her the sheer quantity of wood required to heat all the rooms in the house back then before central heating, never mind the cartloads of candles to light the place. Was there always an underlying chill in winter back then? She pulled herself closer into Cliff's embrace, shivering slightly, and lost herself in the present.

*

She'd brought an overnight bag, knowing she wouldn't be leaving early. In Cliff's bedroom, they undressed each other slowly; any inhibitions from their first time vanished, both of them needy now. Never before had she experienced lovemaking like this. Never before had fingertips across her flesh excited her as much. Caution was dispensed after their first time, and the lovely night at the party had relaxed them more. They added to their repertoire of pleasing each other. As a hint of daylight snuck in through the window, they collapsed into a dreamless sleep.

Chapter Thirty-Seven

January. Another year assigned to history. Guests and family returned to their homes as things slowed and settled. Winter pulled its blanket over Manor Valley, encouraging some well-earned rest.

Daydreaming in her new office, Cassie smiled as she thought back on Vivien's goodbye. "My job here is finished," she'd said. "I must get back to my people." As if she'd just spent two years in Africa finding the source of the Nile and was finally slicing her way out of the jungle and going home. "I've fixed things with you and Cliff and need to get out of here before I catch whatever romantic virus you've got. I caught myself looking at plaid flannel shirts in a shop at the Mall." She said she'd be back in spring or summer to go riding with Leo. As she slung her scarf over her shoulder at the airport, preparing to enter aloof mode for her trip, she said, "If I have time, perhaps you and I can find time for a coffee when I get back."

Her father had his usual political incorrectness go at her the last night at dinner. "You seem to like this Cliff guy, but I can't figure it out," he'd said, a grin on his face. "He thinks that people should work for a living and have personal responsibility. I saw him invading your personal space a couple of times, putting his arm around you or touching your hand. He even said you were beautiful a couple of times. Isn't that politically incorrect? God knows how many times a day he marginalizes or mini aggresses other people. What cave did you find him in?"

Cassie was thrilled; it was her dad's way of saying he liked him.

Routine crept in as the first weeks of the New Year flew by. On her midday jogs, she could see and hear the change of pace in the valley. Boats were being repaired and painted, the stables maintained and spruced up, shops at the Mall refitted with new displays to adjust to changing customer preferences. Smells of sanded wood, smoking chimneys, paint, and damp forest mixed together as she progressed around the jogging trails. Periodically, she'd hear the sound of chain saws clearing deadwood and thinning trees around the lake.

All finishing materials for the final phase of the new wings were on-site or in storage nearby. Cliff spent his time supervising subcontractors at the hotel, expanding the camper parking area next to the boatyard, and doing maintenance on the outside of the Mall. Cassie would bring him coffee and have mini meetings with him wherever he was.

Their evenings were spent together at her place or Cliff's. Despite her best efforts, he had succeeded in conning her to help paint the inside of his home. It was impossible to hide their growing relationship from anyone in the valley, especially Dan and Rita, who were pleased with how often they saw Cliff's truck at Cassie's cottage.

*

And then, before Cassie knew it, spring was waiting at the entrance to the valley. The short, cold winter days were waving goodbye, taking their coats and scarves, and catching a flight to the southern hemisphere. See you in seven or eight months.

Relaxing rides with Lily, Harry, and Clayton became a monthly thing, followed by lunches together at the Pub or the Mall. Mostly she worked. The rides and jogging helped to ease the tension over the approaching opening of the new wings.

It was a Wednesday morning. Cliff tapped on her office doorjamb, walked in with his orange vest, and plopped down on the opposite chair.

"Rita thinks you're working too hard again. I guess I have to take you to San Francisco this weekend," said Cliff. He had completed moving his temporary office from the new wing to an unused storeroom in the main hotel, so the workmen could finish up. Cassie had brought him coffee and a bun from the kitchen.

Cassie still hadn't been to San Francisco.

"Oh, you make it sound *so* romantic," she said as she placed a hand over her heart and feigned a swoon. "I can feel the exciting anticipation dripping off you. Does it have to be this weekend? I'm swamped."

"You're always swamped. Yes, this weekend. Rita gave me tickets to the San Francisco Ballet. They have a condo there, and she has season tickets. My mom or Ethel usually go with her. Dan tries to pass as often as he can. He's forced to go only once a year now. With all his traveling, Rita knows he likes to relax when he's home."

Cassie lit up. She loved the ballet, and had gone once or twice a year in New York. She'd love to have a break and see the city at the same time. "Yes, I'd love it! We can shop for things to put in that warehouse you call a home. Start putting some of your lovely personality into it, now that it's actually got paint on the walls." She'd picked the paint colors and was thrilled with how it was taking shape. When asked for his input, he pretended to be colorblind and left her to it.

*

Cassie thought her first night in San Francisco was ripped from a fairy tale. Cliff sat across from her at dinner in an open-collar shirt and sports jacket. How did he get more handsome? They held hands and were almost late leaving for the ballet a block away.

In the lobby before the performance, they watched a family with two small girls all dressed up for their big night out to watch the magical dancers on the stage.

"Do you want children?" asked Cliff.

"Oh, yes, I do want a family. Aren't they gorgeous?"

It was left at that. Cassie knew the shadow of her two-year commitment was straining their relationship. Their silent pact was holding. Futures were not discussed, 'I love yous' were not exchanged. But it was fraying around the edges. They'd both tried to ignore it, but it surfaced and nipped at them at times like this. How could you talk about family with no future? As was their habit, they each tried to tuck the subject away.

Similar feelings haunted her the next day when they slowly explored downtown. She forced him into the linen department of a department store to buy things for his bedrooms. When she asked for his input, he said he felt like he was coming down with Ebola again. She playfully forced him to make a selection, knowing he'd buy old army blankets if he were left alone.

Leaving the store, Cassie briefly thought about who would be sleeping in the lovely new linens after she was gone. The thoughts were quickly cast aside.

"Is Chinatown nearby?" she asked.

"Three or four blocks away," he said.

"Can we go and walk around? I want to see it. It's where Janet took Travis shopping when they met over a hundred and fifty years ago."

Cliff knew this was coming. She was fascinated by the story of the original hotel occupants. At home, he'd watched her spend hours reading the diaries Lily had lent her.

Exhausted after she'd dragged him through small shops oozing with Asian charm, they finally had lunch—in Chinatown, of course. At the table, she pretended that this was the same restaurant that Janet had taken Travis to.

Another day of sightseeing, where she had Cliff take her across the Golden Gate Bridge and on a boat ride around Alcatraz, and Cassie was convinced it was her favorite city next to New York. Most of the things she enjoyed at home were here. The caliber of the ballet was top notch. The area was loaded with good restaurants to fit anyone's taste. The downtown area, close to Chinatown, offered excellent shopping around Union Square. It was more compact than Manhattan, but the hills and all the views gave it a unique charm. Back in Manor Valley, she missed things from New York: getting dressed up to go out to a nice restaurant; the electricity and energy of Manhattan; all the shows, museums, and other offered diversions. But, like anywhere, how often did you really indulge in these things during your normal weeks? San Francisco was only a couple of hours from Manor Valley. She could come back again with Rita or Lily or Ethel.

And what about Manor Valley itself? Dreading the drastic change of pace when she first arrived, she now realized that she was loving it more and more. The setting was from a storybook, the people all well-mannered and kind. The constant noise level of New York City and the sheer quantity of people going about their daily business was replaced by the soft calm of the valley—the wind and birds, not horns and engines.

That night at home in Manor Valley, before sleep overtook her, Cassie was restless and confused. Like Janet Weaver, she felt a claim being placed on her that she belonged here. She belonged in the valley. She belonged with Cliff. Talking of the future together was awkward and hard at times. She remembered how the sadness had flickered across Cliff's face when he gently stroked her back after they saw those beautiful children all dressed up for the ballet. She'd felt it too. What was to be done?

Chapter Thirty-Eight

By mid-June, as the big opening drew near, Cassie had only been back to New York two times, more out of obligation to her parents than she cared to admit. Soon, the construction's iron weight would be craned off Cliff's shoulders and passed to hers to make the expanded hotel a success. She and Justin were ready.

The fruits of their various promotions, the website Leo had created from her ideas and launched, the blog that Justin and she and Lily had fun with, outlining old and new activities—all paid off. Everyone was shocked at the bookings. Dan suggested keeping it at only half capacity to see how things flowed with staff for the first few weeks. Bookings at the spa, how people were handled at the new pool, and the restaurant's impact all had to be monitored and managed.

In late August, a smooth and successful two months under their belts, Dan had one of the meeting rooms decorated for a celebration party. A long table for twenty was fitted together for the Walkers, the Weavers, all the department heads and their significant others, and of course, Leo.

Cassie had insisted that Justin be included. His contributions had been immense, and he was much too important to her and the hotel to leave out. In the next few weeks, she'd take Dan's earlier advice and bring on another person to help them out. The operations at this hotel were complex to say the least. Both she and Justin agreed that promotion from within would be preferred. They also agreed that Nelly, currently in reception, would be the prime candidate. She'd worked at the hotel through high school and college and knew the flow. She was good with people and terrific at sorting out problems and guests at the front desk. She'd be perfect to supervise the pool, spa, business center, and gym activities and other stuff that was slowly burying Justin.

As the room filled, Cassie, standing with Dan, looked toward the door and jolted as Leo walked in with Vivien.

Dan turned to Cassie. "Leo had told me she was thinking about coming out for the first overnight horse ride into the next valley. I called her two weeks ago to see if she could make it and come a day or two early. You deserve a special surprise."

Cocktails over, everyone sat. Dan got everyone's attention. "Rita and I have had many restless nights over this expansion. I'm pleased to say it couldn't have worked out better. Shop owners, Mall tenants, and concession holders have been calling me complaining. They can't keep up with the business, and we've only been at half capacity. Paid bookings and Rewards Program members from the chain back East are flooding in." He nodded to Leo. "Cassie, Lily, and Leo, are very excited about the new horse safari overnight outing to the next valley they've been working on. They're doing a test run in the next few days, and I'm damn sure going."

Everyone laughed as he turned his attention to Justin and pointed. "That young man has organized our first lake regatta for colleges and universities throughout the state for next spring. This is a big event. We surveyed the town and merchants for their reaction. Support for it far outweighed any negatives. I got tired of listening to him about the level of planning and logistics it will take.

"The way that housekeeping, the kitchen, and the dining room have stepped up to this new challenge can only be called impressive." Dan took a sip of water as a staff member tactfully placed an envelope in front of every department head. "Those gifts are a small thank you for your efforts. Now, let's eat." He raised his glass, and the buzz of conversation resumed.

Cassie wagged a finger at Vivien. "Why didn't you tell me you were coming?"

"You're not important. Going on the first horse safari over the mountains with Leo is. He picked me up in Sacramento. What's your name again? Have we met?" She fanned her face with her napkin. "I almost didn't get my room back. Poor Justin had to do some shuffling when I called to check." She couldn't keep the act up and threw her arms around Cassie. "I'm so proud of you. What an accomplishment. I'm impressed. You fit in around here. I remember when you got that saddle for Christmas, you looked like I did the time Daddy gave me a new Bentley." She ushered Cassie off to the side. "We'll talk later, but after our conversations on the phone, things seem to be progressing nicely with Cliff. Should I tell you the secret to my parents' relationship?"

This should be good, thought Cassie. "Okay, what is it?"

"They go dancing every week—she goes on Tuesdays, and he goes on Thursdays."

*

Leo and Lily had gone ahead to check arrangements for the first overnight horse ride to the other side of the mountain. September was creeping up, but they'd still have time to do two guest trips before shutting it down for the year and be ready for a full season next year. Dan and Cliff would lead the rest of the group since Cassie and the guests had no idea where they were going. A son of one of Dan's friends from the city and his wife joined them on the test run to get an outsider's experience and input on how things worked. It would be a four- or five-hour ride, depending on breaks. Saddlebags were full of snacks and drinks.

Cresting the hills out of Manor Valley, civilization disappeared. Only the panting and snorting of the horses, mixed with the breeze rustling leaves in the trees, interrupted the peace and quiet. They navigated a long game trail high on a ridge before it dropped down into the densely forested neighboring valley. The summit was an excellent place to stop and take a break with a beautiful three-hundred-and-sixty-degree view. As they descended the other side, things changed. This was the wilderness. Various animals darted about, confused by this unfamiliar interruption, while hawks and vultures shrieked at the advancing procession. One of the group pointed between the trees at a bear on a distant slope.

The campsite on the valley floor was out of an old-fashioned movie set. A natural clearing had been cleaned of underbrush and debris up to ten feet behind five tents set up in a circle around a central area. Rustic, natural-wood tables and a large firepit completed the scene. Out of place, five red fire extinguishers hung from posts in the ground behind each tent. The tents had been fashioned after the walk-in type used years ago in mining camps, with two luxurious cots in each. For cool nights, staff had portable heaters for each tent, which they would supervise. Discreet portable showers were off to the side in special tents. For the outdoors, comfort was at the highest level.

Cliff turned to Cassie. He hadn't seen the site before. "Jeez, when I was a kid, we just brought sleeping bags, hotdogs, canned beans, and a couple of six-packs out here."

Cassie patted his cheek. "Well, Dorothy, you're not in Kansas anymore."

Vivien joined them. "Seriously, this is wonderful. Who's bringing my luggage?"

A friend of Leo's, Kevin, was hired as the chef. His crew acted as bearers and waiters, pack-horsing the supplies over the hills and handling setup and cleanup. For years, he had done the big barbeques for all the stable's horse events.

At dinner, Dan said to Leo, "Well, it's all yours now. Your concession just expanded. Good luck."

Cassie knew that the hotel would be getting their small percentage and that Leo was happy with the new challenge.

*

While the men sat by the fire, Cassie and Vivien sat off to the side, catching up. Vivien eyed her friend up and down. "You look terrific. This life out here seems to suit you. What are your thoughts on coming back to New York? It's easy to see things are working well with you and Cliff. You haven't been very forthcoming on the phone."

Cassie looked down at her wine glass. She was glad her friend was here. All of her pent-up, internalized anguish came out. "I'm so confused. I'm in love with him but keep fighting it. The thought of going home is always in the back of my head, and I know Cliff feels the same. Whenever talk about the future comes up, it gets awkward between us. Leaving him would be heartbreaking. You know I want a family, and I wonder how that's going to work. I'm in my thirties now." Her spirits sank as she massaged her forehead. "I'm so mixed up. I try to put off thinking about it all as much as I can."

Vivien looked at her in silence for a few moments. "You know, Cassie, I *need* New York. I need the activity, the hustle and bustle, the crush of the people, the full schedule. I never thought you did. You're more reserved than I. Let's be honest, all you ever did at home was work. I'm the one who forced you to get out. You've been doing so much more here—jogging, riding, supervising your valley, and spending wonderful time with Cliff." She waved her arm around. "Look at you now. Look at how much you enjoy life with him. You say you want a family. Where would you rather raise them, here or in Manhattan or Brooklyn?" Vivien clinked her wine glass with Cassie's and squeezed her leg. "It's time you wrestled with your other option a little more."

And that's what Cassie did on the quiet ride back and over the next few days.

Chapter Thirty-Nine

Though she still had a year left, the shadow of leaving Cliff and the valley had been haunting her, tracking behind her for months. Now it was wrapping itself around her day and night, refusing to leave her in peace.

Working late one evening, she left her office and made her way to the roof of the hotel. After Dan had shown it to her on her first tour of the building, it became one of her favorite places to escape and think, unhindered by ringing phones, interrupting questions from staff, and distracting piles of paperwork. An overcast afternoon was dimming and a cool breeze bit at her, putting her on notice that the seasons were changing. Pulling the sweater close around her, she moved pensively along the maintenance walkway next to the parapet. The view was ignored. A waxing moon, already on its ascent, watched her, peeking out from the moving clouds. A half hour passed, and she knew as she descended the stairs inside that it was time to nudge her life ahead.

*

Late September arrived; it was almost her first anniversary in Manor Valley. *Where did the time go?*

"Can I talk with you?" asked Cassie as she stuck her head in Dan's office.

"You look serious. What is it?" he asked.

It all came out—how happy she was in the job and in Manor Valley, her relationship with Cliff, her doubts about the future. After hurling about more disjointed thoughts, Cassie slumped in her chair and finally got to it. "I guess my question is, would it be possible to stay here as manager and not go back to New York? Is that an option?"

Dan straightened in his chair, tapped his pen on the edge of the desk, and scrutinized the woman across from him. "What did I tell you when you took the job?"

"You said I could go back to New York after the two years and be the senior VP in charge of the entire chain."

Dan smiled and leaned forward. "That's what you wanted to hear, not what I said. I said you could have *anything* you wanted in the company. By now, you're getting the idea that Rita and I want to slow down. I'm sick of all the flying, tired of being away, and exhausted by the stress. Seeing this expansion completed and the new hotel in New York getting ready to open is the high point of my career. You're primed and ready to take over for me back in New York. It was a dream of mine. I'm confident in you and trust you."

Cassie's insides were collapsing as Dan paused and took a sip of water, probably to gather his thoughts after her jolting question. Unfortunately, this conversation was going the way she'd feared. Hope was quickly circling the drain and disappearing. She felt she was disappointing Dan after all the years he'd invested in mentoring her, befriending her, helping her climb her corporate ladder.

His chair squeaked as he leaned back, smiled, and folded his hands behind his head. "On the other hand, having you here would be heaven for Rita and me." He casually flipped his hand in the air. "I can always find a VP for New York or even sell the chain back East. This hotel may be separately owned, but it would always be part of it. Any new owner couldn't walk away from the prestige associated with this place and the Frequent Stayer Program's benefits."

He paused for a moment, as if he were choosing his words carefully. "Cassie, my opinion now is that you belong here in Manor Valley personally, and here at this hotel professionally. You fit in now. I'm glad you're thinking about it. Who am I going to find that I trust and enjoy working with as much as you?" He got up, laughed, and started for the door. "And you keep Cliff in line better than anyone I know. Ethel, Lily, and the rest of us have failed. Come on, let's go down to the dining room, have a cup of coffee, and talk about it. Don't tell Rita, but I'm going to have some dessert too."

*

Cassie Bryant from New York City, age thirty-one, well okay, thirty-two, was euphoric as she drove home. She curled up on her sofa, pulled a comforter over her, and tried to sort out the ramifications of it all. Fall was returning with another overcast day. She thought back to her first week when she'd taken the job a year ago. The scales had changed their balance drastically since then—Manor Valley was now the heavy iron ball on one side, New York the foam pebble on the other. Her decision was made—she belonged here and could stay.

Another problem dropped down from the ether and intruded. How would Cliff react to the news? They'd agreed on the format of their relationship months ago and stuck with it—she would always be leaving. Was he comfortable with the way things were? Could he envision a future with her? Apprehension set in. A family and life together hadn't been the top of their conversation list the past eight months. She realized she'd been focusing on making her own decision, hadn't even thought about his. *God,* she thought, *how do I even bring this up?*

Chapter Forty

It was Saturday and Cliff was working at the allotment, buttoning things up for winter just like he'd done last year when she arrived.

Cassie rode Sonny up in the hills to her favorite overlook of the valley. She sat on the same bench she and Cliff had sat on during her first ride. How different things were now. Now, her whole self surrendered to the surroundings, all fears from that first ride erased. She allowed herself to be enveloped by the sounds, smells, and crisp breeze. Dan and Cliff had been right. She enjoyed going out by herself, embracing the solitude, allowing thoughts to sort out in her head. She took off her riding gloves, tightened her scarf against the breeze, and poured coffee from her thermos.

What a year it had been. How she'd changed. As if reading her mind, Sonny snorted in agreement behind her. The tightly wound, focused, career-driven woman from New York who was content with the narrow confines of her life in Brooklyn and Manhattan had been pulled out of her cocoon. She now loved a man passionately. He'd made humor and happiness a part of her life. He and the people of the valley had forced her to loosen up, enjoy life, and she felt the difference in her bones. All her new experiences expanded her growth. The feared job in the middle of nowhere was now coveted, a part of her new life.

With her second cup of coffee, last-minute thoughts and fears were reviewed. She'd go back down and sort it out with Cliff for better or worse. Their first meeting had been at the allotments, so at the allotments it would be. Other memories tugged at her on the way down the trail and at the stables, probably like Janet Weaver out riding, surveying her domain all those years ago. Putting Sonny away, she thought of her first stable bonding with Old Molly. A murder of crows bursting from a nearby tree made her wonder when the geese would be returning. Was it too early to reserve the hotel Christmas tree?

Memory Lane was turning into a Los Angeles freeway at rush hour.

Molly got her carrots as Cassie talked to her, giving her an update on how Sonny had behaved. She'd forgo her usual cup of coffee chatting with Leo either in his office or leaning against the fence watching a training session.

Cliff was fixing an irrigation pipe and talking to Tank when she walked around the greenhouse, running her hand over the replaced glass panels from a year ago. Memories of Disaster Night forced a half-smile onto her face. No stag was there to greet her, and she thought the tomato plants were trying to dodge out of her way. The two folding beach chairs were against the shed. She sat in one and said, "Can you sit with me for a moment?"

"Sure, could use the break." He plopped down. "What's up? No problems on your ride?"

She clenched her hands in her lap, not wanting him to feel them shaking by reaching over and holding his. "All these months we've been together have been wonderful. I've never been happier. I love you so much. What do you think of me after all this time?"

Okay, it wasn't scripted by a romance novelist but that's the way it came out. Her heart was pounding in anticipation. Sweat building on her neck made her shiver slightly.

A little caught off guard by her serious demeanor but still blissfully unaware, Cliff's eyes widened a little. "Well, your riding has really improved."

Not a facial feature moved; she focused on him until it registered that she was serious, and he spoke again.

He paused for a moment, reached over, and held her hand. "Cassie, of course I love you, have since I met you. You have to know this. The more time we spend together, the more it breaks my heart that you'll be leaving. But that's my problem. I remember what our understanding was. I'll just have to deal with it."

She sensed he wasn't quite getting it and tried again. "What if I stayed in Manor Valley? How would you see our future?"

Cliff squirmed around in his chair. "Wow, I'll remember today at the allotments as much as your first visit." It seemed to be dawning on him. He looked a little shy and nervous. "You're serious? You want it straight?"

"Yes."

"I'd probably propose to you. There's never been anyone else I wanted to be with more than you."

A chill bolted through Cassie's body. *He loves me? Propose?* Dreams of a future with him, long suppressed in the corner of her mind, suddenly danced in front of her eyes. Fear that she almost walked away from this man mingled with her joy. Bordering on shock, she could only manage, "Okay."

"Okay? That's it?" asked Cliff.

She had to get back on track, communicate in a language he understood.

"What is it you cowboys say? Let's see if you put your money where your mouth is—*I'm staying*. I sorted it out with Dan last week." She shyly looked to the side and lowered her voice. "I'm nervous now. I need to know what you think about it."

His turn. "Okay."

Her turn. "Okay? That's it?"

Cliff shrugged his shoulders and got up. He walked a few feet to his neighbor's plot, took out his knife, and stole a lovely blooming cauliflower plant. When he returned, he knelt in front of her and presented the plant like it was a breathtaking bouquet. "Cassie Bryant, age thirty-one... um, thirty-two, from New York City, will you marry me?"

At least with him around, she'd never forget her age. She hoped he didn't have some clever little ditty hidden away about her weight.

Cassie started crying: softly at first as she gazed at the magnificent plant, louder as reality dawned, and louder again as joy raced through her veins.

Cliff started to panic, looking around to see if she was drawing crowds. Tank came over and licked her hand. "Honey, honey, did I say something wrong?"

He was ignored. Unbounded happiness had to be dispensed with first. She pulled him to her and cried into his shoulder. "Of course, I'll marry you."

Cliff allowed Cassie to settle him down after her bawling bout. He thought he was safe, and she was getting back to normal, until she said, "I've been drifting down memory lane all morning. Tomorrow, can we take a nice relaxing drive out to the tree farm and reserve a Christmas tree? I want to be on top of it this year."

His childhood observation was confirmed again: women were wacky. It was only September. Hell, why don't we stop on the way home and pick up some eggs, boil them up now, paint them, and get a jump start on Easter while we're at it? Experience with women in his adult life had taught him that they come up with weird whims like this all the time, and it was best to just go along, follow the discreet path. "Sure, honey. Great idea. Whatever you want."

As they slowly walked up to the parking lot, arms around each other, Cliff said, "It's been a year since your first visit to the allotments. I still can't believe you staged that whole thing just to meet me."

It took them several days for it all to register. An earthquake could have crushed the valley, and the two of them would still be smiling. Yes, she'd move in with him right away. Children? Of course. Learn to ski? What the hell. In for a penny, in for a pound.

The news was shared with those who mattered. They moved her into Cliff's home, which immediately felt like hers since she'd already done most of the decorating, and nearly finished the daunting task of house training him. Tank had never been a problem.

*

The big wedding every girl dreams of was not on Cassie's radar. The thought of planning one exhausted her. A week after Allotment Experience II, she was in the kitchen preparing dinner. She had just put her foot down with Vivien on the phone. "No. You cannot fly out four New York wedding planners."

Cliff walked in with Tank. As if he was doing that backwoods shaman thing again, reading her mind, he announced, "Lily says we should elope to Auburn just like your old buddies Janet and Travis did way back when. She said it would *complete the story* or something like that, said we should get it done and have a party later. She said that you'd understand. Just a thought, what do you think?"

She almost knocked him down, jumping into his arms. She thought the idea was brilliant—just like Janet and Travis did it all those years ago. "Your sister is a genius! I don't want to have a big wedding. Yes, let's do it. A party later, just like the Weavers did. It's a great idea."

Two weeks later, Dan and Rita, Justin and Lily, Leo and Ethel, and Harry and Clayton joined the Walker parents and went to Auburn City Hall. Cassie's parents flew in for the big day. Vivien reluctantly agreed to be her bridesmaid. She was picturing more like a yacht in the south of France, or at the very least, something understated on the top of Mount Kilimanjaro in Africa.

A quiet dinner back in the hotel dining room followed. After toasts, champagne, and a lavish meal, Dan called for their attention. "Rita and I are thrilled. Unfortunately, something has come up, and Cassie has to go on a trip." He looked at Cliff. "If she wants, she can take you with her." He handed Cliff an envelope and shifted his gaze to Cassie. "If you want to run a hotel like this, you'll have to see how others at this level operate. Next week you're out of here to see Claridge's and the Connaught Hotel in London, a few nights in each. Rita and I know the managers, they'll give you a tour. Don't worry, Cassie. Cliff has been there a couple of times. He won't let you get lost." He raised his glass. "A honeymoon present from the Manor Valley Hotel. Enjoy."

Cassie was shocked. She knew these were two of London's top hotels—a city and hotels she thought she'd never see. She started to protest, when Dan's hand came up. "Not a word, Mrs. Walker. Rome won't burn while you're away. Justin and I will soldier through somehow."

It would be their first fight as a married couple. She turned to her husband. "*You've* been to London? Why didn't you tell me? Are there other secrets you've kept from me—another wife, children I don't know about?"

Taking his attention away from devouring Ethel's wedding cake for a moment, he said, "Jeez, honey. London's just like Reno, only a little bigger and farther away."

She was beside herself with the generosity and awe of such a honeymoon. "Are you crazy? A trip like this will require more planning than the hotel additions! What clothes will I need to bring?"

He was focused on stealing Vivien's uneaten cake. "Throw some jeans in a backpack. We'll be fine."

Her head dropped in despair. Mensa wouldn't be inviting her husband to meetings anytime soon.

Cassie looked up as all the women at the table suppressed their laughter and reprimanded Cliff with shaking heads. Lily voiced their opinion. "He's not our problem anymore, Cassie."

About the Author

Jackie Campbell is a writer, an artist, and author of *Crashing Cassie's Comfort Zone*.

Jackie draws on her years of travel, her love of humor, and addiction to romance novels in order to help people have a laugh. She thinks a good romantic comedy novel is the perfect vehicle. When not traveling around looking for ideas, Jackie lives in Marin County, California.

For questions or comments, contact Jackie at:
jackie@jackiecampbellauthor.com